Again Krueger took the microphone. Again he launched into a wearisome chain of platitudes as he described the winner's background, her acting credits, her unbounded enthusiasm for the glittering challenge lying before her . . . Finally he got to her name.

"And now if I may," he started at last, "it is my distinct pleasure to introduce our winner and star of tomorrow, Miss Terri Triano!"

But instead of the expected burst of applause, there was a gasp from several people as they saw Terri Triano stiffen in her chair and struggle to rise. A pained expression tore at her features, and a dry, strangled noise broke from her throat. Her hands leaped up, clawed frantically at her throat.

Then she dropped back into her chair and slumped forward, her head hitting the table with a dull thud. Her body twitched once, then no more. Lying with her left cheek on the tablecloth, she was completely still, eyes wide and staring.

It seemed as though time had frozen. Then two women screamed, and all hell broke loose.

Other books in Eileen Fulton's **Take One for Murder** series:

Take One for Murder

Eileen Fulton's
Dying for
Stardom

IVY BOOKS • NEW YORK

Grateful acknowledgment is made
to Mr. Thomas P. Ramirez
for his editorial advice and counsel.

Ivy Books
Published by Ballantine Books
Copyright © 1988 by Butterfield Press, Inc. & Eileen Fulton

Produced by Butterfield Press, Inc.
133 Fifth Avenue
New York, New York 10003

Back cover photograph: Tom Gates

Library of Congress Catalog Card Number: 87-92142

ISBN 0-8041-0200-7

Manufactured in the United States of America

First Edition: August 1988

To Merrill Lemmon,
who made this book possible
just by being himself.

Chapter One

Tension was heavy in the main rehearsal hall at Meyer Studios. It was nearly five o'clock on a cold Thursday afternoon in mid-February. The day's taping of *The Turning Seasons* had been completed on schedule, at three P.M., and all but four members of the cast of the hugely popular soap opera had left. By the end of a long day of rehearsing and taping the half-hour daily show, the actors were usually only too eager to get away from the studio—and from each other. But today was very different, and the few who remained were the envy of the many who had left.

Several months earlier, the owner-manager of Meyer Productions, Helen Meyer, had demanded that the staff come up with a way to garner more publicity for *The Turning Seasons*. The result was a nationwide talent search for an actress to play an important new role on the long-time hit. It wasn't exactly a blindingly fresh idea, but it had worked.

Soap operas had long since found their public, and the growing popularity of the dramatic form had spread from afternoon to prime time. Soap opera fans now included all sorts of people, not just the stereotypical housewives who loved to experience a little intrigue and romance between the oven and the sink. Market research had proven that

1

TTS, like its rival shows on all networks, was watched by men, women, teenagers, college students, convicts, grandparents, writers, doctors, truck drivers, clerics, drunks, saints, sinners, and (if the letters of a few devoted fans could be believed) an occasional dog and cat.

No wonder the people who appeared on these shows became wealthy and famous; the public idolized them. No wonder so many fledgling actors seemed ready to kill for a role on the soaps.

So the announcement that a genuine search would be conducted for someone to play a role, a new role, an *important* role on TTS was electrifying. The resulting publicity satisfied even the insatiable Helen Meyer, for whom press coverage was only slightly more important than having an attractive man at her side. The Meyer crew had organized a series of regional auditions that were received with near-frenzy by any woman who'd ever dreamed of getting onto a soap. Although the call had been for an actress to play a beautiful, ambitious, conniving businesswoman in her late twenties, the auditionees had included hordes of frantic hopefuls from tubby teenagers to doddering dowagers. Even after the impossible applicants were culled, the judges who had to listen to the three-minute auditions soon found themselves mentally and physically numb. How many impressions of Anne Baxter in *All About Eve* could they listen to?

But inevitably some genuine talent emerged here and there, sometimes in the least expected places. Today the search would be concluded as five finalists gave it All They Had at Meyer Studios in New York City.

The eleven judges in the rehearsal hall were a balanced group representing all phases of the show: management, production, direction, writing, and acting. In addition to Helen Meyer and her chief producer, Horst Krueger, the panel included the director, Spence Sprague, two assistant directors, Nick Galano and newcomer Rob Bryant, the two chief writers, Dave Gelber and Sally Burman, and four of the principal actors. Although all present had a stake in the outcome, it was the four cast members who were most

2

apprehensive. They were the ones who'd have to work most closely with the winner; if she proved to be truly talented, the benefits would be mutual. But if the winner turned out to be a dud who had to be carried, it would be the experienced actors who'd bear the burden.

According to Helen Meyer, the new character of Audrey Lincoln would have most of her scenes with Angela Dolan, Sylvia Kastle, Noel Winston, and—most particularly—Nina McFall, so those four were also present to cast their votes.

Angela, she of the svelte figure, silver-blond hair, and incredible legs for forty-two, or fifty-two, or whatever her age, was draped across an ordinary folding chair as though she were Marlene Dietrich on a chaise longue. To further the illusion, her dazzling mink coat carelessly trailed on the floor. Sylvia Kastle, who had come out of early retirement to join TTS only a few months earlier, had settled into the role of everyone's favorite aunt, regal yet wise. She, too, was on a folding chair, which she somehow managed to endow with the nobility of a throne. *Her* mink, possibly even grander and more expensive than Angela's, played the role of royal robe, worn loosely over the shoulders, its collar caressing her famous neck. Noel Winston, whose previously strained budget had been expanded recently by an impressive windfall inheritance, seemed not so much a loveable grandfather as a Rockefeller who'd wandered into the peculiar scene by mistake, complete with Scottish tweeds and silver-handled walking stick.

Nina McFall, although at thirty-four the youngest member of the quartet, was by any measure the leading player at TTS. At the moment she was also the most apprehensive. Nina had been told privately by scriptwriter Sally Burman that she, as the man-eating business executive, Melanie Prescott, on TTS, would really have the lion's share of scenes with the newcomer. And, since actors can make each other look good, bad, magnificent, or even inept, Nina was more than a little anxious to have a say in who the winner would be. She sat quietly, her nervousness betrayed only by a slight but continuous tapping of her left foot. She, too, had worn a mink coat, for New York was experiencing one of the season's most brutal cold snaps and Nina had been on TTS long enough to know how chilly the rehearsal hall could be in February.

"What the hell's taking so long?" Angela murmured to Sylvia. They had already sat through the first two of the five final auditions. Each of the finalists was required to do a two-minute monologue and then to perform a scene from an upcoming episode of TTS, in character as Audrey Lincoln. The two women who had just finished their auditions were almost interchangeable; both looked to be in their late twenties, both wore form-fitting solid-color dresses (one green, one blue), and both had done well. Either would have made an acceptable Audrey Lincoln— but neither had that special spark Nina was looking for, that indefinable something that would survive the electronic funnel and spring out at viewers from their television screens, making them sit up and take notice, talk about TTS with their friends, and look forward eagerly to the next thrilling episode.

When the third finalist was introduced, Nina's heart went out to her. She was very tall, very thin, and so nervous she could barely walk. According to the resumes for the finalists that had been given to each of the judges, this girl was probably astonished to have reached the finals; her professional credits were extremely slight and her television experience was nearly nonexistent. Even her clothes were wrong—an ordinary medium-brown two-piece dress that did nothing for either her figure or her complexion. Nina guessed that the girl had just thrown up from sheer terror, which might explain her pallor.

She began her monologue in a high, quavery voice and broke out in "flop sweat." She knew she was doing poorly, and she knew that everyone else in the hall knew it, too. Suddenly, in the middle of a sentence, she stopped. She took a step forward and addressed the panel directly.

"That was really terrible, wasn't it?" They were astonished by the girl's directness. "If you want to throw me out now, go right ahead. I won't blame you. But if you don't mind I'm going to start again." No one objected, and she returned to her original position. Again she looked directly at the panel and said in a very low voice, "Stop me when you've had enough." She hung her head down for a moment, and there was an almost audible click as though something shifted inside the girl's mind. Then she began again. She spoke the same words, made the same gestures. But the results were not at all the same. Someone else was suddenly present, someone who hadn't been there a moment ago, someone who wasn't delivering prepared and rehearsed sentences, but someone who was alive and vital, spontaneously expressing these thoughts for the first time in her life.

She finished the monologue and turned her back to the panel. Another one of those silent clicks happened, and then she whirled around and tore through the material from the upcoming TTS script. Now she was mean, conniving, sly, manipulative, and magnificent. At the end, she walked out of the rehearsal hall in silence. Then the panel came to its senses and delivered a burst of applause the girl could have heard even if she'd retreated to furthest reaches of Meyer Studios.

A babble of conversation broke out as the TTS group recovered its wits. "Who is she?" "Millicent Gowan." "Never heard of her." "So what?" "Does she really have the stuff or was this just a moment of desperation?" "Garbage! We saw it." "She did it once, she can do it again." "Maybe so, maybe not. What's she done? Zilch." "Who cares? Did you ever *see* such? . . ." The consensus was that of the three so far, this girl definitely had the edge.

Nina didn't join in the discussion; she was still stunned. The judges were to enter their ratings on a secret ballot, using the standard one-to-ten scale for voice, diction, posture, appearance, spontaneity, believability, and general appeal. Then the ballots were to be tallied by the TTS general secretary, Myrna Rowan, and the results made known the next day, to put the losers out of their misery.

Opinion was divided on the wisdom of taking a chance

5

on somebody so inexperienced. As the debate continued, Nina tried to count sides. At first, opinions seemed fairly evenly divided, but soon the balance began to tilt in favor of the astonishing Miss Gowan. As closely as Nina could tell, only the writers and the new assistant director, Rob Bryant, were hesitant; most of the others seemed to be extremely enthusiastic except Helen Meyer and Horst Krueger, who were oddly noncommital. Nina supposed they were withholding their opinions to avoid influencing the others, which she considered fair and, in Helen's case at least, highly uncharacteristic.

"I don't know why we're going on and on about this now," Helen said. "Have you all forgotten there are two more finalists waiting to audition?" Without waiting for an answer, she gestured to Myrna to proceed.

The fourth finalist was rather good, even better than good, but they forgot her the moment she walked off. Their minds were still firmly tuned in to Millicent Gowan's remarkable performance.

At last the final introduction was made, and again the panel seemed spellbound by the performance. Nina paid very careful attention, not only to the actress auditioning, but also to the other panelists. She knew as soon as the young woman began that the decision was going to be a close call between two finalists: number three, Millicent Gowan, and number five, Terri Triano.

To choose between the two would be difficult. Both gave excellent performances, but Ms. Gowan was almost a neophyte, whereas Ms. Triano's resume listed long experience on stage, in films, and on television. Listening to Terri Triano, Nina decided that her audition was highly professional and would find acceptance among viewers—but it didn't have the sheer electric thrill that Millicent Gowan had delivered. And, she suspected, it never would. Nina's vote was already mentally cast; she wanted very much to work with Millicent Gowan.

* * *

Myrna stood by waiting while the group finished filling in their ballots. The plan was for her to gather all the votes and tabulate the results immediately, at her desk. The results would be announced to the cast and crew the next morning, and to the finalists by phone. There would be a consolation prize for the first runner-up: $10,000 and an all-expenses-paid week in New York, first class. The three also-rans would receive $2,500, to cover their Kleenex bills. The news would be released to a waiting world at a large dinner party to be held Saturday evening, at The Tavern on the Green, where the winner and the runner-up would be introduced. Press coverage was expected to be thorough, not only because of the much-vaunted talent search, but because the ladies and gentlemen of the Fourth Estate knew that when Helen Meyer threw a bash, it was first class all the way. After all, how could they put the news in proper focus if they weren't in the right mood? Hoping to get even more mileage out of the event, Helen also arranged to use it as a celebration of *The Turning Seasons*'s twentieth anniversary as one of America's favorite soap operas.

"Thank God that's over!" Angela said, handing Myrna her ballots and pulling her mink over her shoulders. "I'm ready for a little fortification. Anyone want to play?" Within moments she had organized a group to go around the corner to their favorite local hangout, Corrigan's Pub, where they would doubtless hold a postmortem on the auditions.

"Myrna, before you lock yourself up with those ballots," Helen said, interrupting a whispered conference with Spence Sprague and his two assistant directors, "ask Miss Gowan and Miss Triano to wait."

With no further explanation she rose and headed for her private office. "Would one of you darlings please bring my coat?" she asked over her shoulder.

"I just can't *imagine* which darling that's going to be," Angela muttered as Rob Bryant sprang into action, retrieving Helen's enormous floor-length raccoon coat from the back of her chair and following her, trailed by Horst Krueger, Spence Sprague, and Nick Galano.

"Now I know why she hired a new young AD in such good condition," Sylvia purred. "She knew winter was coming and there just wasn't anyone around strong enough to lift that bearskin." Helen's coat had been a source of much hilarity when she first appeared wearing it. Although she could have afforded a rackful of minks, ermines, and chinchillas, Helen said she opted for the raccoon because it was the warmest damn thing she could find. "You know how I loathe the cold weather. It's bad enough here in the city," she said, putting much disdain into the word "city," "but don't forget the temperature is at least ten degrees colder up in the north woods, where I live."

"The north woods" was her whimsical way of reminding the mink-wearers that when she put on her incredible coat and climbed into her limousine, her chauffeur then drove her to the palatial ninety-acre Meyer estate known as Leatherwing, in Westchester County, where she resided in elegance and solitude. Helen and Morty Meyer had worked hard to achieve the elegance, and ever since his death she'd been trying like hell to get rid of the solitude. It was so convenient to have someone around to tend to one's fur piece. . . .

"Come on, Sylvia, let's admit that Helen wears that gorilla suit because she wants to, not because she has to," Nina said.

"What's this? Nina McFall defending Helen Meyer? Maybe we should put together a news release." Although Sylvia Kastle had been on the show for only a few months, she was well aware of the long-standing antagonism between Nina and Helen. The trouble had begun with Nina's discovery the previous June that Morty Meyer, Helen's husband, had been murdered by his own son Byron (only her stepson, thank God). Then it got even worse in the autumn, when Nina was involved in finding a solution to the May Minton murder. There were moments, many of them, when it seemed to Helen that the very

8

existence of both Meyer Productions and its product, TTS, was threatened by Nina's participation in those events.

Although Nina didn't feel that her position on TTS was truly jeopardized—Helen knew the value of a highly popular star—nevertheless she believed it advisable to keep a very low profile where Helen was concerned, at least for the immediate future.

Holding their furs tight to their bodies against the vicious February winds, Nina, Sylvia, and Angela trouped out of Meyer Studios and made their way up the street to the comforts of Corrigan's Pub. There, in the privacy of a corner booth, the three would treat themselves to a warming liquid or two and undoubtedly tear Helen Meyer and her latest coat carrier to shreds.

"All right, Helen, what's bothering you?" Spence Sprague asked as soon as the office door was closed.

"You're not serious," she responded. Apparently he was. "Good God, Spence, you're the director of this show! Do you mean to tell me you're not the teeniest bit concerned that this girl has next to no experience?"

"Yeah, I thought about that. . . ." he began, but got no further.

"How do we know how she'll react under pressure? We've been doing this for so many years, we don't even realize what newcomers go through. Actors say there's nothing like the pressure of an audition. Nonsense! *I* say there's nothing like the pressure of having to learn a new script four or five times a week, not to mention the last-minute changes we have to throw at them because the idiot writers can't come up with something good until the eleventh hour. And can she keep it up day after day, week after week, month after month, year after year—if she's good enough to get that far?"

Helen paused for effect. She hadn't been around professional actresses all these years for nothing.

"*That's* what's bothering me," she said in a suddenly lowered voice. Then she turned her attention to the two assistant directors. "How do you two feel about it? Nick, what do you think?"

Oh, Jesus, talk about pressure! "Well, Helen. I certainly realize the risks, but I think the rewards might be worth the game."

"*Might*? We can't afford 'might.' Rob? What do you say?"

Rob Bryant had been hired only six weeks earlier, to succeed Bellamy Carter, whom Helen had fired for reasons many of the TTS insiders considered flimsy. He looked from Helen to Spence to Nick and back to Helen. Better play this one safe. "I'm not sure. She could work out well, but she could also be a disaster. Then we'd all look pretty silly. I'm leaning toward the sure thing."

Horst Krueger spoke up for the first time. "I don't understand why we're having this conversation at all," he said. "We agreed on a secret ballot, and the votes have been cast. Let's just count them and get on with it."

"Actually, they haven't *all* been cast," Helen said. "I left mine blank. I wanted to hear your views further before making up my mind."

"Okay, have you heard enough now? This has been a very long day and tomorrow is Friday, not Saturday." Spence Sprague was in no mood to tiptoe around. "You ready to vote yet?"

Helen stared at him, her eyes blazing with resentment at this apparent defiance of her perquisites as owner of the studio.

"No, I am *not* ready. First I want to talk to both those young women, one at a time." Spence opened his mouth, but she beat him to it. "*Privately*."

"Suits me fine. I'm outta here," Spence said. And he was, followed shortly by his two ADs.

"Helen dear, in my opinion, if you don't award this role to the Gowan girl you're going to have a revolt on your hands," Horst said.

"Horst darling, on your way out would you ask Myrna to show Miss Triano in first?"

When the mink-clad trio arrived at Corrigan's, they were pounced on by two more TTS cast members, who were waiting for news of the auditions. Robin Tally, Nina's closest friend in the cast, and newcomer Corinne Demetry listened in fascination as Nina, Angela, and Sylvia related the highlights of the final auditions.

"What do you think's going to happen?" Corinne asked. "Who deserves to win?"

All eyes shifted to Nina, who they knew had the biggest stake in the outcome. "Those are two very distinct questions," Nina said, sipping her sherry on the rocks. Divested of her mink, she was the standout member of a startling group of women. Each of them was a stunner in her own right, regardless of age, and the group was the object of many stares of envy from the other women in Corrigan's.

They looked as though a photographer had spent hours arranging them. Angela's lustrous mass of pale hair was piled high on her head; she wore a form-fitting lilac wool dress and bold chunks of silver jewelry. She had positioned herself at the corner of the booth, to be sure the legs showed to best advantage. Next to her, Sylvia was the essence of sophistication; her figure was even trimmer than when she'd joined the show in a tailored cranberry suit and pale pink blouse with a triple strand of pearls. The two younger women were each knockouts. Robin's pale skin blended with her sheath of winter white, and both were accented by her long dark hair, worn today loose and flowing. Corinne was the tiniest of the group, almost painfully thin but irresistably pretty in a printed silk dress of light gray and sky blue.

Nina, seated center, had decided on simplicity today, since the finalists were the stars of the event. Her scoop-necked jade green dress, adorned only by a simple gold brooch, matched the color of her eyes perfectly, and the contrast to her flawless peaches-and-cream complexion and eye-popping mass of loosely curled red hair was

11

riveting. But the others were used to Nina's dazzling beauty. Right now they were more interested in her opinion than her appearance.

"First, what I hope for," Nina began. "Of the two obvious choices, although either one would be just wonderful—"

"Come on, you aren't trying out for the diplomatic corps," Robin demanded. "Just say it."

"Okay. If it were up to me, I'd choose Millicent Gowan. You don't see that kind of honesty very often. Present company excepted, of course." Nina was determined to offend no one.

"And what do you predict?" Sylvia asked, with a knowing look.

"That's harder," Nina said. "I was trying to read Helen's face. She was being very ambiguous."

"Not only that," Angela put in, "but how did you like that little exit scene, when all the Really Important People went into executive session? Do our votes really count, or were we just going through the motions?"

"If that's the case, why would Helen bother?" Corinne asked.

"To make it look more democratic, perhaps." Nina suggested.

"Or to have someone around to help shoulder the blame if the winner falls flat on her pretty little face," Angela said.

"Do you think they are? Pretty, I mean," Corinne asked a little anxiously.

"Don't worry, sweetie, you still hold the title," Robin assured her.

Pretty wasn't the word for either of the two main contestants, Nina mused to herself. Millicent Gowan was unusually tall and much too thin; her frame as well as her angular face could have used a bit more flesh. Her blond hair was somehow drab. But she glowed from within with a light that was beyond prettiness. As for Terri Triano, she was certainly attractive, but not exactly pretty. Her attraction was somehow darker, more intense and obvious. With her lush figure and jet-black hair, she exuded a Latin

12

quality that would lend itself well to highly emotional scenes—of which there would certainly be many.

Corinne continued a stream of questions about the two contestants, and suddenly Angela plunked down her glass and directed a blunt question at the young actress. "Corinne Demetry! You want that role for yourself, don't you?" It was more of an accusation than a question, and Corinne's instant discomfort was obvious. Angela had intuitively hit a nerve.

"What do you mean? That's silly. I couldn't do that. I'm too young. I have my own role. . . ." The protestations were as endless as they were useless. Nina smiled inwardly. Overreaching ambition was a common curse of actors; they had all suffered from it at one time or another, and there was nothing wrong with it as long as you held on to reality and didn't set your heart on something that was absolutely wrong for you. It was good to reach higher, it was healthy. So let Corinne dream. Where was the harm?

Finally, deciding Corinne had been teased and tortured enough, Angela switched the conversation to the topic they'd all been waiting to sink their fangs into.

"I was thinking about investing in racoon futures," she murmured slowly, and they burst out in a fit of giggles, off and running on the subject of Helen, Helen's fur, and Helen's new fur bearer.

Nina listened as they took turns sharpening their claws, but offered no opinion until Robin asked, in her direct manner, "Nina, what do *you* think about Rob Bryant?"

Nina sent her a smile, shrugging her shoulders. "I've got nothing against Rob," she said calmly. "My only criticism has to do with the callous way Horst and Helen brought him in. To fire Bellamy Carter out of hand as they did—on a capricious whim, in my opinion—was totally wrong. I realize that he was a martinet, unreasonable at times, and that a lot of you disliked him. But he was a good director, all in all. It was cruel to treat him like that. One day he was here, the next he was gone." Her eyes glittered darkly and changed from jade to sea green. "And we all

13

know *who* engineered it and exactly *what* was behind it. If you follow my drift."

"Do we ever!" Robin agreed, an aggrieved twist to her mouth. "There's no fool like an old fool. I thought only men got like that."

The man they spoke of with such venom had arrived on the TTS set less than two months earlier. A chance encounter between Rob Bryant and Helen Meyer at a TV producer's convention in Miami in December had started the whole odious thing. Rob was to have been a temporary backup assistant director, drawing half salary, until a new administrative power base could evolve, while Bellamy Carter, a long-time veteran of the TTS wars, was presumably to be kicked upstairs—to head up publicity, of all things.

But loyalty not being Helen Meyer's strong suit—the illusory budget dragon prevailing as always—Bellamy had received his walking papers on New Year's Eve. He had been sick off and on during December and had been peckish with cast members, and with his bosses, Spence Sprague and Horst Krueger as well. It was deemed sufficient reason to dump him. Carter had gone to the Directors Guild and appealed his case. But in light of Helen Meyer's industry power and the fact that no one wanted to see the show close down, the appeal to management amounted to nothing. Thus, exit Bellamy Carter. Auld acquaintance would definitely be forgot—on the double.

"I can't believe that woman," Corinne said, for once without the virginal smile that had triggered an avalanche of viewer support and made her character, Sherry Payton, a TTS staple almost overnight. "Doesn't she have any self-respect at all?"

From the mouths of babes, Nina thought, even twenty-two-year-old ones. Corinne was an ingenue in more ways than one. "You're new, darling," she explained. "If you'd been around Helen as long as we have, you'd know how ridiculous your question is."

"But," Corinne sputtered, "she's fifteen years older than he is if she's a day!"

"Opportunistic, conniving bastard," Angela fumed. "You know it's a power play on his part. There's no feeling, no real love there at all."

"Isn't there?" Nina said, with an enigmatic Mona Lisa smile. "I'm sure Helen thinks she loves him and that he loves her. And if she's content to live in a dream world . . ."

"Fantasy is the right word for it, all right," Robin said. And after a pause: "So? You haven't answered my question."

"Which was?"

"How are you getting along with Bryant? He works with your group off and on. I've had no contact whatsoever with him yet, other than that ever-present smile of his. He makes me feel all crawly inside."

"Welcome to the club," Sylvia said. "I'd think that Helen would get wise and realize that he's got big eyes for anything in a skirt."

The mysterious smile again. "The eyes of a woman in love can be very blind at times. Selective. They see only what they want to see."

"Does that apply to you and Dino, too, sweetie?" Robin questioned in a deliberately arch manner. They all wanted to know more about Nina's police-detective lover, but Nina refused to rise to the bait.

"We were talking about Rob Bryant," she replied coolly, putting the topic off limits.

"Yes, I was. But you keep changing the subject. What *about* Bryant? Doesn't he make any moves on you?"

"I think he realizes that I'm not available," Nina said. "And that I'm onto him. I'm friendly, but distant. He got that message right from the start."

"Aren't you forgetting something?" Angela interjected. "There's the little matter of that face. Who could resist that face? Kind of like a young Cary Grant, with maybe a little Tyrone Power mixed in."

"You're dating yourself, darling," Sylvia cooed.

"He's a professional," Nina continued, choosing to ignore Angela, "and I'm a professional. We respect that.

15

We don't let our personal lives intrude into that relationship."

"As far as I'm concerned, he can intrude into any damn thing he pleases," Angela breathed, causing Corinne to suppress a giggle and Robin to emit a guffaw.

The tone of the discussion had definitely taken a turn for the worse, and Nina wondered how much of it was genuine antagonism and how much was sour grapes. After all, Rob *was* extremely good-looking, appealingly young, and seemed to have an excellent body. And he was tall. And still tan, from Miami . . . so he smiled a lot; would they prefer a permanent frown?

She didn't know what to believe. Any man as attractive and charming as Rob Bryant could have any woman he wanted. So why would he attach himself to an older woman like Helen? Was he really only sniffing around the Meyer bank book? Hardly likely; even Helen couldn't be that blind. Or maybe he wasn't very talented, and this was the only way he could get a job. On the other hand, his ability as a director was as yet completely unknown. Maybe he'd prove to be nothing but a womanizer, but maybe he'd be a genius who simply liked older women. . . .

"I thought I'd find you here." Nina looked up from her thoughts and saw Myrna Rowan, still shivering from the February blasts that had propelled her up the street from the studio. The group fell silent, waiting for the news.

"Want to guess?" Myrna said.

"Myrna, speak," Sylvia demanded.

Myrna spoke. The role of Audrey Lincoln had been awarded to Terri Triano. Checks and lovely personal notes from Helen Meyer were on their way to Millicent Gowan and the also-rans by messenger.

Damn it and double damn! Nina thought in the disappointed silence that followed Myrna's statement. Helen had played it safe.

Later she realized that safe was the last word to apply to the situation.

Chapter Two

True to her reputation for always going first class, Helen
Meyer sent a limousine to the Biltmore Hotel the next
morning to collect Terri Triano and bring her to the studio
to meet her new colleagues. It was unfortunate that a toss
of the coin had put both the winner and the runner-up in
the same suite at the hotel, and it could have been
awkward. But Millicent behaved beautifully in the face of
defeat, holding back the flood of tears until after Terri left.

At the studio, Terri's entrance into the main rehearsal
hall was timed to coincide with a break in the morning's
schedule, and she was greeted with a burst of applause.
Nina noted the ludicrous contrast between the flashy
electric blue sheath the newcomer was wearing and the
cast's shabby but comfortable rehearsal clothing, which in
some cases amounted to little more than beloved rags.
Helen, elegant as always in basic black embellished by
several diamond scatter pins, escorted Terri, introducing
her to the cast one at a time. The younger members of the
cast crowded around to offer their congratulations and
encouragement. In contrast, the more senior actors played
it differently, preferring to wait until Terri was brought to
them.

Nina wondered if it was accidental or deliberate that she

was the last one Terri was brought to meet. Helen performed the totally unnecessary introductions and then left them, promising to give Terri a tour of the entire studio complex as soon as rehearsals resumed. As the break had already stretched twice its normal length, Nina calculated she'd have about eight seconds with the neophyte. She made the best use of her time by inviting Terri to be her guest at lunch. Regardless of her personal preference, this was the actress Nina was going to have to work with, so she'd better get to know her right away.

Picking up her script as rehearsal resumed, Nina found herself wondering what Millicent Gowan was doing at that moment, and whether she'd be able to get over the disappointment and persevere with her career. Nina decided she'd have to find a way to give her some encouragement; her talent was too promising to be wasted.

Nina decided to lunch with Terri at Corrigan's. Might as well get her indoctrinated into the whole routine at one time. Besides, there was nothing like it in the whole of New York City, and it was definitely off the tourist track, which was a treat in itself.

Corrigan's Pub dated back to the Roaring Twenties; it had survived Prohibition battered but unbowed. To enter the murky bar and grill was to step back into the twenties. It was an atmosphere Corrigan's new owners—engaged in a constant war with New York City's nitpicking corps of building, electrical and health inspectors—fought desperately to preserve.

To the TTS regulars, as well as to other media types who worked in nearby TV and radio broadcasting studios, it was a favorite hangout for lunch as well as dinner and the in-between, post-taping happy hour. The long expanses of ceiling-high mirrors, the marble and oak trim, the dark, nicotine-clouded pillars flanking each end of the high, cumbersome and badly scarred bar—a favorite of such literary greats as Hemingway, Lardner and Fitzgerald, long

18

before television came on the scene—were a throwback to an entirely different age, an age that would never come again.

Corrigan's was crammed, as usual. Nina and Terri snagged the last table in the barroom. The second dining room, a larger area reached by passing through a long corridor on whose wall hung hundreds of autographed celebrity photographs, was also jamming up. Nina saw Spence Sprague at his special table, a phone already plugged in for him, tending to business even as he drank his customary Campari and soda. In another booth, TTS lovebirds Robin Tally and Rafe Fallone had their heads close. Mary Kennerly was down the line wih Corinne Demetry and another young actress, Susan Levy. At the door, still other TTS cast and production crew members were crowding in.

"What a place," Terri said as they crowded behind their half table. "Talk about color!"

"Shhh," Nina cautioned, "not so loud. They'll raise the prices. Isn't it charming? I'll bet Zelda and Scotty's ghosts come out at night. It's our regular hangout. 'Meet you at Corrigan's . . .' It's a catchword. They treat show people like royalty, especially the gang from TTS. It pays off. Loyalty is a two-way street."

As Terri Triano studied the menu, Nina seized the opportunity to covertly appraise the new member of the TTS cast. She loathed Terri's dress, but had to admire her clear pale complexion, which made her mass of black hair gleam. Nina regarded the perfect structure of that lovely face and marveled that the flat, squarish jut of jaw and chin didn't undermine Terri's beauty. But no, it imparted exotic undertones instead. Smaller than Nina, she had a compact, lithe body boasting trim ankles, flaring calves, sassy derriere, and high, surging breasts, all combining to emit a challenging erotic taunt.

But still, millimeters beneath the surface of that soft and curvy exterior, in the tiny lines at the corner of her wide-set, perfectly oval brown eyes, around the edges of her sensuous lips, there existed a jarring counterpoint, a

19

vestigial hardness and world-weariness. The lady's been around the block more than a couple times, Nina concluded.

It was a toughness that Terri, in her speech—slangy, replete with random expletives—made no attempt to conceal. I am my own woman, her manner decreed. Take me on my own terms or bug off.

A good choice, Nina thought reluctantly, for her soap-opera alter image, Audrey Lincoln, who would be an inveterate flirt and troublemaker on the show and who would eventually ingratiate herself with Melanie Prescott's current lover. Maybe Helen and Horst knew what they were doing when they picked Terri after all.

Conversation went momentarily on hold as a perky waitress clad in a white blouse, black slacks, and flouncy red apron, took their orders. Both had Reuben sandwiches, a house specialty. Terri asked for a glass of chablis and Nina ordered mineral water, hoping the unspoken point would get across.

"Do you come here every day?" Terri asked, her eyes darting about the room like lasers. Why, Nina puzzled, is this girl still jittery? Auditions are over. I get nervous watching her. A mild tranquilizer might help.

"Mostly. It's very convenient. Sometimes I switch. I'll take you to some of my favorites in due course. It gets to be a bore eating at the same place every day. But the food is good, and you can keep up on the gossip."

"You got a winner right there." Terri's expression became slightly venal. "Keeps you ahead of the competition. *That* I know about."

Nina sent her a questioning, sidelong look and changed the subject. "So, what do you think of our squirrel cage so far? Getting the hang of things?"

"Oh, I think I'll survive," Terri said jauntily. "Sure, it's a lot to get under your belt all at once, but I've been kicking around Hollywood for years now. Don't worry. I won't embarrass you. This weather of yours is the pits, though. And New York itself! Christ, I thought L.A. was grim . . ."

"Much as I hate to say it, you just have to close your eyes to certain things, pretend they don't exist. And be careful on the streets. I came here from Wisconsin over five years ago, so you can imagine the time I had adjusting."

"I'm on the wavelength, Nina. But finding a place to live is a real drag. The studio's got people looking—I'm in the Biltmore temporarily sharing with Milly Gowan—but most of what I've seen so far is really crappy. And those prices! I thought California rentals were over the moon."

Briefly Nina filled Terri in on choice areas of New York and advised her to get a prestige address early, despite the staggering rental. "Within a year, as your salary jumps, you'll work into it. Then you won't be faced with another move. That can put you over the edge, too. If you want me to go apartment hunting with you, just let me know."

"No thanks," Terri said, sipping at her wine a bit too enthusiastically. "I'm pretty much committed to a place in the West Sixties. But I still shudder at that lease. Gouging's a fine art in the Big Apple, it would seem."

Their food arrived, and as they began to eat, the subject changed. "Tell me about your background, Terri. Are you married, engaged, living with someone?" Nina asked.

"Don't I wish! Nope, I'm on my own. I was married once, but it didn't work out."

"Oh? Divorce?"

"After a fashion." Terri's eyes became wary. "Let's just say we're not an item anymore."

"What kind of things did you do in L.A.? You've got some pretty impressive credits."

"I suppose. If you can count fifty or sixty one-shots. I've tried for years to land a series part, but no way. Tried every trick in the book, short of humping the director, but they kept telling me I didn't have that elusive 'star' quality. I've eaten my share of tuna salad in my time, believe me!" Her smile was sardonic. "So when this *Turning Seasons* promotion hit the L.A. papers, I went for it. What did I have to lose? The loot is first rate."

Nina sent a questioning look at Terri. Again she wondered about the hard-boiled quality. Wouldn't you think, just starting out, that she'd downplay it just a little? And this edginess of hers . . . Something wasn't jibing. "What shows were you on?" she inquired, trying to sidetrack her dubious thoughts.

"Oh, big-ticket dogs like *Blackwell's Ferry*, *The Putnams*, *Embarcadero Beat*, and *Bartoletti and Sons*. Most of them sank without a trace. Once I did a walk-on on *Hooperman*, and I was on *Family Ties* twice—five lines each time. So you can see I'm ready for something bigger."

"Wonderful. That's the kind of enthusiasm we can certainly use. I'm sure it'll work out beautifully for you, and for us as well. This time your natural talent will be noticed." Nina glanced sharply at Terri, thinking, *Will you sit still?* "And rewarded."

"That kind of talk's music to my ears. After all this knocking around, it feels like I'm coming home at last. But I feel bad at the same time. I've gotten to know Milly pretty well, since we're bunking together, and I'm really sorry the kid didn't make the cut."

Nina smiled philosophically. "It's the way things work. I'm sure she's taking it in stride. After all, ten thousand dollars, plus an all-expenses-paid New York holiday is hardly chopped liver."

"I know I'd be resentful as hell, losing out at the last minute like that. When Mrs. Meyer brought me in to talk right at the end, I could have sworn she was getting me ready for the big letdown. Did she say anything to you?"

"No, she didn't." Nina's tone turned edgy. "Helen and I aren't on the best of terms most of the time. I'd be the last person on earth she'd confide in."

"Oh? That kind, huh? And here I thought we were all one big happy family. Tell me, what about this May to December shtick she's got going with that guy Bryant? Already I've heard the talk. Is that for real? She looks old enough to be his mother. Is he really shtupping her?"

Nina was evasive. "Presumably. I've never followed them home."

"If he is, doesn't she know she's being used?"

"We can't be sure now, can we?" Nina said, lapsing into the devil's advocate role. "Some men are intrigued by older women. They feel protected."

Terri regarded Nina dubiously. "Are you pulling my chain?"

Nina's expression was impassive. "You're entitled to your opinion. I'll just wait for the reruns."

"Where'd those two meet up, anyway?"

"Apparently they met at a broadcaster's convention in Miami. Horst Krueger and Helen went down there, and two weeks later, Mr. Rob Bryant turned up. A perfectly good director was let go to make room for him, so he and Helen have been gossip bait ever since."

"Bet you he branches out real soon."

"You mean he's already put some moves on you, Terri?"

"No, just a couple of hard looks. But give it some time. He'll hit on me, wait and see."

"You sound like you know him just by looking at him."

"No . . ." Terri's eyes became excessively jumpy. "I just know the type. Hollywood's crawling with slugs like that."

Nina regarded her more closely. Wasn't there undue venom in Terri's words? "Well, as I always say," she closed the subject, "walk a mile in the other man's moccasins. I'll reserve judgment for now."

Terri smiled skeptically. "You are something else, Nina. I thought Pollyanna types like you went out with the Hula Hoop."

Nina was tempted to address the snide putdown, but luckily the waitress reappeared just then, and both women ordered coffee. "When we finish that," Nina said tersely, "we'd best head back to the studio. Bonita has to do something about my hair."

"Looks great to me, like a flaming halo when the light hits it just right. What kind of rinse do you use?"

"None." Nina said, amazed at the directness of the woman. Small wonder her husband had dumped her. She could become a thorn over the long haul. "I don't use anything. It's completely natural."

"If you say so. Excuse me while I take my foot out of my mouth."

"Not at all, Terri. Lots of people ask me the same thing." Which was an outright lie; Nina was only attempting to be

23

gracious. Long haul, had she said? She was going to have to live with this abrasive woman for weeks, months—for *years* to come. She groaned inwardly.

My mistake, she concluded. Helen's choice for the new role wasn't a good one after all.

Chapter Three

By 6:00 P.M. on Saturday the guests in The Tavern on the Green's Pavilion Room were three deep at the bar. Everyone was in full evening regalia. Helen Meyer and Horst Krueger were gratified to see that coverage for the TTS award party would be heavy; photographers and camera crews were already setting up and taking shots of the TTS principals and the finalists. At the same time, mini-interviews with the show's mainstays were in full swing. It had been agreed that except for photographs, the five finalists were off-limits until after the formal announcement after dinner.

The targets of all this hullaballoo, the actors, fell into two categories: those the press were interested in and those the press were not interested in. The ones who were most sought after somehow affected a modest attitude that implied "God, when will they give me a moment's *peace*?" The other group, those with too many such peaceful moments, stood on the sidelines, nursing agonies of doubt about their popularity and smiling broadly just in case someone pointed a camera in their direction.

Despite the fact that Nina McFall was now, as always, "good copy," it wasn't her idea of a relaxed day off. But such evenings did come with the territory, and she responded gracefully to one inane question after another. Yes, she loved playing a manipulative bitch. No, she couldn't say who had won the role of Audrey Lincoln. Yes, she was sure whoever had won would be wonderful in the part. They were all wonderful at the auditions. Everyone was wonderful. Yes, she was sure the injection of fresh talent would keep her on her toes. (Remember to step on *that* bastard's toes later!) Yes, everyone was enthusiastic. No, she didn't keep a pet python in her bathtub. That was just a silly, silly rumor. . . .

And yes, she certainly needed a drink, which she richly deserved after easing away from one particularly offensive reporter and handing him over to a purring Angela Dolan. Her gesture to a passing waiter was rewarded with a flute of champagne, and she slipped behind a wall of palms to relax in solitude, only to find herself invading occupied territory. Noel Winston was already there, resplendent in a custom-tailored dinner jacket. His silvery hair exactly matched the shade of the pearl onion in his Vodka Gibson, and Nina wondered if the loveable old dear had any idea how attractive he still was. Probably not; he looked a little embarrassed at being discovered.

"Hello, my love," he muttered. "Couldn't take it any longer, eh?"

"Enough. I've done my duty for one night. How are you doing?"

Noel caught the implication nicely. "Three interviews and a half dozen still shots. I, too, have earned my goodies."

She peeked through the wall of palms, noting that the five finalists were being immortalized in various combinations with Helen, Angela, Sylvia, Horst, and Spence, and admired the performance the four losers were giving. She knew she should be out there with them, but she had to give her smile muscles a rest. Her gaze wandered over the scene.

The room was filled with round and oblong tables that seated ten or twelve people each. At the center of every table a tall flower-decorated candelabra complemented the

26

gleaming crystal stemware and exquisite place settings. The red upholstered chairs stood in perfect alignment, ready to receive the guests, and the overhead chandeliers had been dimmed to blend with the thousands of twinkling starlights embedded in the velvety blue ceiling. The overall effect was a shimmering fantasy.

"You know, Noel, this is really a gorgeous place. I can't believe I've never been here before."

"You haven't? Where does that Dick Tracy fellow of yours take you?"

"I'll Dick Tracy you! Dino takes me to a lot of places. . . ." (Actually, he was developing the annoying habit of gravitating to the same two or three restaurants all the time, unless she placed a special request.)

"And where is he tonight, if I may ask? You're far too beautiful to be let out alone in New York on a Saturday evening."

"Why, Mr. Winston, you flattering creature! Such sugary words could turn a girl's head. Detective Lieutenant Rossi is on duty, but I declare, if he heard you say that, he might have to look to his laurels."

"He might have to look to them anyway, judging from my observations," Noel remarked drily.

Enough verbal fencing. "What observations?"

"You can't be unaware of the looks you've been getting from our new assistant director."

Nina didn't want to talk about it. "Come on, Noel, let's find out where we're seated."

Nina, nursing her champagne, and Noel balancing his Gibson, walked around the tables and examined the engraved cards at each place.

"Drat," Noel said when Nina found her card, "I'm not at your table. I swear, if I didn't have bad luck, I'd have no luck at all. Think it'd be kosher if I moved this card to another table, put mine in its place? You don't want to sit next to David Gelber, do you?"

Nina chuckled. "Better leave things the way they are. I'm sure Helen set up the table arrangements herself. You don't want to get in *her* doghouse, do you?"

27

"Heaven forbid! Who knows, I might get drafted to walk her latest pet—Rob Bryant."

Nina felt her stomach tighten. It was becoming an open secret when even a pussycat like Noel took to making wiseguy remarks.

Couldn't Helen see she was making a fool of herself?

"Stop it, Noel," she said. "I thought you were above rumor mongering."

"Rumor mongering?" He made a motion with his head toward the bar area, where an already mildly squiffed Helen Meyer hung heavily on Rob Bryant's arm, looking up at him with a positively lovelorn expression. "Does that look like the real McCoy to you? She'll be pulling him under one of these tables any minute now."

Helen, Helen, Nina agonized, her eyes stricken. *Will you behave?*

Lost in pity for her employer, Nina stood in the middle of the Pavilion Room, drawing more attention than she realized. She was wearing a form-fitting black satin cocktail dress that displayed her figure to magnificent advantage. Wide shoulder straps swept down in front to a daring decolletage that showcased her firm breasts and alluring cleavage. The three-inch heels on her black peau-de-soie pumps gave an extra flare to her long, slender legs, encased in clocked silk hose. Nina was extravagantly attractive from any angle, and at this moment her mass of red hair came alive in the flickering candlelight to form a rose-gold nimbus around her enchanting face. The sparkle from her startling green eyes was echoed in the emerald necklace and earrings she wore.

Noel started to say something, but stopped to regard his beautiful young friend in silence. Several photographers, knowing a photo opportunity when they saw one, were heading toward Nina, and Noel nodded in the direction of their hideaway spot where they retreated again behind the wall of palms.

"Helen will kill me, but I've done my part," Nina said.

"Not to worry. I don't think Helen is concentrating on you at the moment."

Nina really didn't want to get into further discussion of Helen Meyer and young Mr. Bryant at the moment, so she said, "What do you know about this incredible place?"

"Actually, quite a bit. Originally, it was one of those damned government boondoggles," he said. "At least at the start. The work of Boss Tweed, one of the most accomplished grafters in American History." Where The Tavern now stood, Noel elaborated, Boss Tweed had once caused a sheepfold to be constructed, at a cost to the city of seventy thousand dollars. "Chicken feed today, perhaps, but truly big bucks back at a time when a laborer earned two dollars a week. Two hundred sheep were housed here, with separate quarters built in the park for the lucky shepherd and his family. The sheepfold actually existed until nineteen thirty-four, when a parks commissioner decided the parcel should be used as a spot for a popular-priced restaurant. Enter Tavern on the Green.

"Of course," Winston concluded, "the place has been redone several times since then. The biggest renovation was in the mid-seventies, to the tune of almost three million dollars. The rooms over on the north end were part of the original sheepfold building. The rest has been added on. It's unique. No wonder it lures every tourist who ever gets to New York."

"Amazing," Nina sighed. "I'll certainly come again."

Noel Winston's travelogue was cut short as another camera crew discovered the leafy retreat and bore down on Nina. As she answered their questions, smiling until her jaws ached, her eyes wandered. She took in other reporters, other TV cams clustered around Angela Dolan, around Helen Meyer, the founder of the feast, and around Horst Krueger, the show's producer. She noticed that Terri Triano and Milly Gowan were, for the moment, being pretty much ignored, along with the other three finalists. Their time would come. Once the talent-search winners were announced, they, too, would fall victim to strobe blindness.

Now, cut loose momentarily, she approached Rafe

29

Fallone and Robin Tally where they stood near the main table. "Well, lovebirds," she greeted, "enjoying yourselves?"

Robin went into an exaggerated charade of shying away from Nina. "Go away" she whimpered. "You're bad luck. Every time I go to a party with you there's trouble. Keep your distance, I'm warning you."

Nina took the joshing in good stride. "Not tonight, Robin. Not in such a beautiful setting. Everybody's on electroglide. No bad vibes, no loose ends. We're one big happy family."

"Seems I've heard that song before," Rafe joined in. "There were no bad vibes those other times, as I recall. The night Morty died we were one big happy family. And then that party in October, when you drove that man off the cliff . . ."

"I didn't drive any man off any cliff!" Nina cried. "Dino Rossi was the culprit."

"Big deal," Rafe scoffed. "You're a lightning rod, and you know it. Get away from me, woman!"

Then Nina was surrounded by reporters once more. Cameras flashed and microphones were shoved into her face. When she got loose this time, she returned to the bar for another glass of champagne, noticing as she did so, that the wine was already cutting in. But she wasn't deterred; in a festive mood, she was determined to make this a fun night. And if she allowed herself to get the least bit high, so what? Dino's damned duty schedule had forced cancellation of their Saturday night date—she might as well get something out of it. Besides, she'd earned it. It had been a tough week, with an even tougher week coming up. God, she was tired of these camera people!

"All right, gentlemen, that's enough for now. We don't want to wear the lady out, do we?"

The rich male voice was only vaguely familiar, but the words were very welcome regardless of the source. And the tone of authority was unmistakable. The photographers got the message and swirled on to surround Robin and Rafe, who were delighted at the attention. Nina turned

30

to thank her rescuer and found herself looking into the deepest blue eyes she'd ever seen.

They were set in the richly tanned and handsome face of Rob Bryant. He smiled at her, and Nina found herself wondering why he toiled on the business side of the cameras. With a face like that, he'd be a soap opera sensation before the first episode was off the air.

She felt the need to sit down, and they withdrew to a side of the room where the commotion was less intrusive. He flagged a waiter and set a fresh glass of champagne before Nina.

"I didn't mean to intrude, but you seemed to be on the thin edge."

So he had been watching her. But how had he managed to ditch Helen, even temporarily?

"Right you are. Thanks for stepping in. Those boys don't always do as they're told."

"It was a handy moment for me. I was looking for an excuse to come over and tell you how much I admire your dress. It's a knockout."

"Why, thank you, Rob." She couldn't resist a little twist of the shoulders: "Just something I had whipped up—at a cost of hundreds."

"And, of course . . ." his smile became even more ingratiating, "what's in it."

"My, aren't you the soul of gallantry? And what, if I may ask, brought that on?" She regarded his glass. "It wouldn't be the champagne talking, would it?"

"Hardly. Granted, it does tend to endow one with false courage, perhaps even turn a man a bit foolhardy." He winked roguishly. "But dammit, there are certain things that must be said!"

In that moment Nina could certainly appreciate the facets of Rob Bryant's personality that made him so irresistible to women. He had a glib tongue and he knew that flattery—admiration of a woman's costume, comment on some comely facial feature—was the quickest way to command female attention. Beyond that, there was his easy self-confidence, his sense of humor, which—albeit grudgingly—she'd noted on the set before. It was a truism, seemingly carved in stone: Get a woman to laugh with you and you're halfway home.

Perhaps it was her mood, perhaps it was the influence of the champagne, but for some reason she decided, just this once, to play along. Let's see, she mused, just where all this leads. "Rob," she said, adopting an arch Scarlett O'Hara tone, "how you do go on!"

"It's the truth. You look great. Black is your color. It does marvelous things for your eyes, sets that carrottop of yours ablaze." He pulled a face. "Although I can't think of a color you wouldn't do justice to. Those shoes, the emeralds. What can I say? The total picture leaves me weak."

"You *do* know how to turn a girl's head, don't you?"

"Madame, you cut me to the quick. Do I detect a note of skepticism? Don't you recognize sincere admiration when you hear it? Oh, cruel, unfeeling temptress!" he sighed melodramatically.

Nina broke into laughter. "Rob, stop now! What are you angling for?" The honesty of the question took them both by surprise, and they regarded each other for a long moment.

Rob Bryant was a good-looking man by any standard. He was in his early forties, standing five feet eleven, weighing 165 pounds wringing wet. His hair was a tawny mane, streaked with several shades of medium blond, none of them as dark as his neat Van Dyke beard. His shoulders were slightly sloped, lending an easy languor to his movements. And yet he was in physical trim; Nina had heard that he religiously adhered to a three-times-weekly regimen at an uptown gym.

But his eyes, dark-rimmed and heavy-lidded, were his most distinctive feature. They seemed almost unfocused at times, yet penetratingly sharp at others—but always with a gleam of sardonic amusement. There were moments, when Nina caught him looking at her, that she got a distinct bug-on-a-pin sensation; at other moments—as now—she felt the comfortable warmth of sincere male admiration.

32

Nina could easily see why Helen Meyer doted on the man. His ability to make a woman feel special and appreciated must have been particularly welcome to a widow of Helen's age. Nina emerged from her reverie to hear him say, "Maybe we could have dinner some night, Nina. I think it's time we got to know each other better. I'd love to know more about your background. Do you think you'd like that?"

Would I? she thought. She wasn't sure—but she *was* sure of one thing. "Maybe I would. The real question is, would Helen like it? I'm not in her good graces as it is. A thing like that could bring down my curtain for good."

He seemed somewhat surprised that someone could be so dense as not to understand the practical contingencies of his relationship with Helen Meyer. "Well," he said in an almost hypnotic tone, "I'm sure we'd have the delicacy not to bring it to her attention. After all, it's not as if there's anything questionable about the invitation. We'd talk, get to know each other, use our time together as a springboard to a better professional relationship. I'd be a better director for it, and presumably we'd have a better working relationship."

Robbie, baby, Nina thought, you are good. What a smoothie. Small wonder Helen was such easy pickings. "I don't think it would be wise," she said, "I've made it a firm policy never to get personally involved with fellow workers, especially male fellow workers."

"That's a rather narrow view, don't you think? It's not as if I'm suggesting anything the least bit untoward. A meeting of minds, so to speak."

But the sheer appeal in his voice made Nina certain the meeting would go a lot further than the minds. "Of course, Rob," she said, "I understand perfectly. But in light of the fact that you and Helen have an . . . understanding . . . and since I respect Helen so highly . . . I simply couldn't do anything to jeopardize things with her. By the way, she's probably wondering where you are right now. Look, I'm flattered by your interest, I really am. But we'll

33

just have to confine our *knowing* each other to the set itself."

Rob Bryant was no fool. He knew a putdown when he saw it. "Whatever you say," he said, genuine disappointment clear in his voice. "I just think you're making a big mistake. It's never a good idea to refuse to open doors when you don't know what's behind them."

Nina was about to conclude the conversation with the observation that one might find some unpleasant surprises behind those doors, but she suspected he'd have a smooth answer for that, too, so instead she simply turned to walk away. Too late. She found herself looking into the blazing eyes of an avenging fury. Helen had observed the prolonged tête-à-tête and approached unseen by either of them. Nina decided to play it as innocently as possible. Any outburst from Helen would be sure to find its way into the gossip columns.

"Helen, what a fantastic evening! You've outdone yourself," Nina said. "Everyone is raving. You must be very proud."

Helen glared at her in frigid silence. If Nina had suspected earlier that Helen was overdoing the champagne, any sign of wooziness was totally absent now. Helen was in icy control of herself.

"And you must be even prouder of what *you've* done," she said in menacingly low tones, barely moving her lips.

"I don't think I've done anything." True, but why did Nina feel a nagging sense of guilt?

"Never mind what you *think*. We'll discuss that at another time. This is a press party for a new cast member, and you're not going to steal the scene. Or anything else."

"Helen, dear . . ." Rob began, but this was Helen's moment, and she knew it.

"Robbie, I think we're about to sit down for dinner. Shall we find our places?" The invitation was more of a command, and Rob responded accordingly. He took Helen's arm and escorted her toward the dining area, directing only a brief glance toward Nina. But the glance was startling in its clarity; Helen's intrusion was no more than a necessary annoyance, it said. He was seriously interested. Amazing, she thought, how much information a man could pack into a single glance. She took a deep breath. Staying out of trouble with Helen was going to be more difficult than she'd thought.

Despite Helen's reference to dinner, the party seemed to be stuck in the cocktail phase, so Nina found a fresh glass of champagne and cast about for someone to talk to. Someone safe. Someone female. Corinne? No, she was probably still writhing because she couldn't even audition for the Audrey Lincoln role. Nina spotted Millicent Gowan, alone, uneasy, and at loose ends. Nina's mother-hen instinct took over.

"Hello, Millicent. What a marvelous gown!"

And what a lame opening. But what could she say? "Sorry you didn't get the role?" "Are you enjoying the party for Terri that should have been the party for you?" What misery the girl must be in! Anyway, she hadn't lied—the gown was really pretty, an ivory and white creation with silver accents.

"Thank you, Ms. McFall. I'd rather be called Milly."

"And I'm Nina. Whenever somebody calls me Ms. McFall I feel like I've graduated into maiden aunts and grandmother roles. Where did you find the dress?"

"Here, in Bloomingdale's. When I bought it I wanted to make a splash. Now I'm afraid it's too showy for an also-ran."

Obviously she wanted to talk about it. Probably do her good.

"For what it's worth, I thought you were outstanding. Everyone was bowled over. To get off to a bad start like that and then to have not only the courage to admit it but the *control* to go back and start over . . ." Nina trailed off, intrigued by the look on the girl's face.

"Nice bit, wasn't it?"

"Bit?"

"The shaky start, the interruption, the miraculous recovery." She regarded Nina's open-mouthed gaze with cynical amusement. "All carefully rehearsed. I wanted to do something different, not just walk on, say my piece, and walk off again. I wanted to show as many different levels as I could. I wanted to make you all *remember* me."

Nina was astonished. "I don't think anyone who was present in that room will ever forget you."

As Milly Gowan looked at Nina, the cynical attitude suddenly dissolved and sheer misery took over.

"I really thought I had it, I was certain I'd won. Especially after what Mrs. Meyer said when she brought me into her office at the end of the day. I even called Illinois to tell my folks. Oh God, it'll be all over town by now, and they're going to have to take it all back and explain and apologize. That's the worst part, they're going to be so embarrassed!"

"Come on, darling," Nina said, giving her a quick hug, "look at the bright side. It's not the end of the world. You'll be on TV, in the papers, the publicity can go into your resume; it's bound to be a stepping stone to something good—maybe even a chance at another soap opera role. After all, TTS isn't the only soap going. And your name's on file with us. The next time something opens up, you'll certainly get a call."

Milly sighed heavily. "That's easy for you to say, Nina. You've got yours. I wanted to be on *The Turning Seasons* so desperately! I've dreamed of a break like this all my life. Everybody back in Rockford was rooting for me. It was so stupid of me to let my family think I'd won the part. I guess that's what makes this so hard to take. Eating crow is never easy."

The mention of Rockford prompted Nina to sit Milly down and compare backgrounds. The similarities were remarkable. Both of them had come from Midwestern towns, both had starred in high school musicals, both had been active in hometown little theater groups, and both had gone on to repertory groups, Nina in Milwaukee and Milly in Chicago. Most astonishing of all, both had begun teaching careers, grown dissatisfied, and left teaching to pursue their impossible dreams. A strong sense of bonding grew between them as they discovered these parallels, and

Nina had to restrain herself from lamenting aloud that they'd come so close to working together.

Yes, it was grossly unfair that Millicent Gowan had been upstaged by Terri Triano, who—as Nina had so recently discovered—promised to be a problem. Nina yearned to know more about the politics behind Helen's apparent last-minute switch from Milly to Terri. But all Milly said was, "It's too painful to talk about. I've learned my lesson."

Nina noticed that people were drifting toward the tables and the waiters were beginning to serve the first course. As she and Milly went toward the ladies' room to freshen up, Nina caught a glimpse of Rob Bryant in an apparently warm moment with Terri Triano. Amazing, Nina thought. The man was absolutely unflappable. Rejected in one place, he just moved on and set up camp somewhere else. He'd probably have no trouble with Terri, Nina thought. Although at the moment Terri didn't seem to be having such a great time—in fact, she looked worried about something. Probably afraid Helen would spot them and descend like the furies to lay claim to her personal property. But at the moment there was no sign of Helen. Of course not; the pattern was becoming quite clear. Every time Helen's middle-aged back was turned, Rob flushed out another tender young bird and turned on the boyish charm.

Or was it the other way around? Terri was no shrinking violet. Maybe she'd approached Rob; given what Nina knew of her character, it was certainly possible. And given his looks, it was also believable. What woman wouldn't be attracted to that face?

Uh-oh, watch yourself, McFall! Stop thinking about Rob Bryant and start concentrating on getting back into Helen Meyer's good graces. If there was any such thing . . .

When Nina and Milly emerged from the ladies' room and took their seats, the first course was in progress. There was a choice of buttery sautéed sea scallops on a bed of Chinese cabbage, lobster bisque, or tuna carpaccio garnished with scallions, red onions, and slivers of lime. Nina chose the scallops, and for her entrée selected salmon steak

37

in a white peppercorn sauce, although she was strongly tempted to order the venison with truffles. Regardless of her less endearing qualities as an employer, as a hostess Helen Meyer was unstinting; the bill for all this would be staggering.

Nina put all thoughts of Rob, Helen, Milly, and Terri out of her mind as she concentrated on the delectable food and the perfectly chosen crisp Chardonnay that accompanied it. What a treat Dino was missing! But it was probably just as well; he didn't much like wearing formal attire, and he'd probably have been bored with the endless show-biz conversation. Well, later she'd torture him with descriptions of the food.

For dinner companions, Nina had drawn Dave Gelber and Nick Galano. Other cast members at her table were Robin, Corinne, Sirri Ballinger, Susan Levy, Des Folwell, Bob Valentine, and Rafe Fallone. The group was convivial, the wine flowed, and the evening progressed beautifully. Judging from the noise levels coming from the adjoining room where the members of the press were feasting, media coverage of the event would be gratifying.

Finally dessert was served, a concoction called Scotch Old-fashioned. Nina regarded it doubtfully as the waiter set it before her, remembering that she didn't want to have any trouble getting into Melanie Prescott's expensive tailored wardrobe—or Nina McFall's. She dipped her spoon into it gingerly, just to taste, and nearly went out of her mind. Reactions around the table matched hers, and the Scotch Old-Fashioneds vanished in record time. As they ate, they analyzed, deciding it was a mixture of an iced soufflé containing pineapple, oranges, real maraschino cherries, and some very good Scotch, all dressed liberally with a Drambuie sauce. Corinne declared she wanted another one, and they were convulsed when Nick and Rafe actually got up, went to another table, and simply stole three more.

The theft was carried off with such aplomb that the table was convulsed. The timing and the moment combined with the food and the wine to give Robin a helpless fit of the giggles. It was contagious, and suddenly everything was funny. The waiters were funny, the coffee was funny, the sugar and cream were hilarious, and the mildest remark set them howling.

"It's like laughing in church," Robin burbled between fits. "The more you want to stop, the funnier everything gets." And that sent her off on a fresh wave. Nina was afraid they wouldn't be able to control themselves when the awards program began, particularly not if Helen or Horst began to deliver pompous remarks.

"We're beginning to attract attention," Nina observed, and it was true. Heads at other tables were turning in their direction. Was it annoyance, or was it envy? Then Helen Meyer rose from her center position at the head table, tapping on a glass with a spoon. It was clearly not a look of envy she threw toward the offenders, and Nina forced herself to think dark thoughts in an effort to quiet down. In light of the little predinner scene with Rob, Helen would be apt to blame Nina for anything that went wrong, from a noisy table to a chipped coffee cup.

"We wish to welcome you all," Helen began, "the *Turning Seasons* family, as well as members of the press. We trust that you all enjoyed your meal, and are now ready for the main event, the real reason we've all gathered here. For not only are we gathered to celebrate the twentieth consecutive year *The Turning Seasons* has been on the air, but we've also come together to welcome a new member of soap opera's royal galaxy. To proudly introduce the winner of the '*Turning Seasons* Introduces' talent competition."

She proceeded to provide far too many details on TTS's struggling first years, on how much advertising revenue the show generated, on how many homes tuned in daily, the Neilsen share. Next she went on to describe how the contest itself had been conceived and executed. The press group grew restless. Now she told how difficult it had been to narrow down the entries to tonight's finalists. "Portfolios were received from all fifty states," she rattled, "and when these were evaluated, five finalists were flown in to be interviewed, to audition for the *Turning Seasons* panel consisting of—" And she introduced each member of the panel. When it was Nina's turn to stand and acknowledge the applause, Robin nearly slid under the table to stifle her laughter.

"Each of these five talented young ladies acted in specially written scenes wherein the aggressive and unorthodox character of Audrey Lincoln would be introduced to our millions of loyal fans." Helen went on to tell what a challenge lay before the new actress—playing opposite the brilliant and popular Nina McFall would be a tough and demanding task for the lucky newcomer. Of course there were plugs for some of the other TTS anchors—Angela, Noël, Sylvia, Rafe, Robin—as well.

Keep it up, Helen, Nina thought. "You've nearly got them sleeping in the aisles.

"And now," Helen announced, "to present the awards, here is our own Horst Krueger, a recognized giant in the TV industry. Horst, if you would be so kind."

Krueger, a frustrated ham, blew another five minutes before he got down to business. He introduced the five finalists individually, and the photographers dutifully immortalized each one. They were named alphabetically, starting with Julia Burns and ending with Ingrid Willowski. Milly was second, and Nina thought she looked radiant. She seemed to have lost her mournfulness and taken on a hopeful glow, as though she still believed she might by some incredible fluke of fate be the winner. Was this another flash of brilliant acting ability, or had the Scotch Old-fashioned taken over? Whatever the reason, Nina was glad to see Milly looking happy.

Terri Triano was fourth in the introductions, following Marguerite Perch. Nina wondered if Terri would bother to hide the fact that this was all a sham and she was already the winner. But when Terri stood to take her bow and be photographed, she looked like anything but a winner. Her eyes seemed slightly glazed, her face was pasty white, and little beads of perspiration lined her upper lip. And despite her long-sleeved velvet gown, she looked chilly.

I don't care how much wine you've had, Nina thought,

you *can't* be sick. Not now, not here. She glanced over at Robin, who was stuffing a napkin into her mouth. The thought of Robin's reaction if Terri were to throw up in the middle of Helen's banquet was almost too much for Nina. She quickly bit hard on the inside of her mouth and felt the tears spring to her eyes as the instant pain quelled the urge to giggle. Helen, you'd never believe the things I do for you, she thought.

Finally Horst got to the main event.

"And now, introducing the runner-up in *The Turning Seasons* talent hunt. She will receive a ten-thousand-dollar reward, plus an all-expenses-paid holiday in New York City. In addition she will realize a lifelong dream and visit the TTS set, mingle with the *crème de la crème* of the soap opera industry. Ladies and gentlemen, I present Millicent Gowan."

A glowing Millicent rose and graciously accepted an engraved certificate and an empty envelope representing the check that was already tucked into her purse. When asked for some appropriate words, her remarks were brief and gracious: "This has been one of the most exciting and gratifying experiences in my life. I've enjoyed tremendously the opportunity to meet you all, to watch you at work. It has been a thrilling and fun-filled time for me. I will cherish these memories always, and return home filled with fresh hope for my future career. In addition I want to wish the winner all the best of luck, and long happiness as a member of this wonderful and talented TV family."

Again Krueger took the microphone. Again he launched into a wearisome chain of platitudes as he described the winner's background, her acting credits, her unbounded enthusiasm for the glittering challenge lying before her . . . Finally he got to her name.

"And now if I may," he started at last, "it is my distinct pleasure to introduce our winner and star of tomorrow, Miss Terri Triano!"

But instead of the expected burst of applause, there was a gasp from several people as they saw Terri Triano stiffen in her chair and struggle to rise. A pained expression tore at her features, and a dry, strangled noise broke from her mouth. Her hands leaped up, clawed frantically at her throat.

Then she dropped back into her chair and slumped forward, her head hitting the table with a dull thud. Her body twitched once, then no more. Lying with her left cheek on the flower-patterned tablecloth, she was completely still, eyes wide and staring.

For a moment, there wasn't a sound in the room. Even Robin had stopped laughing.

Chapter Four

It seemed as though time had frozen, with everyone in the room locked into the position and attitude each had held when Terri Triano collapsed. Then two women screamed—Nina never discovered who, but it didn't matter—and all hell broke loose as a babble of excited cries and shouts erupted. Pandemonium reigned. The people who were sitting leaped to their feet. The people who were standing pressed toward the head table for a better look. The people nearest the head table began to shove away from the frightening sight. And the press came to life, scrambling for position with cameras held high, shutters popping in all directions.

Within seconds, several cameramen were pushing toward the exit, eager to scoop the competition.

Clinging to the back of her chair for support, Nina felt the need to stop the cameramen before they could get out. She believed instinctively that was what Dino would do if he were there. Damn that duty schedule for keeping him away! "Stop them," she called out to no one in particular, fearing the possibility of vital witnesses and essential evidence somehow being compromised.

"Hold it!" Spence Sprague was standing on a chair, his

43

unamplified voice louder than Horst's had been over the p.a. system.

"QUIET!" he demanded. "No one leaves this room! *Do you understand!* Not until we get a doctor in here, not until the police have been called. "Rick," he called to Rick Busacca, a robust six-footer, "you and Rafe block that door. See that no one, and I mean *no one* gets out." He had chosen the two tallest and sturdiest young men in the room.

By that time Nina, along with Nick Galano and Rob Bryant, had reached Terri Triano. Rob lifted her head from the table and eased her back into her chair, his fingers sweeping along her throat, testing for a pulse. His face ashen, he said, "I don't think a doctor's going to help. There's absolutely no pulse. Nick, help me get her on the floor. I'm going to try CPR just the same."

As he worked—a seeming expert—Nina stood at the edge of the human circle, watching gravely. A wave of déjà vu crashed over her; she felt as if her bones had turned to milk. Please, Terri, she pleaded inwardly, *live!*

How could such a thing be? Only a little while ago she'd been on top of the world. Before dinner she'd seemed fine. But she wasn't fine at all; death had been hanging over her shoulder. Nina remembered the way her complexion had changed from flushed to pale. Had that been an unheeded warning signal? Of what? A heart seizure? An allergic reaction, a backfiring drug, a blockage in the windpipe? Poison? An image of Mortimer Meyer lying dead on his own living-room floor at Leatherwing chilled Nina.

One of the Tavern waiters intervened just then. "The management has a doctor on permanent call. He's located nearby. Shouldn't we call him?"

"By all means," Spence said. He called to Rick Busacca, pointed at the waiter. "Let him out! He's going for a doctor."

At that moment Rob Bryant looked up from his lifesaving chores, a haggard light in his eyes. "Might as well. We'll need a doctor eventually. But this lady's gone. She

44

isn't responding one bit." Still he turned back and recommenced his efforts.

Nina knelt, tugged at Terri's skirt and brought it back down over her knees. Grant her that last dignity anyway, she temporized, wanting to scream with frustration. Why, she wailed inwardly, on the edge of tears, do these things keep happening to people around me?

Now, possessed of a sense of maddening uselessness, she rose and approached Spence, noting that Horst was standing helplessly next to Helen, who sat holding her head and shaking it in stubborn denial of what had just happened. "I'll call the police, she offered. "Something's terribly wrong here. Terri didn't die of natural causes, I know she didn't. I want to call Lieutenant Rossi."

"Yeah, I guess you better," Spence Sprague said. He caught Rick Busacca's eyes and pointed to Nina. Rick nodded.

As Nina moved toward the door, she could almost feel a rising tide of resentment aimed at her. The news people, chafing at the delay in filing their stories, were grumbling. Her own friends were sending jaundiced here-we-go-again looks in her direction. But she had to call Dino. Terri's death had happened within his precinct, and he'd undoubtedly be the chief investigating officer.

Then she realized she was about to make a big mistake. Leaving the scene of a possible crime right after it happened? How stupid could she be? Dino would never forgive her. Send someone else to call him. She had to stay there and be his eyes and ears, keep her part of the bargain they had sealed months earlier, when he'd first enlisted her aid.

Never mind that the bargain applied originally only to the studio, where he couldn't be all the time. He couldn't be here right now, either, and this was where something important could be happening, right under her nose. She had to look hard, listen carefully, and remember everything.

Moments later, Robin was allowed to leave the room with Dino's number scrawled on the piece of paper she clutched, and Nina was busily piling up mental snapshots of anything and everything that might prove important. But what should she look for? Who should she watch?

Helen was still sitting at the head table, apparently numb. Horst was still standing by, patting her gently as though she were a little girl who'd just been told her favorite doll had died.

Rob and Nick were standing near Terri's body, having given up the valiant but hopeless CPR effort.

Spence was over by the press group, explaining for the fourth or fifth time why they couldn't leave the room.

Milly and the other finalists were huddled in a far corner, terror written all over their pretty young faces.

The rest of the crowd had broken down into groups and were gathered around various tables, talking quietly. It could have been a sedate, restrained continuation of the predinner party. Only two things were missing: laughter and the sound of ice cubes.

Which made it a wake.

Oh, she felt so brainless! Nothing looked odd, nobody was acting strangely, nothing seemed to be out of order. Later, when she'd be alone with Dino, what would she have to tell him?

Lieutenant Dino Rossi was the chief investigating officer for a Special Operations Division unit that was sometimes referred to as the "Silk Stocking Squad." Working out of a separate squad room in a midtown-north precinct, the team concentrated on "celebrity" crimes almost exclusively. Any crimes involving theatrical or literary types, business tycoons, politicians, diplomats and visiting firemen fell to them. While at first the establishment of such a unit within the complex chain of command of the NYPD had been deemed some sort of practical joke, now the unit was definitely high profile, a much respected arm of New York City law enforcement; an amazingly successful track record had seen to that.

The man who instantly took charge entering the Pavilion Room a half hour later, who quieted the feisty news-men with a single, baleful glare, stood six feet two. His trim waist and heavily muscled chest and shoulders combined with his demeanor to dare anyone to buck him. And yet, venomous as his stare could be, Rossi seldom raised his voice. There was an inherent toughness about him that sent out the warning, "This is no man to hassle." Rossi was accompanied by his chief assistants, Charley Harper and Bruno Reichert. Rossi addressed the crowd briefly, telling them that Harper and Reichert would take their names and any other statement they wanted to make. He wouldn't detain them any longer than was necessary.

Then Rossi's eyes skimmed the Pavilion Room until they found Nina. A guarded, reassuring smile from her, signal that she was all right, was enough for him. He sent a brief smile of his own and abruptly turned back to the business at hand. "Okay, Charley," he snapped. "What've you got?"

"Death by unknown causes. We got us a mystery, all right. The house doc's already looked at her, and he hasn't got clue one about the cause of death. It could be a heart attack, an embolism, a reaction to something she ate." His tone turned sarcastic. "It could be respiratory. Like she just stopped breathing, you know?"

"Spare me the humor," Rossi shot back. "What about the crime-scene unit?"

"They're on the way. But what they'll find in this mob, I have no idea. I'm keeping everybody back from the table area as best I can. These reporters are a pain in the butt. A hundred questions a minute."

"Get their names first, ask them the pertinents, and clear 'em out. Christ, that's all we need, a bunch of newshawks looking over our shoulder while we work. An autopsy, do you think?"

"Definitely."

"Call the Medical Examiner's office first thing. Have Doc Berger stand by."

These last comments Nina McFall, working her way close to the officers, heard clearly. "Hello, Lieutenant Rossi," she said, hewing to their previously agreed-upon code of formality when together in public. "Good of you to come so quickly."

"Ms. McFall. This seems to be habit forming. We've got to stop meeting like this."

Nina's eyes were bleak. "It isn't funny, Lieutenant. She was a friend, of sorts. We were going to work together. For a long time, I thought. I still can't believe it. I had lunch with her just yesterday, I spoke to her briefly tonight. And now she's gone."

"So," he said quietly, looking searchingly into Nina's eyes, the barely hidden intimacy glittering there, warming and reassuring her, "what do you think? Is it murder?"

She shook her head dazedly. "I don't see how it could be. There are no marks, no signs of foul play whatsoever. There was no way it could have been done without dozens of people seeing something." She sighed deeply. "And yet . . . I know you'll laugh . . . I've got one of my hunches again."

His expression was wary. "Well, I'm not about to knock it. Your hunches have proved out before." He glanced up, caught Bruno Reichert passing by.

"Bruno," he ordered, "get a brief statement from the casual witnesses first, dismiss them quickly. Then concentrate on the people who were at the table with the deceased. Let's clear this place out as fast as possible, give the Crime Scene Unit all the elbow room we can."

"Check, Lieutenant." He ganced at Nina admiringly. "I take it you'll be interviewing Ms. McFall personally." His grin was faintly snide.

"I'm doing that right now, Sergeant." Reichert recognized the warning tone in his boss's voice and quickly went about his business. Dino turned back to Nina.

"Okay, what've you got?"

"Not much. You already know the headlines. I'm just bothered by a lot of little things. You know—loose ends."

"Anything that adds up to a motive?

"No, not a thing."

"You're overlooking something, Nina."

"What's that?"

"Who stands to gain by Triano's death?"

"I have no idea."

"Sure you do. What happens to the prize?" She looked blank. "The role, the part. Who's the understudy or the standby or the runner-up, or whatever you call it?"

Nina was stunned at the thought. "Milly Gowan, I suppose. But that's impossible!"

"Nothing's impossible, Nina. Suppose this Milly was more than a wee bit ticked over losing out. Maybe landing a slot on *The Turning Seasons* was more important to her than most people would suspect. Important enough to kill for, maybe?" He sent Nina a sly look. "There are people like that, people who put their careers above anything else in the world. Maybe your Milly wasn't exactly dying for stardom but didn't mind if somebody else was."

"Dino, I know that girl, and you're on the wrong track. For that matter, you could also say that any of the other also-rans are suspects, out of pure jealously. Or Corinne Demetry. Angela Dolan told me Corinne would have killed to . . . Oh stop! It's just a figure of speech, and you know it."

"Yeah, I know it." But his expression told her he was far from ready to dismiss the thought. "Anyway, I think a talk with Milly Gowan might be very useful."

"Dino, be easy on her. She's had a bad time. She was sure she'd get the part, and it was an awful shock when she didn't. . . ." She realized what she was saying and hurried on. "But that's nonsense. Milly was nowhere near Terri before dinner, and they were at opposite ends of the table. She could no more—"

"Whoa, take it easy, I just want to talk to her—along with a lot more people as well. I'll call you at home as soon as I finish here. Okay?"

"Yes, sure."

Nina watched as Dino strode quickly toward the table where Milly Gowan and the other three girls were sitting. He spoke to them briefly and then took Milly, weeping and plainly terrified, to a separate table. Nina didn't want to watch any more and went toward the cloakroom where she ran into Robin and Rafe, who had just been released.

"I never dreamed that anything like this . . . would happen," Robin said. "Not again. God, I feel like I'm caught in some kind of time warp!"

"You and me both," Nina replied ruefully. "Never in my wildest dreams . . ."

"What do you suppose," Rafe cut in, "this'll do to our shooting schedule? Gelber and Burman will go crazy. And who's going to take Terri's role? I suppose, by rights, it goes over to Milly Gowan."

"Hard to say," Nina said absently. "It would be the logical thing to do. She *was* the runner-up, after all . . ."

Nina's heart did a quick flip-flop and her pulse quickened. Could she be wrong? Could Milly have had something to do with Terri's death? If there had been a slow-acting poison of some sort involved, wouldn't she have had time to administer it, in the hotel room, before they'd headed out for the awards dinner?

Impossible! she scolded herself. A woman like Milly? Never in a million years. And yet—why was she even entertaining such off-the-wall conjectures?

She allowed her gaze to return to Rossi. Already finished with Milly Gowan, he was bending over Terri's body, apparently intent on something he saw on her left arm. When he came up he was frowning, but Nina made no move to rush over and ask him what he'd found. That wouldn't do at all. Rossi was the prime investigator, and she'd defer to that hard-won status.

When he was ready, he'd tell her. But damn it, she'd rather stay with him.

"Want a ride?" Robin said. "If you're allowed to leave, that is. We've already had *our* third-degree. It looks like your guy is going to be pretty much tied up the rest of the evening."

"Thanks," Nina said absently, "I'd appreciate that, since you're heading my way anyhow. . . . No, I don't think Dino will be needing me any more tonight. He's in his element. He's forgotten I exist. Let's get out of here."

Nina sent a last glance back at Rossi. But, dedicated cop to the last, and busy with another interview, he never saw her leave.

As she reached the door, Helen Meyer's voice came across the room. "That does it," she told Rob Bryant, who was struggling with her massive raccoon coat. "I'll never throw another party again as long as I live! Every time I do, someone dies. What did I ever do to deserve such a thing?"

Tell me about it, dearie, Nina thought, her heart feeling like it was cast in lead. And by the way, what did *Terri* ever do to deserve it?

Back in the calm and order of her own luxurious apartment, Nina took a long, hot shower and put on her warmest robe and fuzziest slippers. Outside the winter winds screamed relentlessly around Primrose Towers, clawing at the windows. She drew all the drapes and made a cup of soothing herbal tea, then sat down to think and to wait for Dino's call.

But her thoughts went in circles, leading nowhere. Why? how? and who? chased each other like squirrels in a cage.

It was nearly two hours later when the phone rang.

"Hello?"

"Hey, babe. Did I wake you?"

"No, I've just been sitting here trying to sort it out. What happened after I left?" The question that was really in her mind was "What did Milly Gowan tell you?" but she thought she'd better just wait and let Dino say what he had to say.

"The usual routine. We finished the basic questioning, the photographer took his shots, and now we wait for the ME's report on the cause of death. Could be anything from a heart attack to terminal indigestion. That was a pretty heavy meal."

"Dino, just before I left I noticed you were very interested in something you saw on Terri's arm."

"Yeah—I think your talent-search winner was on something."

"Drugs?"

"I've seen enough track marks to bet a month's pay on it."

"That's horrible! You think she overdosed?"

"Go easy, you're jumping all over the place. Just because you see a needle hole in somebody's arm, you can't decide they overdosed. That'd be like figuring everybody who has a garage owns a car."

She chuckled at his analogy. "I take your point. A needle hole proves nothing beyond the fact that something shaped like a needle made something shaped like a hole. Anything else is an assumption."

"You got it, babe."

"Including the conclusion that Terri was on drugs, of course."

"Hey, not bad. You studying to be a trial lawyer?"

"Okay, go on. What else?"

"Something kind of interesting came up in my talk with your friend Milly. Did you know she was rooming with Terri at the Biltmore?"

Oh God, had she forgotten to tell him that? "Don't tell me I left that out! Did I?"

"That's okay, it was a crazy night. But it might be important, especially if the two women were together just before the party. Getting ready in their room, and all that?"

"Yes, meaning what?"

"Meaning I'm just trying to get the total picture, that's all. Milly Gowan was so broken up I couldn't get much out of her. I'm going to drop in on her tomorrow morning and see what else I can find out. She's got to know more than she said."

"She's a nice girl, Dino. She's very ambitious, but she's not hard, the way Terri seemed to be."

"Anything more you can tell me about what went on tonight? If I know you, you had your bright eyes open every second."

Nina related her observations before dinner, when she'd

seen Terri talking to Rob Bryant, and of how she'd seemed anxious even then. She described the obvious distress that overtook Terri as dinner ended, the paleness of her features, the fact that she'd barely touched her food. So much for terminal indigestion.

"I credited it to the drinking," she elaborated. "Maybe she'd had too much. Some people get to an open bar, and they just lose perspective. Terri could have been like that, I suppose."

Rossi was quick to leap on the comment. "Why do you say that? Sounds a bit harsh to me."

"As I told you, we had lunch yesterday. I got to know her a bit, and I couldn't help getting some antsy feelings about her."

"What kind of feelings?"

"Like there was something she was keeping from me. I felt she was guarding some sort of secret, that she was one tough lady, and that's she'd been through the mill. Pushy is the word."

"Somebody said she was in Hollywood for a long time. They play hardball out there, don't they? Can't hardly blame her for being on the tough side."

"I can't put my finger on it, Dino, but there was something else. I felt she was deliberately steering the conversation away from something in her past, something she didn't want to talk about." She let out a frustrated sigh. "It bothered me then, but I dismissed it. Now I'm not so sure."

"Don't try to force it. Just put it on the back burner for a while. It'll come."

"I suppose . . ."

"Honey, you sound tired. If you haven't got anything else to tell me, why don't you turn in? I'll drop by to see you for a while tomorrow afternoon, okay?"

Just "drop by for a while"? She was ready for more than that.

"Okay. Good night, love."

But instead of uttering the tender parting words she expected, he abruptly tore into Jagedorn for some deviation from procedure, and the line went dead. Well, he'd had a hard night, too.

As she went around the apartment dousing lights, she kept thinking there was still something else about the evening she'd neglected to share with Dino.

Just before drifting off, she remembered what it was. The whole strange conversation with Rob Bryant before dinner. Well, it would keep until tomorrow. Meanwhile, there was a murder to solve. Never mind that the ME's report wasn't in yet. It was murder all right, she was certain of that.

Nina's dreams that night were an odd blend of audition scenes, sea scallops, Scotch Old fashioneds, videocameras, needle marks, empty garages, and Van Dyke beards on handsome faces.

Chapter Five

Dino Rossi arrived at the Biltmore Hotel at eleven o'clock the next morning, showered, shaved, and grumpy from very little sleep. He'd telephoned Milly Gowan an hour earlier to arrange the appointment; her voice over the phone sounded thoroughly exhausted, and her face, when she opened the door of the suite she'd been sharing with Terri Triano, matched the voice. Yet there was an attitude of tightly suppressed exuberance that Dino found curious. And she was fully dressed as though planning to go out. He'd expected to find her in a robe.

"Hello, Lieutenant Rossi. Please come in."

"Good morning, Miss Gowan. Apologies for bothering you so early."

"That's all right, your call didn't wake me."

"Bad night's sleep?"

"I don't think I slept more than ten minutes at a stretch without waking up. Have you found out anything?"

"Not yet. But we will."

"I hope so. This is so horrible. . . ." For a moment Dino thought she was going to start crying, but she got control of herself. "What can I do to help?"

What a good question, Dino thought, because he was certain that she *could* be of help. He just didn't know exactly how. And until he had the ME's report in hand, he didn't want to waste his shots.

"I need to look through Ms. Triano's things." She looked startled. "It seems coldhearted, I know, but it's necessary. You understand."

That little phrase usually helped get over the bumpy spots when people seemed hesitant about cooperating. "You understand" was somehow appealing; people rarely liked to admit they didn't understand something.

"Of course. I started to gather her things together, but then I thought better of it." She indicated a partly-packed suitcase and two of the four drawers in a bureau. "Actually, I began to get squeamish about touching Terri's clothing. Anyway, I realized I wouldn't have known what to do with it."

Dino looked at the suitcase, standing open on one of the beds. "Did you pack it?"

"Some of it, from the top drawer. Some of it was still in the suitcase. Terri didn't bother to unpack completely."

"Sounds as though she didn't expect to stay very long."

"No, it wasn't that. Terri just wasn't very organized."

Dino began to look through Terri Triano's belongings, and soon realized he was probably wasting his time. There was nothing unusual, just what a young woman would bring on a trip to New York. The suitcase contained mainly underwear, pantyhose, and blouses. The rest of Terri's clothing was still in the bureau and the closet, and her toiletries were still in the bathroom and scattered over the top of the bureau. Milly's, he noted, were grouped neatly on a small side table.

What he found was of no significance; as he searched, his interest became more and more sharply focused on what he failed to find.

"As far as you know, Miss Gowan, has anyone else been in this room since you left for the awards dinner last evening?"

"No—only room service when I ordered breakfast this morning."

"What time was that?"

"About eight-thirty. After eight, I gave up trying to sleep."

"And then did someone come back to remove the cart?"

"No. I wheeled it into the hall. Was that all right?"

"I beg your pardon?"

"I mean, is that what people do when they're finished eating? I don't usually stay in hotels, particularly hotels like this."

The innocence of her question was irresistible, and he grinned broadly. "That's exactly what people do."

"Good. I hate to make a fool of myself."

"Don't we all. Miss Gowan, what are your plans now?"

The trace of exuberance Dino had noted earlier suddenly flowered and the color rushed into Milly's face.

"I can't help being excited! I know it's terrible, it's not the way I wanted it to happen, but I'm going to play the role on *The Turning Seasons* after all!"

"When did this happen?"

"Right after you called. Mr. Krueger phoned and said he'd been in conference with Mrs. Meyer, and since the decision was such a close one anyway, they'd agreed to take a chance on me!"

"Congratulations. I'm sure you'll be wonderful."

"They're drawing up a contract now. I'm going to meet them later." Suddenly she seemed conscience stricken, and the excitement faded away as rapidly as it had erupted. "Oh, how can I feel this way? If this hadn't happened to Terri, I'd just be the runner-up, heading back to oblivion."

"Well, don't think of it that way. You're just a by-stander."

"But it's so unfair," she said mournfully, collapsing into a chair by the window. "When I arrived here I was so frightened and nervous, and she took such good care of me."

"How do you mean?"

"Oh, she realized I was terrified and she reassured me, she really backed me up. She was so kind to me. She knew that I was just one of the competition and she could have ignored me, let me worry myself to death. But she

57

encouraged me to have confidence in myself. In just a few days I felt we became really good friends. We promised each other that no matter what happened, we'd support each other. But then . . ."

She paused, not sure of her words. "Then what?" Dino prompted quietly. Just a small nudge was sufficient; it was clear she wanted to talk.

"Then she changed. Just during the last two days before—before Saturday. I overheard her arguing with someone on the phone, and she'd disappear for an hour or so at odd times. That was all right, except that she never told me where she was going or where she'd been."

Dino waited. That was it? "Did you hear anything specific? Any names? Places?"

"No, nothing like that. She seemed to be very careful about me overhearing. I didn't hear any words at all, just this angry *tone*."

"I see. Miss Gowan, do you know where Terri Triano's home is? Or where her family lives?"

"No, she never told me anything about her background. All I know is she lived somewhere on the West Coast."

"She told you nothing else? Isn't that strange, for someone who was becoming such a good friend?"

"I guess so, but it didn't strike me that way at the time. I had so much to think about, and I was just so glad to have someone to talk to. I suppose she did most of the listening," Milly concluded weakly.

"Anything else? Did she mention any boyfriends?"

"Only that she was once married, but that it didn't work out." Milly stood up and seemed to gather her courage. "Lieutenant, I have to meet Mrs. Meyer and Mr. Krueger soon. If I can think of anything else, should I call you?"

He'd been dismissed, hesitantly but definitely. On the way out of the hotel, reviewing what she'd said and her contradictory feelings about Terri Triano's death, he remembered something very important: he was dealing with a very good actress.

* * *

Staring down on New York City from her nest on the thirty-sixth floor, taking in the winter smog, the wet streets, the soot-stained snow, Nina was not reassured. It was 2:30 P.M., and, warm and snug inside her superplush Riverside Drive apartment, she awaited the arrival of Dino Rossi.

She hadn't slept well. The tape of Terri Triano lurching up from her chair, her hands at her throat, then slumping over the table had played in her brain, looping nonstop all night long. In addition to this, surrendering to uncharacteristic pettiness, Nina resented the fact that she'd been locked out of last night's investigation.

She was being childish, she knew. Dino *was* a police detective, for God's sake. How would it look to his fellow officers if he conferred with his girl friend on every single detail, as though he didn't trust himself to make a move without her? There was protocol, after all, and appearances must be maintained. It was all part of her general malaise, she grudgingly conceded. Another gloomy Sunday. She'd get over it.

And where other people—Robin Tally, for instance— could look forward to a lazy, directionless day with their significant other, what did she have? Again the specter of murder hung over her—over her *and* Rossi. Again there was an incessant welter of speculation, of nonstop doubts. What-ifs and how-comes and whys and who-did-its. Until it seemed her brain had been thrown into a rolling drum, a drum that never stopped.

Was this any kind of life for a basically provincial, peaceful, and sensitive person like Nina? What should happen was that she and Dino should spend the day together, with no demands, no deadlines of any kind allowed to intrude. They could have lunch, either in her apartment or at a cozy restaurant. Then they could simply talk, have a few drinks, or listen to music, kiss and cuddle to their hearts' content. They could let the mood take them wherever it chose. And if certain erotic volcanoes just happened to erupt . . .

Afterward they would regroup, return to square one. She and Dino could run her lines for the next day, play

Trivial Pursuit, watch an old movie on the tube. Then it would be time to catch dinner at some low-key, neighborhood haunt, maybe with Dino's twelve-year-old son, Peter. And finally—back to the apartment for afterglow, Scotch for Dino, Sambuca for her. Should it just happen that lightning struck yet another time, so be it. They'd still have an early evening. She'd be in bed by ten, ready to rise at six in order to meet her eight o'clock call at the TTS studios Monday morning.

But that wasn't how it went at all—not very often, at any rate. There was always a case. A case that invariably broke on a weekend—and forced cancellation of any plans they'd made. Why did criminals favor Saturdays and Sundays so heartily? They never *had* gotten to the north country for the autumn colors last October.

And even if Dino did manage to get away, there was always a lurking sense of disaster, the feeling that he could receive a call at any moment. Otherwise he was often moody and preoccupied, his mind not on the moment—or her—at all.

Nina struggled to break out of her demoralizing funk. Drop it! A bad mood, that's all it is. Maybe you're coming down with something. Dino's a good man, a careful, considerate and exciting lover. Stop trying to read more into your upset than is really there. You are getting to be some kind of a drag.

At that moment her intercom phone rang. "A Mr. Rossi is here to see you," Willie, the doorman, announced from the lobby.

"Send him up, please." She ran to the bathroom, fussed with her hair a last time, rechecked her makeup. A fleeting look at herself in the full-length mirror assured her that the purple velour lounging suit set off her rust-gold hair to perfection, and the sexy, mid-heel pumps were appropriate for an afternoon visitor. Then she heard the buzzer, and ran to the door.

As they kissed and clung to each other, Dino holding her painfully close, Nina felt her resentment and tension begin to fade. Just maybe, she thought, a quick heat making itself known in her body, once last night's business was out of the way—It was a whole week since they'd been together. There was definitely time to be made up for. Lord knows, she mused, working her lips hungrily against his, I am a growing girl, possessed of healthy female needs!

"Well," he said as he pulled away, looking down at her admiringly, "that's what I call a *warm* welcome!"

Nina produced a tissue and dabbed at the lipstick on his face. "More than you deserve," she said with a snippier tone than she'd intended.

"Oh? Is that right? Am I in the doghouse for something?"

"You are. And I think you know why."

His brow furrowed. "Give me a clue."

"You could have asked me to stick around last night, just on the off-chance that I might have been of some help."

"Oh, I see. Feeling left out, are you?"

She realized instantly how foolish it sounded. "No that's not it at all, it's just that—"

"That's it exactly. I know you, you insecure little gorgeous, bird-brained, sharp-witted bundle of contradictions." He certainly did know her. "Now come here and calm down. We both know you're not being left out of anything. Am I always at the studio when something is popping? No. I rely on you. You're my eyes and ears, remember? So when you can't be on the scene, for whatever reason, maybe you could return the favor and rely on me. Partner."

As he spoke, his arms around her grew tighter and tighter and his tone sank lower and lower. Then he moved her down onto the couch. "Darling," he murmured huskily, "I've missed you this week. God, but you feel good! So warm, so soft! This velvet thing." His fingers slid hungrily up and down her trim, taut back. "So smooth."

She moved under his weight. "If you think *that's* smooth . . ."

"You are shameless."

"Yeah," she agreed, "I guess I am. What kind of punishment did you have in mind?"

"You're so adorable. God, how I love you! How I ever got along without you . . ."

"You suffered a deprived youth. Admit it."

Now his lips slid up her elegant, fragrant throat, nestled behind her right ear. "Yes, I did, love," he said, his voice husky. "I was only half alive before you came into my life. I realize it more every time I'm with you."

Nina's breath caught. "Dino, what a lovely thing to say. Oh, what that does to me, when you talk like that!"

He struggled up from the couch, "No more. Not right now, anyway. A guy's got just so much will power."

Nina assessed his dark, rugged handsomeness, and tried to assess his mood. "What makes you think you need willpower?"

"I've got to check in at the precinct in an hour or so. The beat goes on."

"Dino, no! I thought we had the afternoon. I had the cutest little place picked out for dinner. . . ." Resentment flooded back and shot down her playful, happy mood. "Oh, damn, damn, and double damn!" She went to the window for moment, then turned abruptly back to him. "All right, this is a workday—let's work. What did you find out at the Biltmore this morning?"

He was somewhat taken aback by the sharp shift in her attitude, but welcomed the chance to keep his mind focused on the case.

"Not a whole hell of a lot. Your friend Milly had a lousy night, too. Seems really sorry about what happened. Sounds as though she and Terri were getting to be good friends." Dino related the gist of his conversation with Milly. Nina listened silently until he described the mutual support pledge and Terri's behavior during the last two days of her life.

"Wait—that's odd. Why didn't Milly tell me about that last night, before dinner? It was the ideal moment—she was letting it all hang out . . . Well, maybe there wasn't enough time."

"No, there's always time when you want to say something. Maybe she didn't tell you about it because she hadn't invented it yet." Nina greeted this idea with surprise and doubt. "Maybe she made it up when she needed it, for sympathy."

Nina recalled Milly's story of her preparation for the "spontaneous" false start at the audition and related it for Dino's benefit. When she finished, he said, "One way or another, she was really anxious to get that role. And now she's got it. Milly told me Krueger called earlier. She's going to play the part on your show."

"That's no surprise at this point. Wait'll Corinne hears. She'll have a fit. So you didn't really learn very much?"

"Oh, yes I did. I looked through Terri's things."

She rushed across the room and slid onto the sofa beside him, their personal situation forgotten for the moment.

"What did you find?"

"It's what I *didn't* find that interests me. No address book, no airline tickets, no stubs, no receipts from department stores, no credit cards. Nothing more personal than a lipstick."

"How can that be? People don't travel that way. Maybe she had those things with her last night, in her purse."

"No, forget it. So far there isn't a single indication of Terri Triano's background. We don't even know who to notify that she's dead. Before leaving the hotel I checked on her phone calls—strictly local. It's like a smokescreen, like she rolled off the assembly line the day she hit New York for the final auditions. You know what I think? I think I wasn't the first person to go through Terri Triano's belongings. I think somebody got there before me and made a clean sweep of anything we could use."

"But who?"

He laughed. "You ask the big ones, don't you? So far, it looks as though our two biggest leads are negative. First, there's nothing to tell us about Terri's background.

"And second?"

"Second, the ME hasn't been able to find the cause of death."

She sat up straight, glaring at him, then snatched a sofa pillow and beat him across the chest with it.

"You heard from the ME and you didn't tell me?"

"Calm down, Sherlock. One thing at a time." He paused for effect. "It looks like Terri Triano was definitely on drugs. This is more than an assumption now. This is according to the ME. And there weren't just a few needle holes—she had track marks all over both arms. It looked like she liked her heroin pretty well."

Nina's eyes narrowed. "Well, that explains something."

"What are you talking about?"

"When I had lunch with her the other day, I told you, she was acting funny. All jumpy and stuff. She couldn't keep her mind on things for two minutes at a time. Maybe she was hurting for a fix but holding off because of winning the part, or being with me." Nina smiled sadly. "How do people let themselves get so messed up?" She switched tack, became all business again. "So are you saying that she died of an overdose? That it wasn't murder?"

"Nina, you make such giant leaps. I never once, last night, admitted that it *was* murder. No, it wasn't an overdose. In fact, Doc Boyer found only traces of heroin residue in her system."

"I don't understand. One minute you say she had a habit, and the next you say you found little or no heroin in her system. How did she die? What *did* the ME find?"

"It gets crazy. And while we're both willing to concede that there's the faintest possibility that maybe somebody . . . Terri herself even . . . might have injected something deadly into her veins, we still aren't buying any murder angle. Even if we were . . . and here's the puzzler . . . Boyer found absolutely nothing of an even remotely toxic nature in the body."

Nina sent Dino a mystified look. "Then you're saying she had a stroke, something like that? She *did* die of natural causes?"

"That's all we can assume at this time. Even though the autopsy indicates a blood clot in the brain which should, by rights be considered an embolism, Boyer still isn't buying it. the woman was young, her organs showed no marked deterioration, there was no reason for her to go out just like that. If it had been drugs . . ." He broke off impatiently. "Hell, no! He found no strong traces of drugs. I tell you, it's got us both going around in circles."

Disappointment registered in Nina's eyes. "I can see how frustrating that could be."

"Boyer's giving it another hard look right now. That's why I'm going over shortly. He's got some other tests he wants to try. And if they don't pan out . . ."

"Then it means that someone's just got away with murder."

"Look, we have to face the possibility that there's nothing wrong here. What we have is a body. We don't have a cause of death, a tangible weapon, or a solid motive. All we *do* have is a lot of suppositions. So suppose this: suppose everything we know is exactly the way it seems at face value. Suppose Terri Triano died of unusual but natural causes."

"Do you really believe that?"

"I have to go on facts! You can't spend your whole life thinking everything's murder just because you've got a hunch about something."

"It's more than a hunch. Terri was acting so funny on Friday at lunch; there was something unnerving about her attitude. And now . . ."

He sighed wearily. "All right, let's run through it again. Tell me exactly what you saw last night. You said you thought Terri wasn't looking well just before the dinner."

"She was standing near the head table, talking to Rob Bryant. And I got the feeling that they were closer, personally speaking that is, than they'd like the world to know. It was then that I noticed that her face looked kind of funny, there was a glazed look in her eyes."

"And you attributed it to the booze."

"Yes, that was my first thought. But I don't know if that's so. She had some wine at lunch the other day, and it didn't bother her in the least. Then I got the impression that she'd become angry with Rob."

"And later, at the table? How did she look then?"

"She was kind of quiet, staring straight ahead, even when Nick Galano was talking to her. Then, when it was time to announce the prize winner . . . she got sort of pale. She was slightly flushed before, but now she had this pallor—you know, the look you get just before you throw up."

"That sure sounds like she was reacting to something internally to me. Food allergy, too much to drink, whatever. Even a poison of some sort . . ."

"Then when she grabbed her throat—it all happened so fast—I remember thinking that she must be choking. But she never coughed or turned blue or anything. It was all over by the time I fought my way through those newspaper people. Vultures! They were hanging over everybody, taking picture after picture . . . instead of trying to help her."

Rossi turned thoughtful. "What, exactly," he asked finally, "does anyone on the set know about this Triano gal?"

"Not a lot. As I said, she gave me a feeling of being secretive, especially about her past. She was married, she got divorced. Or maybe just separated. Even there, she seemed deliberately vague."

"And you didn't press her?"

"Really, Dino. If people are reluctant to talk . . . Even I'm not that pushy with someone I've just met. I let it go."

"This Rob Bryant fellow. He's the one who shaded Bellamy Carter out of the picture? He's thick with Helen Meyer?"

Nina laughed. "Thick? That's the understatement of the year!"

"Is it obvious to everyone?"

"Oh, yes. She had a necklock on him that night you wouldn't believe."

"So what was he doing with Ms. Triano? Do you honestly believe they were involved, too?"

"I got a creepy-crawly feeling when I saw them together. I thought, Oh, no, not Terri, too! Not this fast. She'd only been in New York four days." Nina winced. "But then, Rob Bryant is that kind of a guy. Women find him very attractive. I gather."

A dark look, verging on fury, crossed Rossi's face. "Has he ever made any moves on you?"

That old-world possessiveness, Nina recognized, feeling a small thrill run through her. He cares that much. I *am* his woman! She related her encounter with Rob Bryant, toning down the steamier aspects. "But of course. What am I, chopped liver? He pitched me at the awards dinner, in fact."

Rossi's eyes took on a fanatic glitter. "I'll kill the bastard! If he so much as . . . You keep away from that creep, hear? You tell me the next time he bothers you. I'll break every bone in his head!"

Nina sent Dino a sidelong look. "Honey, I've never seen you like this. I'm beginning to think you really *do* care."

He stared through her. "What did you tell him?"

"I told him to peddle his papers elsewhere, that I was spoken for. But in a nice way, of course. After all, he *is* a boss of sorts. He could make things unpleasant for me on the set if he chose."

Dino stared through her for a moment. "If he ever creates problems for you, just let me know." He spoke quietly, but his tone was chilling. "You'll only have to tell me once."

Nina was genuinely awed by his controlled rage. "I'll tell you. I promise."

He paused. "Is it possible that this bastard would have any reason to kill Terri Triano?"

"Hardly. They just met this week. Even if he managed to coax her into bed that fast, she couldn't have been *that* bad."

Rossi's sour mood deepened. "I don't like it when you talk like that, Nina," he said sullenly. "You make it . . . passion . . . seem like something cheap and sordid. Like it really doesn't count for anything."

Nina had sense enough to pull in her horns. Time to switch channels. "It counts for a lot, especially when it's

67

between the right two people." She came close, snuggled her face into his throat. "You know I'd never give another man so much as a second look." She giggled. "Why should I? When I have a grumpy old teddy bear like you to keep me warm?"

Rossi refused to be jollied. He lapsed into a brooding silence, mulling private thoughts, remembering his former wife, a woman who wasn't above welcoming attention from a man other than her husband. Furthermore, he pondered the depths of his feelings for this redheaded charmer. He *was* blaming the wrong person.

"Sorry, honey," he murmured. "I didn't mean it to sound like I was accusing you of anything. It's just that guys like that make me see red. It's like they've got to sample every woman on earth. And some women are just dumb enough to go along with it."

Nina nuzzled again. "Present company excepted?"

"Present company excepted." Abruptly he became restive, glanced at his watch. "I've gotta be going. Boyer'll be blowing a gasket."

Nina was hard put to hide her disappointment. "I'm sorry your visit was so short." Her eyes turned mischievous. "I had such *interesting* plans for the afternoon." She played with his ears. "Perhaps another time."

"Yeah. Just perhaps."

He rose, and shrugged into his topcoat, pulling the Gucci scarf Nina had given him for Christmas snug about his neck. "We'll be at the studio tomorrow morning, asking questions. You may as well know I intend to bear down on Millicent Gowan. And I want the truth, not a performance."

"I still think you're offbase with that one. Milly couldn't kill anyone. I just know it. It simply isn't in her nature to do such a thing."

"It's a moot point. As things stand now, it'll be routine, to say the least. And if Boyer closes us down this afternoon, I'm gone." He came close to Nina, leaned for a good-bye kiss.

"You could come back afterward, darling," she said

softly, momentarily quelling her antagonism. "We could eat in, maybe, have some time to ourselves . . ."

"I'd love it, Nina, you know that. But I just can't. I still have all those interview sheets to go through tonight if I'm going to be on top of things tomorrow." His face moved close again. "Take a raincheck?"

The kiss was perfunctory, to say the least. Just barely civil. And Rossi sensed it. "If I hear anything, I'll call you," he said distantly. "Take care."

Again Nina was alone in her apartment. Angry, bitter, and more than a little bit frustrated. Hadn't he realized how much she needed him this afternoon? Of all times for him to play Mr. Big New York City Detective!

What now? she asked herself. Glancing at her telephone, she had a fleeting thought of Rob Bryant. *He'd* come running if I called him. He'd drop everything, Helen Meyer included, to spend the afternoon—or longer—with me. Transient sex, was that what Dino said?

There was a lot of that going around.

Nina smiled faintly, but down deep she didn't find her cynical attempt at humor the least bit funny.

How much of Dino's sudden jealousy was justified? She wasn't sure. After all, Rob was extremely attractive and highly intelligent to boot. He and Nina spoke the same language, moved in the same circles.

Was Dino laying it on a bit thick, macho-man style, or did he sense a real threat?

And if he did—was he correct?

Chapter Six

The 8:00 A.M. announcement on Monday by Horst Krueger that Millicent Gowan would replace their recently departed castmate was received with scarcely a murmur by the TTS cast. Gathered in main rehearsal for group lines, they pasted quick smiles on their faces, and shammed "welcome to the family" greetings which none under the grim circumstances sincerely felt. There was a small spattering of applause, and a few of those closest to Milly leaned over to congratulate her.

"I know," Horst went on, "that you all join me in extending our deepest regrets to Terri Triano's family and friends."

"Whoever and wherever they may be," Nina murmured to herself.

"I request that you all give Milly every possible consideration," Horst continued, "that you pitch in and help her during what must be a most difficult transition period for her. And for us as well. Remember, we're professionals. When we experience traumatic events like this, we are resilient and flexible. We bounce back, made even stronger by adversities. We . . ."

He might as well have saved his breath. The cast was little better than shellshocked. They'd barely recovered from the murder of May Minton. Adversity, yes. But one adversity after another? Was *The Turning Seasons* jinxed, a lightning rod for disaster?

After Horst dismissed the group they moved about like zombies. Though there had been no official report on the cause of Terri's death, the majority of the cast and crew were conditioned to expect the worst. Dark, suspicious glances were exchanged; whispered speculations were rife.

It was immediately clear that Milly was being given wide berth. Those absolutely unable to avoid her exchanged a few stiff words and quickly remembered an errand elsewhere. They were, of course, neither blaming, nor accusing her of anything. And yet who, if not Millicent Gowan, had prospered because of this latest disaster?

Nina McFall, working closely with Milly Gowan, quickly saw what was happening and strove twice as hard to fill the vacuum the others were creating. When not deep in their scenes, she kept Milly talking, straining for lightness and wit, anything to keep her mind off Terri Triano's death and the cast's behavior.

At about 9:15, glancing through the open door of the rehearsal hall, she saw Dino arriving with Charley Harper in tow. He gave Nina a quick glance as he passed, in observance of the public fiction that they were no more than acquaintances. But she knew him too well not to recognize even the traces of a cautious smile as he went by, had there been any. Okay, it's strictly business, she thought, wondering if in the future they might arrange a little secret signal for such times—perhaps a smoothing of the left eyebrow to mean "Hello darling, I love you"? Or maybe a tug on the right earlobe, signifying, "Sorry I can't speak to you at the moment, sweetheart, but I'm longing for your loins." No, she doubted if Dino would go for such an arrangement. Actually, it would be more Rob's style. . . .

Not many minutes after Dino disappeared into Horst Krueger's office, Myrna came out to summon Milly. Would she please step in for a moment with Lieutenant Rossi? Immediately, all the self-confidence that Nina had worked to instill in Milly vanished. Visibly trembling, the girl went into Horst's office as the producer and his secretary withdrew, obviously irritated by this interruption in the day's work.

Nick Galano, who'd been working with Nina and Milly, was also annoyed. He flung down his script, called a break, and stamped off to complain to Horst. Great, Nina thought. Now I'll have a teary-eyed scene partner and a grouchy director the rest of the morning. And we don't need a break, we need to concentrate on this scene. Might as well work on my lines in the interim.

Taking a chair into a far corner, Nina began again at the top of the scene in which the scheming Audrey Lincoln would be introduced to the plot. But no one, least of all Melanie Prescott, as yet had any reason to suspect young Ms. Lincoln of ulterior motives. Even though Melanie Prescott eventually used everyone who crossed her path, first she had to get on their good side. So keep it light, Melanie, keep it light. . . .

"Hello, Nina."

She looked up, startled to hear the voice so close. She'd thought there was no one nearby.

"Oh, Rob. Hi."

"On a break?"

"Unfortunately. Di—Lieutenant Rossi is questioning Milly Gowan, and Nick is off on a sulk."

"Which gives me the lucky chance to talk to you alone."

She knew that should make her feel uncomfortable—and she also knew it didn't, not in the least.

"Have you heard anything new about Terri?" he continued.

"Not a thing," she lied smoothly.

"Horrible mess, isn't it?"

"Unbelievable."

"Well, I don't suppose there's anything we can do. We'll just have to watch and wait."

"Yes, that's right. I hope you didn't get into hot water Saturday."

He chuckled, showing a slight dimple. "Not to worry.

73

Helen was somewhat fuzzed by the wine. She apologized later."

"Helen Meyer *apologized?* You should have had the tape recorders going!" He smiled, keeping his eyes locked on hers. "Well, maybe we were all a bit fuzzed."

"I wasn't. I know exactly what I said to you, and I meant every word of it. According to the schedule Spence has worked up, I'm going to be working more and more on your scenes. We really need to get to know each other better."

How could any one man have so damned much charm? "For professional reasons?" Nina asked casually.

"Yes. To start with, at least. Is there anything wrong with that?" She couldn't resist a glance toward Horst's office, where she knew Dino was still questioning Milly. "You're not, as they say in drawing room comedies, 'attached,' are you?"

Terrific, he was putting her on the spot. "Well, yes and no. At least, not officially," she said lamely.

"Good. I think we should have lunch and talk about the character of Melanie Prescott. *Officially.* You know, you have a great advantage over me, having played Melanie for so many years. If I were to go into the vault and rerun all those tapes, it would take me months."

"Why do you feel you need to do that?"

"To catch up on the plot. It's pretty complicated to a new-comer. I really ought to know more than just the bare bones of it."

"You mean you haven't been watching *The Turning Seasons* every day for the last ten years?" Nina affected high dudgeon.

"Guilty. Just don't tell the boss," Rob whispered.

They broke into laughter at the thought.

"Okay, your secret's safe with me. And relax, I can fill you in on the plot in no time at all."

"I'd be very grateful. When's a good time? How about today?"

Smooth, smooth, smooth, she realized. Having failed to score with the direct approach, now he's using Melanie Prescott to get it done! Well, it was damned flattering to have someone work so hard to get her attention, especially since Dino was pretending she didn't exist.

"No, today I'm busy. Maybe the day after tomorrow. I'll check my . . . calendar." She'd been about to say date book, but it sounded wrong.

"I'm sure it's open. And if it's not, I'll open it," he said in a lower tone of voice than was strictly necessary. And then his mood abruptly changed as he looked toward the far end of the rehearsal hall. "Uh-oh . . ."

Nina turned and saw that Helen had just come in and was engaged in intense conversation with Nick. Obviously she wanted to know why rehearsals weren't in progress. Nick's answer clearly aggravated her; even from a distance they could read her body language very clearly.

"I think we'd better do a quick fade in opposite directions," Nina said quietly, still looking at the gesticulating Helen, whose voice was beginning to carry clear across the long room.

But when she looked up for corroboration, she found she was already alone. Nina wasn't the only one unwilling to cross paths, words, swords, anything else with the testy Helen Meyer.

When rehearsals resumed shortly thereafter, Nina found the scrambled schedule gave her an unexpected free half hour, so headed for her dressing room, planning to shut the door and hunker down with her lines. But the fates seemed determined to keep her from her script that day. Passing Milly's dressing room, she heard the unmistakable sounds of stifled sobbing.

Keep going, pass it by, she told herself. Don't get involved again.

So, of course, she knocked on the door and went in.

As Nina expected, Milly was a crumpled mess, slumped over her makeup table with tears flowing down her face, eyes red, nose runny. How could anyone expect her to create the character of a conniving little bitch when she'd just been reduced to blubbering jelly? What had Dino said to her to get such a reaction?

Quickly shutting the door, she took Milly into her arms, crooning, "There, there now, honey. It's not that bad. It's going to be all right. What happened? What's wrong?"

"That police officer," Milly blubbered, burying her face in Nina's shoulder. "He called me into Mr. Krueger's office, he interviewed me, asked all those awful questions. Lieutenant Rossi . . ."

Anger blazed in Nina's eyes. What had that bull-headed man done now? "What about him? What did he do? You can tell me, hon."

"He's acting as if he thinks that Terri was murdered. He thinks . . ." She broke into fresh sobbings.

"What? Tell me. What does he think?" Yes, Nina thought, exactly what? Did this mean that the ME had come up with something solid?

"He thinks . . . he implied . . . that I had something to do with it. I thought she died of a heart attack or something like that. I never *dreamed* . . ."

Dino, you clod, Nina seethed. And after I told you to take it easy on her. "Now, now, Milly, calm down. I'm sure he didn't say anything like that. He's too much of a professional to out and out accuse someone . . ."

"Maybe he didn't exactly *accuse* me, but his meaning was clear enough." Milly pulled away and plucked a handful of tissues from a dispenser on her dresser. "I'm not that green that I don't recognize when I'm under suspicion. Murder? I can't believe it. Who'd want to murder a wonderful girl like Terri?"

"Tell me exactly what he said. I'm sure you must have misunderstood. All this has been a dreadful strain on you."

Line by line, as completely as Milly could recall it, she recounted the interview. Rossi had opened with the usual casual questions—name, date of birth, birthplace, what her parents did, how she got interested in show business. Loosening-up stuff, Nina realized, to soothe the subject, win her trust. Then he'd zeroed in on her feelings about Terri, asked how they'd gotten along in their shared

76

quarters, about possible competitive vibes existing between them. He'd recreated an hour-by-hour accounting of Saturday. What time they got up, what they did first. And next? And next? Did Terri have any visitors? Was she seeing anybody in New York? Had she received any phone calls? The questions had come faster and faster and Milly had become more and more confused.

"How could I remember all that? Sure there were calls. I already told him that. How could I tell where she went nights or even during the day? I was busy with my own things. I only remember Friday night, and she was home before eleven that time."

"Did you tell Lieutenant Rossi that?"

"Of course." Milly's eyes were an open book. "I told him everything I could. But that wasn't enough. He kept coming back to Terri and me competing for the part. He asked if I was angry when I learned I'd lost out. Was I mad enough to do anything about it? Did I even *consider* doing something about it? Did I want to get even?" She verged on fresh sobs. "He kept coming back to that, over and over, like he was deliberately trying to mix me up."

Which he was, Nina conceded silently. That was standard interview procedure. Rossi probably hadn't meant to be overly harsh; it was only Milly's naivete that made it seem so. To coax Milly from her paranoia, to calm her so she could get through the upcoming rehearsal, she began to tease in a breathless voice. "And did he force you to confess everything? Tell him all the gory details of how you killed Terri?"

"Nina! That's not funny!"

"I'm just kidding, darling. Come on now. Dry those tears. Let it go for now. Shrug this police nonsense off for now. Who cares what Rossi thinks? He was only doing his job. I'll bet he lays that same line on everybody he talks to, even Helen Meyer. Come on, now, fix your face. Rick will be calling us soon, and it'll be final tape before we know it."

But the reminder that there was a scene to be worked on only brought forth a flesh flood of tears. "I can't do it," Milly wailed. "How can I get through all these lines now?"

Nina seized the opening and ran with it.

"If you're having trouble with a tricky set of lines," she advised, "do what I do—stay cool. Get a general idea of what the scene's all about, and mentally run some words of your own that will convey the same basic meaning so that if you go blank, you can improvise. The writers go berserk, but it works. If the person you're playing against has any smarts at all, he or she'll pick up on it without a hitch."

"Easy enough for you, Nina," Milly said, a self-deprecating smile on her face, "but I just panic. I've had some stage experience, but the idea of throwing in new lines is terrifying. I'll just have to take my chances with the teleprompter."

"Don't start," Nina insisted. "It's self-perpetuating. Once you get into the habit, you can't break it. You lose confidence in yourself. It's like drugs. If you never start, you can't get hooked. If I had my way, those idiot rolls would be outlawed."

Nina was encouraged to see that Milly had stopped crying and seemed to be getting her mind off the session with Dino Rossi and onto the business at hand.

"Nina, you're so good to me. I know what you're trying to do, and I'm grateful. I won't let you down, I promise. I'm going to put all this horrible business out of my mind entirely and do you proud. I swear I am!"

Just do yourself proud, Nina thought. You have an entire career in the balance.

Nina had spoken the truth when she told Rob Bryant she had a lunch date that day. She and Dino settled into a booth at the English Garden on West 66th Street, one of their habitual haunts.

"I asked you, Dino," she said as soon as the waitress walked away with their orders, "not to be rough on Milly Gowan. She's not involved, I just know it. She was in tears after you questioned her. It took me half an hour to calm her down. Was that really necessary?"

"First, I wasn't rough on her. It was standard questioning. Second, it's my job to get information out of her, whether she—or you—like it or not. We often get the really good stuff out of people who are so innocent they don't even know they have important facts in their possession. And third, I don't buy it."

"You don't buy what?"

"That meek-little-lamb act. It doesn't compute. Even though Boyer and I can't prove it's murder one yet, we're both convinced that it is—there are too many loose ends. But when we do get something solid, I'm going after her. She knows something she isn't telling. And even if she's innocent, maybe she can lead us to the guilty party. I'll just keep hammering at her until she cracks. I think she was nursing a real grudge against Ms. Triano. She wanted that part bad enough to do anything to get it."

"I don't believe it," Nina said sharply. "I tell you, Dino, she'll do something drastic. You're scaring the liver out of that poor girl!"

"That's what I intend to do. I'll drop back on her tomorrow. And the next day. And pretty soon . . ."

"She'll get a lawyer and you'll have a nice, fat harassment suit on your hands. I'll tell her to do that, Dino, I swear I will. Unless you have some hard evidence."

"If I'm prejudging," Rossi retorted, "then what do you think you're doing? Just because she'd managed to sell you on her Bo Peep image . . . She's hiding something, I tell you."

"What? Do you have any ideas on whom this phantom suspect she'll presumably lead you to might be?"

"Not yet. But . . ."

"You don't even know how Terri died. What did your Dr. Boyer have to say yesterday? You were going to call me back later. But, of course, you didn't."

"I got tied up, honey," he alibied. "I lost track of the time."

"That's the story of your life. You're always getting tied up. But you don't care who else *you* tie up."

Rossi regarded Nina dourly. "Boy, you really *are* on a tear today, aren't you?"

"Well, when you go chopping away at a poor little thing like Milly, I see red."

"Will you get off that kick? I was not unduly harsh with Ms. Gowan," he insisted. "If she's led that sheltered a life maybe she's in the wrong business."

"See what I mean? Now you're insinuating that she's out of her depth. Murder, indeed. *Skip it*." There was a long pause. "What about that ME report?"

Rossi's face fell. "Zilch. We can't get off of square one. Boyer has a few more tests to run—something about blood protein—before he can isolate whatever it was that did Triano in."

"So you take out your frustration on poor Milly with no evidence whatsoever. Typical macho behavior!"

"Hey," Rossi said, his mouth set in an angry line, "knock it off. This kind of stuff gets old in a big hurry."

Another pause while the waitress served their food. "Okay, I'll get off your case for now," Nina said. "But if you could have seen Milly crying . . ." She fell silent and began on her salad. "And what about some other suspects? You must have some ideas."

"Milly mentioned some phone calls Terri received, and some calls she made from the hotel. Milly came out of the shower once, caught her shouting at someone on the phone. Right away she clammed up, acted like it was a gag. Then there's the thing about her being out with someone on Friday night."

"Are you making a federal case out of that? Terri was a big girl, kind of a swinger, in my opinion. It's only natural that she'd know people in New York, that she'd want to see them."

Rossi shook his head doggedly. "No, there's something there. No matter what you say, Milly Gowan knows something she isn't telling."

"You are a real Johnny-one-note on that point, aren't you? First you say you can't even prove it's murder, and next you're all over Milly again. I don't know about you, Lieutenant." Again Nina paused, stabbing at a lettuce leaf. "What about those interviews you were going to review last night? Anything turn up? I sure hope you're going to give Rob Bryant, Nick Galano, and Horst Krueger as hard a time as you gave Milly. And speaking of Rob, did you ask Milly about the possibility that he and Terri might have gone way back? Maybe he was Terri's mystery caller."

"She never heard the voice. Terri jumped on the phone like a shot whenever it rang. The one time Milly was in the hotel room alone and the phone rang, whoever it was hung up when she answered.

"As for the preliminary interviews," Rossi said, his expression a dead giveaway of his own self-doubts, "there's nothing there that ties anybody in with anything. We're out in left field so far we'll never get back. And until forensics comes up with something . . ." He drummed his fingers on the table. "That's the real nut."

"So, for the time being we're in limbo." Nina wrinkled her nose. "Okay, I can live with that. Maybe it'll mean we'll have a little more time for each other."

"Don't count on it. I want you to keep your eyes and ears open on the set, hon, just like before. At the least inkling of something helpful, pass the word. I know I can depend on you."

"I'm still your head stool pigeon, huh?" she sighed. Nina took a deep breath, fighting to regain her cool. "Eternal patsy. Nice to know I'm good for *something*."

Nina arrived back at Meyer Studios at 12:25, leaving herself five minutes to wash up before the scheduled run-through. Lord, how she hated those early lunches, even though most days she was starving by 11:15, when the meal period began.

She went into the main rehearsal hall as others were straggling in from various directions. She saw Milly enter from the hallway that led to the dressing rooms, pause at the doorway and scan the room as though looking for someone. Nina noted that she was carrying her script and bore no traces of the emotional upheaval she'd been through earlier. Good, she thought, heading for her dressing room. Maybe the afternoon would be smooth sailing after all.

Before entering the hallway Milly had come from, Nina looked over her shoulder and saw her in intense conversation with Rob Bryant. She was probably conferring with him on some point in the script, Nina imagined. Good again; buckled down to business. That was what distinguished the amateurs from the pros.

She hung up her coat, thoroughly brushed her teeth— she was always careful not to create a problem for the people she had closeups with—and headed back for main rehearsal.

". . . not to tell me my business! Furthermore . . ." Oh, God help us! Helen's voice was rising like a flood tide. Who has done what now to offend the Almighty? Nina wondered, grateful that she had no part in it.

But her heart sank when she entered the rehearsal hall. Helen had two figures cornered and was going at them hammer and tongs, mindless of the scene she was creating.

"You are to work with Mr. Galano *exclusively*," Helen seethed, glaring at a trembling Milly Gowan, "and if you want to survive in this business, you'd better learn who's in charge! And as for *you*," she said, turning her fire on a cool Rob Bryant, "you already have your instructions as to what you are to work on, and with whom!"

"I bet he does," Robin muttered, coming up behind Nina. "And I imagine some of his biggest scenes are rehearsed outside the studio, over and over and over. . . ."

"Now let's get moving!" Helen snarled to no one in particular.

Sorry, Milly, Nina thought. So much for smooth sailing. Better check your lifejacket.

Chapter Seven

"I want you to give Audrey Lincoln just a little more edge here, Milly," said assistant director Nick Galano. "She should come off with more authority, maybe let just a flush of her innate bitchiness out. Advance on Melanie, affect an implied threat with your body. You follow me?"

"I think so. You mean like this?" Milly Gowan moved toward Nina, the beginnings of a steely look on her face. She slid her hands to the back of Nina's chair, leaning slightly toward her. "I hardly think that's necessary, Ms. Prescott." She delivered the line with just the right amount of force. "I'm not exactly a novice when it comes to corporate ad copy. I did head my own department at Bancroft International, after all. Don't treat me like a trainee."

"I'm sorry if I offended you, Ms. Lincoln," Nina came back as Melanie Prescott, mild hauteur evident. "I simply wonder why this doggy copy was ever sent out. Layouts like this went out in the fifties. This *is* your sign-off, isn't it?"

"Great, Milly," Galano broke in. "That's exactly what I had in mind." He called to the cameraman, "Move in a bit, there, Jerry. Try a midshot, so we can see the sparks fly between these two, instead of flip-flopping on the close-ups. . . . Yeah, like that."

It was Thursday morning, and a week that had started out on a very shaky note was stabilizing nicely. Some of the trauma of Saturday night was fading; the sleepwalker ambience on the set was becoming a memory.

The fact of the matter was that Millicent Gowan had turned out to be one hell of an actresss; the swift adaptability shown at the auditions and just exhibited in the scene at hand was impressive to all. Behind her back Galano had winked, sent Nina a grinning high-sign, to which Nina had smiled a broad I-told-you-so.

"Take fifteen," Nick Galano said now. "I've got to talk to Burman about the next scene. It's at least a minute short."

As Nina and Milly threaded their way toward the dressing rooms through the welter of camera, sound, and power cables, they talked softly. "How was it, Nina?" Milly asked. "You think I'm improving?"

"There was nothing to improve, Milly. You had it right from the start. I told you the first day that all you had to do was ease up a little. You're a pro, and class will tell."

"You don't know how good that makes me feel. Thanks ever so much."

"Nothing to thank me for. I'm only telling it the way it is. You're good, Milly. And you're going to get better. I foresee a long run for you on TTS."

"I sure hope so." She paused. "I just want you to know, Nina . . . how much I appreciate your friendship. You're about the only one. Most of the others on the set treat me like I've got the plague."

"Milly, don't be too hard on the gang. You know what the pressure's like on the set . . . everyone concentrating on his own lines, his own character's problems. It takes time before they accept you. Don't take it personally."

"I hope that's true. I feel like such an outsider."

They reached Nina's dressing room. "Want to come in and talk awhile?"

"If I won't be keeping you from something . . ."

Milly, Nina thought, will you stop putting yourself down?

"Only some fail mail I've been avoiding. It's really piling up. I'll have to request a second dressing room if I don't clear some space soon."

"I should be so lucky to have that problem," Milly sighed.

"Your day will come." Nina made a wry face as she surveyed a mound of letters on a side table. She had already sorted out the two-week backlog; those letters destined to receive a form letter—which would be handled by Myrna Rowan and the secretarial staff—were in one pile, while those requiring a more personal response waited in another.

"My goodness," Millicent said, "all that mail! I had no idea the fans cared that much."

"Oh, yes, soap opera viewers are very devoted. Some people—especially retirees and shut-ins—spend the whole day watching them. These people take their soaps seriously. You'd be amazed at the things they write. They give Melanie Prescott all kinds of advice on how to conduct her business affairs, her personal life. Some dear souls even tell her to watch out for this character and that character on the show, warn her they're up to no good."

"I had no idea. How long does it take to build up a following?"

"If you start off as a 'meany', no time at all—but it took about a year and a half before my fan mail amounted to anything. Now I get two to three hundred letters a week. There are times when I wish they didn't love me quite so verbally. But then, fan mail helps the paycheck. Management keeps a running count. The more popular you are with the fans, the more valuable you become to the show."

"Any problems? You know, psychos writing in or something?"

"Oh, yes, we get our share of crank letters. People write to tell you their troubles, they request loans, or beg outright for money. There have been some threatening letters, too, but some send in prayers and religious medals.

We get letters from all kinds of people: college kids, mechanics, priests, nuns, housewives, female executives like Melanie, teachers, people in nursing homes. And you wouldn't believe how many men watch soap operas. I've even had occasional letters from prison inmates. Some are just lonely, some are hostile, and others are convinced that they've fallen in love with me and beg me to write back. I turn those over to Myrna."

Nina's expression turned regretful. "I hate to do it," she admitted. "I'd like to write a few personal lines myself to everyone, but that's totally impossible. So I make sure to sign each letter she's typed up myself. I owe them that much."

Milly pointed to a small pile of packages on the floor beside the table. "What about those?"

"Another benefit of being a soap-opera queen. The fans send us presents—handmade sweaters, aprons, pot holders, ceramic animals, recipe books. Scrapbooks they've made about us. They send costume jewelry and ask us to wear it on the show; some of it is really quite lovely. One woman even sent her daughter's wedding dress, insisted that Susan Levy wear it when her character got married on the show." Nina smiled at the memory. "There's no telling what the fans will do next!"

"Well, so long as they confine it to letter writing."

"But they don't. There isn't a day that passes when there aren't a few fans waiting out in front of the studio, wanting autographs, giving you story ideas, ready to tell you their personal problems. And then there are the Bible-bangers who swear you're headed straight for hell. It gets hairy at times—two years back, Angela Dolan actually got waylaid by a fan who thought she was being too tough on Buffy Kingston. You know, Robin Tally's role? The woman clobbered her with an umbrella and put Angela in the hospital for a few days. Horst Krueger persuaded her not to press charges; it would have been poor publicity for the show."

As Nina drew up a chair, methodically scanning and relegating letters, already machine opened, to their separate piles, she and Milly carried on a running conversation. Nina stopped here and there to read particular selections aloud. "Here's one from a woman in Minnesota that'll give you a chuckle: 'Dear Miss McFall,' she writes, 'I want you to know that I never miss a single episode of *The Turning Seasons*. You are my favorite actress on the show. But I am not your greatest fan. I know you won't believe this, but my dog, Biscuit, is crazy about you, too. Whenever the show is on, he sits beside me on the couch and watches. And when you're not on, he loses interest and goes to sleep. . . .'"

Milly giggled, then fell silent, content to watch as Nina continued sifting through her mail. But abruptly, out of the blue and in a hesitant tone, she said, "Nina?"

"Huh?" she replied preoccupiedly. "What is it, Milly?"

"Something's been bothering me—something I feel a little bit guilty about. And since you're the only real friend I have around here . . ."

Nina came instantly alert. "I'm glad you consider me a friend. But the only one? What about Rob Bryant? You and he looked pretty thick the other day. Doesn't he count?"

"Oh Nina, I don't know what to do! I'm so crazy about him I can't think of anything else. I know what you say about Mrs. Meyer is true. She could fire me in a second if she saw me as a threat. But I think I'm falling in love with him." The girl looked miserable.

"When did this happen?" Nina asked.

"It started the first time I saw him. I thought he was the most gorgeous man I'd ever seen, but I assumed he was out of reach. Such beautiful men usually are. I didn't dream there could be anything between us."

"Sounds like you're dreaming now," Nina murmured.

"I can't help it. He's not only so handsome, he's so *nice*. I never met such a nice man. And he really seems interested in me. That's the wild part. I know I'm no raving beauty, but he really *likes* me!"

Nina recognized the feeling. Did Rob have that effect on every woman he came near? "What are you going to do?" she asked quietly.

"I don't know. I'm so afraid of Mrs. Meyer. She goes into such rages. She doesn't much like me anyway, and it wouldn't take much for her to fire me."

"Milly, relax. Helen rages on, but believe me, if you're good for the show, she's not going to dump you. Why do you say she doesn't like you?"

Milly set her mouth in a thin line and wrestled with her conscience for a moment. Then she spoke. "Why else would she have changed her mind about me at the last minute, after the final auditions? She all but told me I'd won. When the letters came the next morning and I found out Terri was the winner, I couldn't believe it. I was more surprised than Terri. Later I talked about it with Rob, and he agreed."

Something was wrong there. "You mean Terri wasn't excited at winning?"

"Well, she was happy about it—but she just didn't seem surprised. Maybe Mrs. Meyer told us both the same thing. Could she be that mean?"

"No—no, I doubt that. There must have been some misunderstanding somewhere. . . ."

Something was very wrong. The memory of her lunch with Terri flooded back into Nina's mind. What was it Terri had said about her eleventh-hour interview with Helen? *I could have sworn she was getting me ready for the big letdown*, or something like that. But in that case, why wouldn't Terri scream in surprise at the news she'd won? Was it possible that Milly wasn't telling the whole truth? In either case, why would Helen Meyer have played such a cruel joke? Or had she?

The break ended, and as they wended their way back to rehearsal, Nina decided to be extremely cautious and observant from then on in regard to Milly Gowan.

The rest of Thursday went by in a kaleidoscopic blur, with crisis following crisis, keeping the cast, the directors, and the production crews in a perpetual sweat.

Finally they reached the final taping. Nina and Milly

were alone on the Marston Corporation set, waiting for their scene when Milly glanced at her watch, said, "Forgot something up in my dressing room," and dashed off the set.

The camera crews were almost set up now, spots and floods were blinking to life. They'd be on in less than three minutes. What is she doing? Nina wondered. She knows we're on standby. This is no time for anyone to rush off a set, least of all a beginner.

Seconds later, off in the distance, carrying from the downstairs corridor between the massive soundstage and the main rehearsal hall, came a single, piercing scream. Then there were loud male voices and Nina became aware of footsteps running from all directions toward the site of the outcry. Immediately she was on her feet, running after them.

Even as Nina fought her way through the crowd, she had a sudden awful premonition of what she'd find. After one glimpse she turned quickly away from the bloody, crumpled figure on the cement floor, the skull crushed like a squash. . . .

Revulsion shook her body as she huddled against Rafe Fallone's shoulder. The voices receded momentarily, then became louder. She began to tremble convulsively. "No, no, no . . ." she heard her own voice crying in a singsong refrain.

"It's Millicent Gowan," said one of the voices in the confused welter of sound. "She must have fallen from the top landing there. Christ, that's a hell of a drop!"

Nina looked back for a moment. She saw Spence Sprague kneeling over the body, his shoulders mercifully concealing the shattered remains of Milly's head. "Nothing we can do," he grunted, his face ghastly white. "She's gone for sure. She's dead. Somebody better call the police."

Walking in a trance, not feeling her hands or feet as she moved along the corridor toward Myrna Rowan's office, Nina dredged up Dino Rossi's precinct number. Moving like a robot, she slowly began punching in the required digits.

Chapter Eight

The day's taping, of course, was wrecked. Spence Sprague, going crazy by inches, stared about wildly, trying to come up with an alternative plan—an evening taping, perhaps. But he knew that whatever he tried wouldn't work. The best he could do was to hope to pick it up the next day, and shoot around Audrey Lincoln's part until a new actress could be found—or an entirely new script could be prepared.

Milly's body had been draped with a length of canvas by the time Dino Rossi arrived, accompanied by four squad members. He approached the corpse, lifted the improvised shroud briefly. He looked down impassively for a moment, then dropped the canvas.

His second look was for Nina. She was standing at the end of the hall, her face haggard and pale, her body slumped in bewildered dejection, and he was seized by an urge to take her in his arms and grant what small comfort he could. But all he could relay in that fleeting second's glance was a deep sense of sympathy and concern. She saw it and understood. For the moment it must suffice.

Dino approached Spence Sprague. "If you'll have everyone . . . production people as well as actors . . . gather in one place, please. I don't want anyone moving around at all until my men have finished their work."

"The main rehearsal hall would be the best spot," Sprague offered in a defeated voice. "Good God, is this stuff never going to end? Another one of these and I'll be ready for the rubber room!"

"This will probably take a couple of hours," Rossi cut him short, knowing he needed to establish the whereabouts of every single person at the time Millicent Gowan went over that railing.

"Are you regarding this as murder?" Sprague said, his eyes haunted. "She could have fallen. It could be suicide for all we know."

"Suicide? Do you have any reason for thinking that?"

"The woman was strange. She wasn't fitting in here. I'd venture to say that she might have been kind of depressed after Terri died. Things could have ganged up on her. So she decided to take a header."

Rossi's mouth formed a disdainful line. "A header? If she was thinking suicide she'd find a better way than that."

"Well," Sprague bristled. "An accident then. Accidents do happen. Just don't go off half-cocked and call it a murder before you even take a second look."

"Tell me, Mr. Sprague," Rossi said, hard put to conceal his growing irritation, "when was the last time someone *accidentally* didn't see the railing around that landing and took a tumble?"

"Well, never," he grumbled. "But that doesn't mean it couldn't happen. There's always a first time."

"Who found the body?"

"Myrna Rowan, our office administrator. She was just coming back from the copier . . . running tomorrow's scripts . . . when she found Milly on the floor. She let out a yell, and everybody came running."

"Okay, I'll start with her. Now if you'll get your people into that rehearsal room you spoke of . . ."

While Spence Sprague began herding a stunned and shaken staff through the door into the main rehearsal hall,

Rossi, flanked by Charley Harper and Bruno Reichert, stared upward at the towering steel stairway, trying to see just how a body could have been pitched over the double-railed landing without someone downstairs or moving about in the dressing room corridor being alerted. They asked themselves how the body could have landed so far out—practically against the opposite side of the corridor—unless it had been propelled by some force.

"Bruno," Rossi commanded, "go up and check the room that fronts on the landing. Someone could have clubbed her in there first, then tossed her over the rail. It would take some shove to launch her like that."

Reichert, short, balding, slightly roly poly, started up, taking pains not to touch the railing.

"Is that door open?" Rossi called up to him.

"No."

"What's behind it?"

"The card on the door says Sirri Ballinger. Must be a dressing room."

Rossi looked around, beckoned for Spence Sprague. "Get Sirri Ballinger. We want to look at her dressing room."

"Sirri isn't in today, Lieutenant. She was written out."

"Written out?"

"No scenes for her in the script. She's not here."

"I guess that lets her off, doesn't it? Anyone else have a key?"

"There's a master. And Horst Krueger keeps all the dupes locked in his office."

Moments later, inside Sirri's room, Dino searched for signs of violence, for scuff marks on the carpeting. "So how would anybody get in here?" Sprague demanded.

"People have been known to have duplicate keys made," Rossi said, irritated by Sprague's continued challenges. "Friends get keys. Friends of friends get keys. It happens every day." He called off Reichert, who was prowling the floor on his hands and knees. "It's clean, Bruno. Nothing's been bothered in here. Let's go downstairs." And to Sprague, he said, "I'll need some empty office space, where we can question people privately."

Rossi summoned Nina McFall early in the session. In the privacy of Rob Bryant's office, he held her trembling body in his arms, ran his hands gently up and down her back.

"We don't even know the answer to Terri's death," her voice broke, "and now, another one."

"I'd be willing to go on record that Milly Gowan was dead before she fell from that landing."

"She was *pushed*." Nina said. "I'm certain. She had so many things to live for and I can't think of a single reason for her to want to die."

"Guilty conscience?" he offered.

Nina released herself from his arms. "Dino! You don't still think Milly killed Terri, do you?"

"I can't rule it out just because Milly is dead. Sometimes people can't live with guilt, and then they crack. Look, I've got to talk to a lot of people. I just wanted to touch base with you first, to—"

"I know why, and thanks," she said, giving him a soft kiss on the cheek. "I'll wait around until you're finished. Then we'll pick it up again."

"It'll be hours."

"Don't you want me to wait?"

"What do you think?"

Why the word games? she thought. Why can't he just say, "Yes, please wait for me"?

"I think I'll wait."

He spoke again just as she opened the door. "Nina?"

"Yes?"

"Ask Helen Meyer to come in first."

"Good idea. She's probably climbing the walls."

But Helen was unexpectedly calm. She entered Rob Bryant's office, the picture of dignity and resolve.

"Lieutenant Rossi, I'm beginning to think you should be on my payroll, not the city's."

"Mrs. Meyer, the necessity to upset your production schedule once again is regrettable."

She took a seat and lit a cigarette. "Yes, yes, of course it

94

is. Tell me something, how long do you think it will take you to conclude your investigations?"

"That's impossible to say. It could be today, it could be months from now. Why do you ask?"

"Because I have made a decision. I have decided to sell Meyer Productions and *get away from this insane business!*" Her voice suddenly rose two octaves and the calm, collected executive was replaced by a wild-eyed gesticulating fury. "Ever since last June we've been plagued by these crimes! Someone is out to ruin me! Someone hates me enough to destroy everything my husband and I built up! Who'll be next? I can't stand any more of this! You've got to do something about it!"

"Please, Mrs. Meyer, try to be calm. We're doing everything we can."

"As far as I can see, you're doing *nothing!* Do you know yet why Terri Triano died? No, of course not. And now you have to find out why Milly Gowan died. It's a plot, someone is plotting against me!"

Enough of this garbage, Dino decided. "Mrs. Meyer, I won't keep you long," he said smoothly. "Can you tell me what you were doing when Myrna Rowan discovered the body and screamed?"

The question brought her up short. "That's the most insulting thing I ever heard in my life! Do you think I'm sabotaging my own show?"

Easy, boy, easy; she's the type to go straight to the Commissioner and complain about Gestapo tactics. "Nothing of the sort, Mrs. Meyer. In circumstances like these, we simply have to establish the whereabouts of every single person who was on the premises at the time. If Ms. Gowan's grandmother were here, I'd ask her the same question."

"I see. That means you'll have to find out where Ms. McFall was, too, doesn't it?"

"Yes, of course. No one can be left out."

The answer seemed to satisfy her, or perhaps it was his suddenly steely tone. "I was in my office, going over our ratings."

"Alone?"

"Yes, alone."

"Did anyone see you enter your office?"

"Are you harassing me, Lieutenant?"

"No ma'am, I'm establishing your alibi."

"Oh. Oh, I see. Well, you should talk to Rob Bryant. He was there with me not long before the scream was heard. We were discussing . . . production values." He nodded solemnly. "If you don't believe me, ask him."

"Thank you, Mrs. Meyer, I will. That'll be all for now."

"I'll let you know if I plan to leave the city," she said sarcastically, moving toward the door.

"Are you? Planning to leave the city?" he asked politely, and was rewarded with a slam of the door.

Helen Meyer thought she'd told Dino Rossi nothing. But she was wrong. She'd told him something that could prove to be extremely significant. He knew from her exaggerated fury, her ridiculously overdone indignation, that she was hiding something. Probably something important, or else why hide it?

Dino called next for Rob Bryant.

The interview with Rob was brief and uneventful. He said that he'd been with Helen Meyer in her office for approximately twenty minutes; he'd left shortly before Myrna's scream was heard—maybe five minutes.

As for his own whereabouts, Rob said he had gone from Helen's office directly to Corinne Demetry's dressing room and had been with her when the commotion started.

Later, when Dino asked Corinne where she had been at the fateful moment, her statement not only corroborated Rob's, but she also unexpectedly verified Helen's claim that she'd remained alone in her office after Rob left.

"When we heard the scream, Rob and I ran out of my dressing room. We didn't know where it had come from, and people were running around in all directions. We ran right into Mrs. Meyer coming out of her office, and then we followed somebody else. I think it was one of the cameramen, but I'm not sure. It was all so hurried and confusing."

"And that's the way it went all afternoon," Dino told Nina much later in her dressing room, where she'd waited for him until the last statement had been taken, the CSU unit had come and gone, the inevitable photography of horrors had been completed, and the body removed.

Nina had been filling the time trying to answer fan mail, but with little progress; images of both Milly and Terri invaded her thoughts constantly. Now she wanted nothing more than to get away from the studio.

"I've got to get out of here," she said, standing and reaching for her coat, and waiting for him to pick up his cue.

"We'll be on this all night," he muttered. "Might as well take a break now and get something to eat. You want to grab a bite?"

How could she resist such a romantic overture?

"Are you any closer to finding out what killed Terri?" she asked after one of the desultory silences that punctuated the meal. They had exhausted the subject of Milly's death for the moment, and in desperation were back to Terri's, raking through some very stale ashes.

"We're still out in left field. The ME's doing more blood work, trying to find out what could cause a stroke in such a basically healthy young woman."

"You're sure it was a stroke?"

"Boyer says it was textbook. But he can't figure out what made it happen. That's what's driving me nuts. And those needle tracks leave the game wide open. Somebody could have put something into her and we wouldn't know one needle hole from another."

"Sure," Nina scoffed. "And Terri would just sit there and let someone stick a needle in her arm and go off to the party as if nothing happened. Fat chance."

"Which brings us back to our original idea. She injected the stuff herself, not knowing what it was. But what did she shoot up on? How did her murderer . . . if she *was* murdered . . . engineer a tricky move like that?"

"What's happening to the body?" Nina asked.

"Another mystery. We can't run down any relatives anywhere. So for the time being, pending further notice, she's still on ice. Literally."

"She made that vague comment about an ex-husband in the woodwork. Any trace of him?"

"Yeah. A guy named Freeman Collier. But that's another dead end. Can't locate him anywhere. And if she mentioned a divorce, that's phony, too. No paper on that at all. He was listed at an L.A. address. But he's long gone from there. Why would she lay out that line of bull if it wasn't so?"

"Good question. Maybe it wasn't bull."

"Good answer. . . ."

Coffee appeared and then disappeared, accompanied only by the sounds of spoons clinking against the sides of cups.

"Time for me to get back to work," Rossi said, covering the check with a few bills. "What's going to happen to the show?"

"I don't know. Unless I'm informed otherwise, I'll just arrive tomorrow morning at eight, as usual. There are really only two choices, as far as I can see. They can scrap all the stuff with the Audrey Lincoln character and get some new plot line to substitute—which might just cause Dave and Sally to tell Helen where to stick her Neilsens. Or they can recast, again, and we'll all just have to scramble to catch up."

"That sounds easier."

"Could be. But you know how superstitious actors can be. I don't know that I'd be thrilled to accept a role after the first two people cast in it were carried out feet first."

"I see what you mean."

Outside the snow had begun again, and Nina wrapped her fur coat tightly around her while Dino hailed a cab. She wondered if he'd find the time to see her home, maybe even come up for a little while before getting back to the investigation. . . .

But he only deposited her into the cab and gave the driver her address, promising to call her later, or the next day. He gave her the kind of kiss he might have planted on the head of a pet spaniel and waved the cabby on. She resisted the temptation to succumb to anger. Don't be selfish, she told herself. Now he has two deaths to figure out. And who knows if that'll be all? Despite the heat in the cab and the layers of mink around her, Nina shivered uncontrollably.

When Nina let herself into her apartment, she found the red eye on her answering machine beckoning with its tireless wink. She pushed the buttons and waited. Rob Bryant's voice floated into the room, still silky smooth despite the electronic assaults of the tape.

"Nina," he said. "Scratch tomorrow. Helen and Horst have decided to recast and have a special catch-up session on Saturday. We'll see you at eight A.M. Sorry if you had weekend plans. Get a good rest tomorrow. Take care, stay warm, and stay well."

Was he worried about her? That was sweet of him, but he needn't have worried; she had every intention of staying very well.

Chapter Nine

Everyone was in a foul mood. If half the grumbling and grousing could be believed, enough weekend plans had been wrecked to throw the American tourist industry into bankruptcy.

Huddled in her dressing room to stay out of the lines of battle, Nina mulled over the ironic solution to the casting crisis that Spence Sprague had come up with. If there was any comely, competent talent on the loose in New York City, Sprague knew where to find it.

Contract negotiations alone normally consumed as much as a month's time, yet less than forty-eight hours after Milly Gowan's death, Christy Hall found herself cast in the role of Audrey Lincoln. Despite the increasing notoriety of the part—or maybe because of it—it was a chance that any aspiring actress would give her life for. And considering that two young woman already had, Nina wondered if Christy Hall had a death wish.

But then, Christy was not exactly an aspiring actress. Over the years she'd played a variety of scheming young women in several soap operas. In fact, her agent had very energetically pitched her for the role of Audrey months earlier, before anyone even thought of the talent-hunt idea.

Too bad he didn't succeed, Nina thought. If he had, Terri Triano and Milly Gowan would probably be alive now.

She knew Christy Hall's work, and she was sure she could play the pantsuit off Audrey Lincoln. She wondered if her failure to win the role originally was her fault or her agent's. Sam Baylog was one of the best-known agents in New York, but for all the wrong reasons. People remembered him because they couldn't forget him—no matter how hard they tried. He'd do anything to get a client a job (and at the same time get himself a healthy percentage, of course).

Sam Baylog had been accused of literally kidnapping a name actor once so that his client, the understudy, could go on. He'd been known to produce screaming fits in normally low-keyed casting directors by his persistence on getting roles for his clients. Not auditions, screw auditions—he wanted *roles*. He'd been discovered late one night in the office of the typing service used by the biggest writers, sitting there feverishly reading scripts to find out what upcoming parts he could put his clients into. He often reduced unemployed actors to tears by tearing into their offstage behavior as unprofessional and shouting that he wouldn't represent them for one hundred and ten percent.

Casting directors hated him. Producers hated him. Other agents loathed him. And actors hated him—all except his own clients, of course, for whom he would fight, bleed, and possibly die. Nina wondered fleetingly if Sam Baylog would kill for his clients, and immediately dismissed the idea. Audrey Lincoln wasn't *that* good a role. Besides, Christy Hall never lacked for work. Actually, Nina was relieved to hear she'd been signed, and looked forward to working with the lovely, sharp-featured brunette. With her understated sexuality and her 120 pounds nicely distributed over a slim and curvy five feet six inches, Christy Hall would be an ideal substitute for her unfortunate predecessors. Best of all no break-in, no introduction to the specialized world of soaps would be necessary for her.

But even an accomplished pro like Christy Hall needed

time to learn moves and lines; teleprompters couldn't do it all. Which was where she was at that moment: in her dressing room, gallantly committing Audrey's scenes to memory. While the Saturday session would cost a small fortune in overtime (a full camera, sound and lighting crew, an assistant director even now waiting on Christy's quick study), it was a pittance compared to the alternative of writing Ms. Lincoln out of the script and starting from scratch.

Despite Nina's loyalty to Millicent Gowan, it was impossible to dislike Christy. She was witty, wisecracking, effervescent, and totally flexible—the dream actress Nina would have wished for a Marston Corporation colleague from the very start.

It was now 10:45 A.M. and Nina was at her makeup table, going through the motions of relearning the more difficult lines in her part and establishing blocking cues, but she was unable to concentrate. Her thoughts kept veering back to the unexpected phone call she'd received from Dino at the end of the unwelcome day of restlessness that Friday had turned into.

"Murder one," he'd said tersely over the phone, and she promptly misapplied his meaning.

"You found out what killed Terri?"

"No—Milly. She was strangled before going over the edge." Nina sat down hard, her pulse pounding. "You okay?"

"Yes, okay. It's just the surprise." How could anyone do that and not be seen? Or at least not be missed by anyone?

"I figure she probably had a date to meet someone when she left you on the set that day," he said.

"But everyone has an alibi."

"Hey, that's easy. Either there was somebody in the studio we don't know about, or somebody lied."

Of course. Now all they had to do was figure out who. It was enough to make Nina suspect that an outside influence was at work, that someone other than a cast member had committed Milly's murder. Maybe Milly Gowan had inherited Terri Triano's phantom slayer. Were the two deaths really linked?

Before concluding the conversation, Dino said that Milly's background was being closely checked: police information nets between New York and Rockford, Illinois had been activated. Her parents had arrived; a discreet way would have to be found to ask them some leading questions.

Nina fidgeted and tossed the script aside. Concentration was impossible. She'd have to rely more than she liked on paraphrasing and the teleprompter. And damn it, there was no telling how long today's taping session would last. More than likely, if the present turtle's pace gave any clue, it would run well into the evening. Late enough, at any rate, to cancel her standing Saturday night date with Dino. Granted, his workload was an obstruction as well, but there had been a faint hope of getting together until this latest emergency had surfaced. Now she would be tired, peevish, no fit company at all. Rain check, please.

Downstairs the skeleton production crews drank coffee and played poker or pinochle to mark time while the cast and directors honed lines and movements to razor edge. Nina wondered if she could scare up a bridge game. Sometimes total distraction was the best way to clear the head and let jumbled thoughts rearrange themselves in more orderly sequences.

It was at that moment that the cat appeared. Nina had left her dressing room door slightly ajar, and it was through this opening—bunting his squarish, mottled head, then his bulky shoulders through—that the animal entered. He was a marmalade shorthair, his white front and paws dingy. No longer in his first youth, a little scarred and battered, he must have weighed at least fifteen pounds, Nina conjectured. Advancing confidently on Nina, he plunked himself at her feet and looked up at her with a self-satisfied smirk. "Purp?" he said.

"Well, hello, kitty," Nina answered cautiously, sidling away from him. She had never been at ease with cats. "Where did you come from?"

Where he had come from was the alley. The production crew, to alleviate the heat of the set lights, had wedged open a fire door, and the cat had apparently slipped in. A dark spot on the bridge of his nose gave him a roguish air. His mouth was seemingly set in a perpetual smile. He was a disreputable-looking creature, all brawly tomcat. And yet, obvious stray though he was, a gentlemanly sedateness remained. Noting the subtle indentation in his ruff, indicating a missing collar, Nina suspected that somewhere there existed a loving and grieving owner.

Her heart went out to the animal, who sat patiently, looking up at her with intense, yellow eyes. Lost, she thought, her familiar kneejerk compassion taking over. His person was probably out looking for him at this very moment. We'll have to run an ad, she thought, gazing at the cat, see if we can find out who he—

Abruptly her eyes widened in surprise. Could it be? She leaned forward, staring harder at the cat and took in the stately, proffered paw. Was he actually offering to shake hands? Obviously he was. This had to be someone's cat. They had taught him this trick. Goodness, and I always thought cats were untrainable! Nina thought, astonished.

The animal stared gravely at her and continued offering his smudged paw. Despite her distrust of cats, Nina leaned down and gingerly took his paw in her hand. She shook it lightly, feeling foolish. "Well, pleased to know you, too, kitty," she said.

She no sooner released the paw than the cat offered it a second time. "Ohh," Nina said, "I bet I know what you're up to, you little beggar. Food, that's what you want. I'll bet you get a reward every time you shake hands."

Nina opened the bottom drawer of her dressing table and drew out the brown bag lunch she'd brought along. Cast and production crews had agreed to eat in today in hope of speeding up the retakes. "You're in luck—I brought tuna today," she told the cat. "Talk about perfect timing."

Nina chose a section of the morning paper and spread it on the floor. Opening the sandwich, she used a discarded coffee stirrer to scrape tuna from the bread onto the newspaper. Immediately the cat dove in, his motor rumbling nonstop.

Nina leaned back to watch and felt some of her tension slide away. Good therapy, she conceded. Nothing like watching an animal to take your mind off your problems. Better than cards. No finicky cat this, he lapped it all down, garnish, mayonnaise and all, and looked around for more. Nina shrugged and gave him the tuna-smeared bread, then watched him demolish that. Poor thing, she thought, he's starved. I'll have to try and find something else.

She remembered Horst Krueger's posted string of no-nos, with pets on the set ranking high on the list. Well, just for today. Good thing both Horst and Helen are off somewhere. Lord knows we could use a cat on the set—there are always mice running around downstairs.

He was an attractive animal, she thought, and not all that dirty considering his alley wanderings. How long had he been on the loose? She looked at his face, wondering who he reminded her of. Then it came to her. The Chesapeake and Ohio Railroad logo, of course. Chessy the cat. Perfect! She offered a timid hand. "Here, Chessy. Come, Chessy, that's a good boy . . ."

The cat abandoned the last of his bread scraps and came mooching over, leaning hard against her ankles and allowing her to scratch behind his ears. He twined himself around her legs. Next he hopped up on her lap and bunted at her face with his head. As Nina continued to pet him, gaining more confidence by the moment, the arrogant puss settled into her lap where, purring happily, he made himself perfectly comfortable. Chessy had found himself, his furry brain deduced, the perfect patsy.

As she continued petting him, assessing his hard, wiry frame beneath the thick orange fur, Nina wondered how she could have ever been afraid of cats. Yes, they were aloof, and sometimes didn't come when called. So what? Nina knew a lot of people like that. And Chessy was certainly an exception to the rule, so friendly and loving.

Well, she decided, the least I can do is sneak out this

afternoon, find him something else to eat. Surely Corrigan's Pub owes me some scraps. She would leave him in her dressing room and feed him late that afternoon, just before putting him out for the night. Until his owner claimed him, that would be the extent of her ministrations on his behalf, Nina vowed. But in the meantime, he needed a cozy place to sleep. She remembered an old cashmere sweater in one of the drawers, and took it out.

"Chessy," she said, rising carefully and lowering the heavy brute to the floor. "Here—how'd you like to sleep on this old sweater? I'll put this little rug under it, and you'll have your own bed. Won't that be nice?"

Chessy cocked his head quizzically. Then, as though deciding to go along with Nina's foolishness, he settled lazily into the fluffy nest. Some people, his expression said, really know how to treat a cat! He never once stopped his deep, rumbling purring.

Rick Busacca went past in the hall. "Troops are assembling," he said, rapping on her door.

"Coming." Nina gathered her script, gave Chessy a last pat on the head and started out. But if she thought she'd desert her new friend, she was mistaken; he was at her heels in a flash, frisking and rubbing all the way down the hall. Nina shrugged. It would help to lighten the day.

"Well," Christy Hall laughed, registering approval, "who's your furry friend?"

"Gang," Nina replied, "meet Chessy. He's auditioning for the part of studio cat. Think he's got the stuff?"

"Looks great to me," Bob Valentine said, leaning down to pet him. Chessy tolerated his touch only momentarily, then strolled away and wound around Nina's ankles again.

"Just keep him out of the way when we're on camera," Rob Bryant said. "He's a husky brute, isn't he? Should be in a zoo."

"Harmless as a kitten," Nina defended, lifting Chessy into a chair that wouldn't feature in the take. "Now you stay there, Chessy. *Sit*. That's a good boy." And regarding her colleagues: "Want to see something? Watch this. Chessy, want to shake hands?" Instantly a gentlemanly paw came up. The actors oohed and aahed, delighted by the trick. Master Chessy had found an appreciative audience.

"Okay," Rob Bryant cut in, "if we can get back to making money. Those lines, Christy? got 'em this time?"

"Like a lock, Rob," she replied confidently. "Ready when you are."

"Places, everyone. Close in, Valentine. Lights. Camera. This is a take." The stick boy shoved the scene board in front of the number one camera. Clack!

The long day went on.

It was perhaps the fourth or fifth time Nina had worked under Bryant's direction. Before the day was out, she found herself marveling over his competence, and was forced to admit that he was developing into one hell of a director. He had a feel for the mood of a scene and he could be light and flip when necessary, but he could be just as cutting when someone fouled up. The cast responded well, and the episodes kept piling up, with surprisingly few problems.

Looking around her as they worked into the late afternoon, Nina saw he'd cast his spell on the rest of the ensemble, males as well as females; she'd never seen Bob Valentine respond so well to direction before. Christy also took to the bearded, lazy-eyed man, giving an excellent performance. Where does it come from? Nina mused. Why do some people seem to have a complete corner on charm?

Rob took a special liking to Chessy and made a genuine fuss over him. It was he, in fact, who disappeared briefly at midday, returning with several cans of cat food in assorted flavors. At least Chessy would face his outdoor weekend with a full tummy.

Shortly before eight, the last episode of the Marston Corporation wrapped up, and all hands were dismissed. It was as Nina reluctantly edged Chessy through the fire door and emptied the last of his rations into a bowl she'd found in the property room that she looked up to see Rob Bryant standing behind her. "Why don't you take him home with you?" he laughed. "You two redheads make a great pair."

"Oh, no," Nina said, suppressing a tingle of pleasure at his unexpected appearance, "I couldn't do that."

"Why not? You've seemingly fallen in love with the creature. Does your building have a no-pets rule?"

"No problem on that account. It's just that I've never owned an animal. I wouldn't know how to care for him. Beside, I have to consider my apartment. He might turn into Attila the Hun and claw up all the upholstery. No, it's best this way. I'll place an ad, try to find his owner. But aside from that . . ."

"Good night, Chessy," Rob said brusquely, closing and locking the fire door. "See you Monday. We hope."

"Good night, Chessy," Nina sighed. At that last moment, seeing the cat staring up questioningly at her (the temperature hovering under the forty mark and headed downward) she almost had a change of heart. Then, reasoning that it wasn't really her concern, that he'd managed to exist without her help up to this point, she shut him out of her mind.

The voices that floated around the studio were rapidly diminishing, and Nina hurried back to her dressing room to gather her things. She didn't want ot be the last one out.

Struggling into her fur coat, she suddenly heard a man's voice raised in anger. Whoever it was, he was really furious, and with the thinness of dressing-room walls, it sounded as though he was right in the room with her. Actually, he was two doors away, the room Christy Hall was sharing with Susan Levy.

"I don't give a crap what they said!" the voice raged. "You gotta stand up for your rights in this lousy business! I can't be here to look out for you alla time! What the hell are you, some lousy green kid? The contract says 'private dressing room,' you gotta have a private dressing room! You think it was easy to get a private dressing room out of that cheap Meyer broad? I hadda stand on my head! I hadda spit nickels! I hadda *bleed!*"

The response was a tinkling laugh and the words, "Cool
109

down, Sam, you'll last longer. My room wasn't cleaned out yet, so I'm sharing."

Nina recognized Christy Hall's voice and knew she was overhearing a conversation between the new Audrey Lincoln and her infamous rep, Sam Baylog. She suddenly felt like an eavesdropper and began to move with stealth, wanting to get out of the studio without being seen. All she needed was a run-in with an abusive gent.

She turned out the lights and began to open her dressing-room door, but drew back into the room. Christy and Baylog were just coming out into the hallway. She glimpsed his mountainous frame and almost gave herself away giggling. He was wearing a fur coat! Men's fur coats had always struck Nina as funny, but this one was hilarious, ballooning around his thick frame and coming to way below his knees. She retreated back into her dressing room, muffling her bubbles of laughter with her scarf. They'd have to pass her door to leave, and she stood motionless.

"The private dressing room will be ready on Monday, Sam. They promised."

"Yeah, famous promise number three, right after "Your check's in the mail,'" he spluttered. "And you know what the other one is."

Another peal of dismissive laughter came from Christy, and Nina wondered how she put up with him. Still, if you needed someone to fight your battles, you could probably do worse than Sam Baylog. She waited for a moment, to be sure they were gone, then emerged from her dressing room.

"Stand on my head!" the voice boomed. "I'm tellin' ya, I hadda stand on my head! That cheap Meyer broad! I shoulda stood on *her* head!" Nina yelped in surprise and whirled around. She could have sworn they were gone.

And they were. The accurate imitation of Sam Baylog had come from Rob Bryant, who was standing at the end of the corridor, grinning at her. She burst out laughing.

"That's wonderful! You have a sensational ear!" she told him.

110

"Baylog's easy. All broad brushstrokes. The hard ones are the people who don't have any particular mannerisms. You should hear my Dustin Hoffman. Now *that's* a work of art."

"It must be," she said, as they walked down the corridor toward the exit, and then she burst into a fresh fountain of laughter at the memory of Rob's impression.

"Hey, it wasn't that good," he said modestly.

"I wish I had it on tape. We'd break the place up Monday morning. Oh, do it for them, please, they'll love it!"

"You think so? Sure, why not?"

Outside, there wasn't a cab in sight and February was still doing its worst: the wind sliced down the street like a carving knife. Nina again began to regret putting Chessy out into the alley.

"Would you like a ride home?" Rob asked.

"Oh, I'll catch a cab on the corner."

"Nonsense. There aren't any cabs. Anyway, I'd be more than hapy to see you home. It's the least I can do. Repay you for the yeoman job you did today. I wonder if you realize, Nina, what a good influence you are on the rest of the cast? You just seem to bring out the best in them. I think it's the professionalism you bring to your work."

"Rob," she warned, her heart lifting at the compliment, "don't start now."

"I mean it, Nina. I'm amazed at the *esprit de corps* you inspired on that set today. Other groups I've worked with don't have it at all." His smile was sincere, disarming. "Let me drive you home, please? Better yet, let me buy you dinner." He raised a conciliatory hand. "At Corrigan's. Neutral ground, how's that? I certainly can't get out of control in a setting like that. I promise to behave. How about it?"

Why not? Her date with Rossi was off; there was nothing urgent waiting at the apartment. "Scout's honor?" she insisted.

He raised his right hand in the universal Boy Scout symbol, smiling puckishly. "I will be courteous, kind,

111

thrifty, brave, clean, and reverent. And I will help old ladies across the street, whether they want to cross or not."

His sheer good spirits won her over. "Okay, Rob," she agreed. "You're on. Corrigan's. But just for a quick bite, promise?"

"I promise! I promise! Famous promise number nineteen! And you know what the other eighteen are!" he shot back, allowing Sam Baylog another appearance.

They entered Corrigan's on gales of laughter.

Dinner was a joy. Corrigan's was half-deserted, a murky sanctuary in the gathering storm; none of the regulars were present. Against her better judgment Nina drank two gimlets before dinner. She ordered a spinach salad and a loin lamb chop, and surrendered to the temptation of a butter-drenched baked potato. And as they drank, then ate, there was delicious, witty conversation. Rob was on a tear, making her laugh nonstop. Talk touched on cast antics, on the Miami drug scene, on music, literature, politics—everything but religion. Things turned serious when he got onto the subject of poetry—a first love of Nina's—and she was all but seduced by the soul-touching that took place.

For not only could Rob cite poets and poems, he could also discuss the sonnet form and the impact of new young moderns. Most surprising of all, he could rattle off verse after verse of such favorites of Nina's as "Elegy in a Country Churchyard," "Thanatopsis," "Stopping by Woods on a Snowy Evening," and "The Highwayman." To which Nina countered with lines, verses, whole poems she'd committed to memory as a child and during her college years.

"'And still of a winter's night,'" they recited in quiet unison, "'they say, When the wind is in the trees . . . When the moon is a ghostly galleon tossed upon cloudy seas . . . A highwayman comes riding, riding, riding—'" Nina actually shivered. "Oh, I *love* that! The mood, the meter. You can just hear the horse's hooves, see the highwayman racing to meet the landlord's daughter." She

112

paused and stared at Rob. "What is this?" she asked with a deprecating laugh. "Crazy. I haven't talked to anyone like this, about things like this, in ages. And now, tonight, with you . . ."

"Don't stop," he said. "I'm loving every minute. It's so seldom that *I* can share thoughts . . . feelings . . . like these with anyone." His voice became almost reverent. "Oh, Nina, you are so special."

Something in his voice warned her that she was venturing into deep, troubled waters. Take it easy she told herself, back off, before it's too late. And she forced herself to shift gears, to steer the conversation into less seductive, less personal channels. Quickly, while she still had the will power to listen to her instincts. She blurted out the first thing that came to mind. "Isn't it terrible about Milly?" The words, jarringly out of synch, destroyed the warm, lulling rapport instantly.

His eyes chided her, fought to regain ascendancy. "Now what kind of a thing is that to say, Nina, when we were having such a nice time? Are you sure you want to talk about it?"

Nina forced some muscle into her words. "I . . . guess I do, Rob. Milly was my friend. I've taken her death—her *murder*—pretty hard. I want to find out anything I can that might lead to her killer. I . . ."

Something clicked behind Bryant's eyes; he frowned almost imperceptibly. "Murder? Is that what the police are saying? I'd understood that it was considered an accident. How come the police are confiding in you?"

Nina recognized her blunder immediately. "The police didn't tell me," she lied. "Scuttlebutt on the set. Nobody's *ever* fallen over that railing before. Talk, you know? I happen to believe it's true. It couldn't have been suicide. Milly had too much to live for; she'd gotten over the shock of Terri's death, and she was beginning a promising career. She wouldn't have killed herself just when things were beginning to look up for her."

Nina lowered her eyes. "She told me . . . that last day . . . that she'd been seeing you. She led me to believe that it had gotten pretty serious, if . . . you know what I mean."

Bryant smiled slightly, running his fingers over the back of Nina's hand. "Milly tended to overreact at times. She was badly shaken when Terri died. I held her several times when she broke down. There's a lot of comfort to be had from the warmth of a hug. But there was nothing between us beyond that."

Nina wanted to believe him. "If you say so, Rob. Only . . ."

His shoulders sagged, and he looked away in misery. "And you think that I had something to do with Milly's death? Is that it?"

"I didn't say that, Rob. I'm saying that you were . . . *close* to Milly at the last. Her only other friend on the set, really. I can't help thinking that perhaps you might know something about her that would prove helpful." Her eyes took on an apologetic look, pleaded with him not to misunderstand, not now, not when they were just getting to know each other so well.

"Maybe you can tell me what she told you," he said. "We can make that our jumping-off place."

Nina decided there was more to be gained than lost. "All right," she said, "What about her claim that she, not Terri, was originally first choice for the Audrey Lincoln role? That she was scratched at the last minute?"

"She told you that? It's news to me." His eyes registered astonishment. "But if it's true, then who was behind it? Who has the kind of power to make a decision like that?"

"Helen Meyer, of course. She *does* sign all our paychecks, after all. But why would she change her mind at the last minute?" Nina wondered aloud.

He pondered for a moment. "Talk about mysteries . . ."

Nina persisted, "You're *sure* she never mentioned that to you? It was eating her up. She was sure that the last-minute change was somehow related to Terri's death."

"And did she mention this to your favorite lad in blue?"

114

The unexpected reference made her uncomfortable. "What are you talking about?"

"Come on, Nina. I've been on the set long enough to hear the talk. I know you've got something going with Lieutenant Rossi. Give me a little credit, will you?"

She remained defiant. "Even if it were so," she said firmly, "I don't think it's relevant here. I'm asking you about Milly, for any background information that might shed some light on her murder."

"So you can run back to Lieutenant Rossi with it?" It was Bryant's turn to be defensive.

"He *is* the investigating officer, isn't he? Why not?"

He took a deep, long breath and let it out slowly. "Believe me, Nina," he said, "I told Rossi everything I knew about Milly, including the fact that we were *not* intimate. And now could we, please, talk about something else? I was enjoying our previous conversation so much." He smiled, and the earlier, more welcome mood began to reassert itself. "Read any good books lately? Now *there's* an original line for you."

Deciding that discretion was the better part of valor, Nina went along. "I'm reading all the Ann Tyler I can find. Do you know *Dinner at the Homesick Restaurant*?"

"Loved it. One of her absolute best. It was one of those books you never wanted to see end . . ."

They were off again. Once more the soothing, warm intimacy built. Nina found herself deliberately trying to dispel the bad vibes of a few moments ago. And soon, a warm ease rebuilding, Nina felt as if she'd known Rob Bryant all her life.

It was almost eleven o'clock before they drew into a parking space close to Primrose Towers' main entrance. As Rob switched off his engine and killed the lights, he said, "It's been a lovely evening, Nina. I hate to see it end." He permitted Alan Alda to join them for a moment. "I don't suppose you'd invite a guy up for a nightcap?"

Nina giggled, confused by warring emotions. She, too, dreaded to see the evening end and briefly toyed with the idea. She couldn't remember when she'd had so much fun, when the conversation had flowed so spontaneously, so wittily. To have a man listen, really listen, and treat her like an intellectual equal! There were times when Dino was unable to surmount that not so subtle macho barrier. . . . She did a mental double take. Whatever am I thinking of? she asked herself. Bring Rob up? Not under any circumstances!

"No," she said lightly, "I don't think that would be wise, Rob. You are simply too charming for your own good—or mine. I don't think I'd be up to it." She offered her hand in good night, instantly embarrassed by the gesture's staginess. "It's been a marvelous evening."

In one smooth move his fingers closed around her wrist and firmly pulled her toward him. Their faces were dangerously close. "And you are too much for me to resist," he said softly, tilting his head to kiss her. Nearly in a trance, Nina allowed him to draw her those extra inches closer.

"Rob, don't," she whispered. "I don't think . . ." The rest of it went unfinished as his lips, sensuous, warm, slightly moist, closed on hers. His hand tightened on her back and drew her body tight to his. She found herself melting, dazedly wondering why his beard wasn't as bristly as she'd imagined. His cologne carried to her nostrils; the touch of his hand on her back soothed and aroused her at the same time.

Nina struggled for a moment, not with Rob but with herself. Relax and enjoy this, one part of her was saying. You know it's nice, don't you? You know you like it. He's so delicious. Just relax—see what develops.

A delightful torpor built within her, coupled with a dazzling heat and urgency. Just a little longer, a seductive voice murmured somewhere deep in her psyche. Let's see where this leads. You can always stop if he goes too far. You can . . .

His hand reached smoothly between the heavy folds of her coat and closed on her right breast. It moved in a maddening, will-robbing motion, an attention Nina allowed for the slightest extra second—then the final warning bell exploded into a deafening clangor.

She pulled away and flung herself toward the door. "That's enough, Rob! Do you hear? Stop it!"

He shook his head, and the glazed look lifted from his eyes. "God, Nina, I'm sorry! I didn't mean to do that, not with you. I was going to wait . . . for a more opportune moment. But then everything seemed to fall into place. I thought maybe you were enjoying it as much as I was."

"You thought wrong, Rob," Nina lied. "I'm . . . I'm not interested in anything like that."

He smiled at her. "Well, in case you're passing out rain checks . . ."

"I'm not! Now, if you don't mind . . ."

"I can wait, Nina. For a woman like you I'd be willing to wait a long, long time." Rob's voice took on a lulling tone, quiet and supremely confident. "Because in the end . . . I intend to have you, Nina. We're good together. We're going to belong to each other."

"Rob, it's not going to happen. Now, if you'll just let me out . . ."

"I'll see you to the door," he offered.

"That's not necessary, Rob."

As he came around to open her door, he tried to draw her into his arms, to take another kiss. Nina whirled out of his grasp, her heels clattering on the frigid pavement as she hurried toward the lobby door.

She looked back and saw him standing beside his car, the familiar boyish grin on his face.

Then Nina was inside the building, heading for the elevator. As she started up to the thirty-sixth floor, she slumped against the wall in a daze.

What is there about that man? she questioned. Good God, for a minute there I almost—

Shamed, she couldn't even finish the thought.

Chapter Ten

It was 2:35 on Sunday afternoon. Nina had spent the morning clearing the decks, seeing to minor household chores, getting Monday's lines under her belt. Icing the champagne . . .

And now Rossi was there. Haunted by thoughts of the night before with Rob Bryant, Nina was eager to get her hands on Rossi, to renew their relationship and erase the memory of what had nearly happened.

But life doesn't always follow the script. Dino declined the champagne and seemed oblivious to her mood. He just wanted to talk about the case.

"So?" Nina said to Dino. "Terri has been dead a week already. Milly's gone three days. And we still don't have an angle on either one. I just don't understand why, with all the high-powered police technology available, no one can come up with a breakthrough of some kind. Is there anything new on Terri's West Coast connections?"

"Still slogging," Rossi answered, settling down into the raw silk cushions of Nina's sofa. "A little here, a little there. Phone calls to various past acquaintances of Ms. Triano. Calls to various directors she worked with."

"And?"

"She was an extremely talented actress, ambitious to a

119

dangerous degree—read 'knife in the back.' Not a pretty picture. I meant it when I said acquaintances. She seemingly had no friends. There are some pretty bitter people out there where Ms. Triano is concerned. She was very secretive—confided in nobody from what I can gather."

"Sounds like Terri all right."

"I called the LAPD, and asked them to track down the address we got from the Screen Actors Guild. The rent was paid up, but they came up empty there, too. A most unsentimental lady, Ms. Triano. She wasn't big on souvenirs at all. Can you believe, not one single photo of her ex."

"That *is* weird. Anything new on him?"

"They were married about three years back. The guy named Freeman Collier is even more elusive than Terri. When, and if, they got divorced, were separated, or whatever, is definitely up for grabs. He was supposedly in insurance, although there's no trace of any company he ever worked for. I've got some strings out in Washington, via Social Security, to see if we can get a current location on him. And there's supposed to be an aunt of Terri's who lives in Detroit, *maybe*. The PD there is trying to run her down."

"Still no clues on the cause of Terri's death?"

"Zilch. It's got Doc Boyer stumped. But Earl's a bulldog when it comes to forensics; he'll break it down sooner or later. And when he does, things will start to fall into place."

"Have you thought about Milly's claim that she was supposed to win the role in the first place? I think that might turn out to be important. What'd Helen say?"

"Haven't asked her about that yet. She and Horst are in San Francisco for some convention this weekend. Spence Sprague begged off. The world was falling around his ears Friday. I'm talking to him tomorrow. I got to Gelber, though."

Helen Meyer in San Francisco? Nina mused. That explained why Rob Bryant was on the loose last night. But she didn't want to think about that. "And what did David have to say?"

120

"Not much. He wasn't aware that there had been any commitment one way or another before the final decision was made. But he pointed out that he was not included in the closed-door session that Helen held after the final auditions. I got the impression he was less than candid."

"Meaning?"

"He may be covering up for someone. Could be he was forced into something unsavory, something he's not proud of. I'll be ready when I talk to Sprague tomorrow. I'll jar something out of *someone*."

Nina sipped thoughtfully at her champagne, eyed the level of Rossi's scotch and water. How would she pose her next point without incriminating herself? She began in a thoughtful, faraway voice, "When you interviewed Rob Bryant on Friday . . ."

"Yes?"

"Where did you tell me he was when Milly died?"

"Going through a last minute runthrough with Corinne Demetry, in her dressing room. She's the one who took Valerie Vincent's place, isn't she?"

"Right."

"And her statement checked with his. What are you getting at?"

"Something's nagging me. On the day she died, Milly told me that she was beginning to get involved with Rob, that he was being very supportive and protective toward her. In fact, she said she was crazy about him and terrified that Helen would find out."

"So?"

"But just yesterday he denied it."

Dino focused sharply on her every word. "Exactly what did he say?"

"Not all that much. He said that he'd tried to comfort Milly, and that she overreacted, and there was nothing going on. But it wasn't what he said, it was how he said it. . . ."

"Tell me about that."

Nina recalled Rob's attitudes of the day before and searched for exactly the right words to describe them.

"Nick was out sick, so Rob directed several scenes yesterday, and it was amazing. Dino, he's really very good. Everyone responded beautifully, which was a miracle in itself, considering what a rotten mood we were all in. Then later on, he was so different, so relaxed—until I mentioned Milly. That was when he tensed up. He denied they were involved, but he sounded very defensive to me. A few minutes later, when we got off the subject of Milly, he relaxed again."

Dino set his drink on the coffee table and regarded her for a long moment. "What do you mean, 'later on'?" he finally asked.

She looked back at him, the picture of innocence, but her mind was racing at top speed to find a way to cover up the slip. It would be a vast error to let Dino know she'd had dinner with Rob Bryant. So she said, "Later on, in the afternoon—we were chatting during a break. It seemed like a good time to pick his brains regarding Milly. Do you think it means anything?"

He relaxed and picked up the drink again. "I don't know. Could be, but . . ." He paused for a moment. "Are you telling me you were with that guy all day yesterday?"

"Relax, there were at least twenty other people around the whole time. And a cat." An additional decoy couldn't hurt—get him further off the scent.

"A *cat?*"

"Yes—he's the cutest thing. I call him Chessy." Nina wrinkled her nose playfully. "He followed me home, Daddy. Can I keep him?" She briefed him on the appearance of the stray tomcat. "Maybe when we go out for dinner, we can drive by the studio? I'd like to leave him some food. If he's around, you'll actually get to meet him."

But Rossi wasn't so easily sidetracked. "Get back to Bryant. What are you suggesting?"

"I'm suggesting we'd better keep an eye on him." Nina was both uncomfortable and puzzled by the ambivalent feelings the put down caused her. "Either he or Milly were not telling the whole story. Another thing: He knows

122

that you and I are an item; he suspects that my interest in the case is more than casual."

"You did have yourself quite a little talk, didn't you? I hope you didn't blow your cover too much."

"He says he's been hearing things about us from other people on the staff. God knows, it's no secret anymore."

"Anything else?"

"Yes. Something that didn't ring true. I mentioned how Milly had been led to think she'd won the role over Terri. He said it was news to him. But on Thursday Milly told me that she'd discussed that development with Rob as well."

"Did she tell you that outright?"

"Yes. Unless my memory's completely on the fritz."

"You couldn't be mistaken about that?"

"I could be, but I don't think I am."

"Strange. Maybe you can question him again on that tomorrow. Come at it from left field. See how he reacts. Sounds like you had yourself quite a busy day yesterday. Cats. New actress. Rob Bryant . . . By the way, where were you last night? I called several times. Got done with my paper work early, thought maybe we could have dinner after all. You still weren't in at eleven. That's when I gave up for the night."

No, Nina thought, hard put to keep her expression neutral. I wasn't here. I was out in Bryant's car, struggling with him—and with myself. "We didn't clear the set until eight. Then I went to dinner with Christy Hall. We yakked it up at Corrigan's for hours. She's a great gal. She's going to work out just fine." Enough. Too much and he'll start to get suspicious.

She jumped up in an attempt to further smokescreen her anxiety. "Freshen your drink? Good God, that sounds like I'm trying to seduce you!"

"Aren't you?"

Don't drop a beat, she told herself. And *keep it light*.

"Guilty as charged, officer. Take me away. Book me. Print me." She grinned, "You dope. Any other man would've been all over me by now, instead of all this shop talk." *Especially Rob Bryant*, she thought.

"A time and place for everything," Rossi said.

She dropped fresh ice into his glass, then drowned it in Scotch and added a drop of water. Topping off her champagne, her thoughts drifted again to the incident in Rob's car. What did it mean? she asked for the hundredth time. Was the lady simply ripe for dalliance? Was she already tiring of Dino? Impossible! She loved him; theirs was definitely a forever-and-ever arrangement. It would be his place to throw her out, if and when things went sour. Then if it wasn't that, what? Was she a more sensual creature than even she realized? Did she have a sense of time running out, of life passing her by? She'd read about things like that.

If not, then why last night's close call? Just because Rob had wrapped her in a web of starshine the likes of which she'd seldom encountered before, played her like a virtuoso, plucking all the right strings? Her stomach felt hollow all of a sudden and a hot urgency rippled through her body.

She advanced on Dino, carefully balancing the brimming glasses. If something doesn't happen soon . . .

"Darling," she said as she put the glasses down, "I've missed you so terribly. It's been two weeks now." She gently shoved him back into the cushions, her lips closing on his. The tip of her tongue invaded his mouth, began to explore the familiar yet foreign territory. He responded and brought his right hand to her breasts. Yes, her mind raged, now!

"Wow," Rossi sighed, when finally she pulled away. "What did I do to deserve that?"

"Don't talk," she murmured just before she replaced her mouth on his. "Just hold me, kiss me, love me . . ." Rossi's gentle talented hands turned her body to living flames.

She pulled away, rose, and started from the room. "Bring the drinks, darling," she crooned. "Come with me. I can't wait one minute longer." He stood up slowly, tugging at his tie, his eyes fastened on her as though he'd never seen her before.

124

"Hurry, love—unless you want it to happen without you!"

She disappeared into the bedroom and he followed quickly, leaving the drinks behind.

As time passed, his scotch became diluted and her champagne grew flat. Later they poured fresh drinks and sipped them slowly in the gathering darkness of her bedroom.

February could be a beautiful month after all. . . .

Chapter Eleven

"One minute there!" Spence Sprague called, stopping Nina dead in her tracks at the studio the next day. "Just where do you think you're going with that thing?"

Nina glanced at the heavy load of orange cat contentedly draped over her right shoulder and said innocently, "What thing?" Then she turned on 100 watts of radiant smile. "Oh—this cat, you mean?"

"Yeah, that cat. You know the rule about no animals on the set."

"Well, we can't always take such things seriously, now can we, Spence? Rules are made to be bent a little. Besides, I've got a mouse in my dressing room." She smiled fondly at Chessy, who'd been patiently waiting for her that morning when she'd opened the fire door on the north end of the soundstage. "And Chessy's just crazy about mice."

"C'mon, Nina," Sprague growled. "You know we can't go starting this. If I allow your cat in, next thing you know everybody in the cast will want the same privileges. We'll have a zoo here!"

"This isn't *my* cat," Nina said, fluttering her long lashes in playful guile. "He lives in the alley. He's a stray that I'm keeping in my room until I can locate his owner." She put Chessy down on the floor, where he immediately began twining around her ankles. "Chessy isn't just an ordinary cat, Spence. Look at this." She addressed the animal. "Here, Chessy. Will you shake hands?"

The cat dropped his ample bottom onto the floor and lifted his right paw. "Well, I'll be damned!" Sprague said. "I never saw anything like that."

"You try it."

"C'mon, cat," he said gruffly. "Shake."

Chessy was no fool. He approached Sprague, sat down and again offered a large, furry paw. And after Sprague took the paw and gravely shook it, he began his little love dance about his legs as well. He kept it up until the man squatted, giving him a few grudging pats. "Friendly, isn't he? Built like a damned tank."

"I'll keep him in my dressing room, Spence. He won't bother anyone. I just can't bear to think of the poor guy out in the cold all the time." She indicated the bag in her left arm that contained cans of cat food, a can opener, bowls, and a carton of milk. "I'm all ready to take care of him. Come on, Spence—don't be a grouch. I'll put him back out tonight. And we *do* have mice, you know. He won't be in anybody's way, I promise."

As Chessy, the eternal promoter, continued to twine around the man's ankles, Spence relented. "Okay, Nina. But he goes out every night, fair weather or foul. Otherwise, he's history, understand?" He patted Chessy one last time. "Now get going. You've got group lines in a few minutes."

Up in her dressing room, Chessy purred like a tractor as Nina spread newspapers on the floor and set out Chessy's breakfast. Then he did a thing that endeared him all the more to Nina. Instead of greedily pouncing on his food, he continued dancing around her feet; he wouldn't be content until she picked him up again. When she did, he bunted her face with his nose, and snuggled his head into the hollow of her neck. Finally, once the ritual was concluded, the clever feline deigned to eat. As Nina watched him she thought, What have I let myself in for this time?

Robin Tally and Corinne Demetry stopped by and when

Nina displayed her new buddy and had him do his trick, the Chessy Fan Club began to grow. Angela Dolan, a dedicated cat-nut herself, charged in. Chessy offered her a gentlemanly paw, and she was enthralled. After which, sedately haunched, he regarded the women with a smug look, obviously ruminating on the fact that it never hurt to have as many allies as possible.

There were those who grumbled when the inquisitive cat managed to escape the confines of Nina's dressing room and appeared on the set. But once Nina had him do his trick, the mood changed. Mr. Personality moved from person to person until he received a pat from each.

On the Marston Corporation set, Bob Valentine, an avowed cat-hater, determined to hold out. Deliberately keeping his hands in his pockets, he ignored the animal. Finally Chessy bounded up on the couch beside him, nudging at Bob's wrists, coaxing nonstop to unwedge them. At last Valentine, amazed by his persistence, was forced to give in. "Did you see that?" he marveled. "That fool cat just wouldn't quit until I gave him a pat." It appeared that he and Chessy were well on the way to becoming the best of friends.

Learning fast, Chessy stayed out of the way of the cameras, prowling the dark corners of the soundstage, hunting mice. Then he found an empty chair and caught up on his sleep. When awake, he groomed himself tirelessly until his paws and the wide bib under his chin were gleaming white.

Nina had hoped that Nick Galano would be back this morning. She simply couldn't face Rob Bryant after Saturday night's scene. But Nick was still down with the flu. Even yesterday's fiery session with Dino hadn't completely blotted out the memory of her reaction to the man. Yes, she'd stopped him in time. But a nagging thought persisted: had Rob not taken "no" for an answer, would she have found the will to resist?

But Rob was remote and thoroughly professional, Nina had to admit. Still, there were moments when his look

129

penetrated to deeper levels. Or so Nina thought, guilt still preying on her mind.

"How was your Sunday?" he asked as they gathered for the day's first blocking session. "Get rested up?"

Nina, remembering the three separate events with Dino, allowed a lazy, enigmatic smile to surface. "In a manner of speaking," she said, content to let Rob think what he would. "And you?"

"Sacked out all afternoon," he replied. "Took in a movie in the evening. Quiet. *Too* quiet." His meaning was unmistakable.

"I was thinking about some of the things we talked about," she said, checking to make sure no one was eavesdropping.

"Oh? What? The poetry session maybe?" His look became a shade heavier. "The road not taken?"

Nina ignored his quotation from Robert Frost. "No— Milly Gowan. Something you said about her bothered me."

His eyes became wary. "That woman's beginning to haunt me."

Nina pondered the wisdom of confronting Bryant just now. *Maybe it would be better to wait.* But a steely resolve formed. No time like the present. "When I told you about the dirty stunt Milly said Helen Meyer pulled on her . . ."

"Yes?"

"You said that it was news to you."

"Yes, it was."

Nina fixed him with a hard stare. "Later on, I distinctly remembered Milly telling me that she'd discussed it with you." Nina tried to keep it light. "You wouldn't be keeping something from me, would you?"

"Hardly, " he said calmly. "I think you're mistaken, Nina. I don't remember anything like that at all. As I said Saturday night, Milly was a great one for jumping to conclusions. She may have thought she told me about it, but I can assure you she didn't." He turned away abruptly, waved Christy Hall and Bob Valentine forward. Had he done it deliberately to get off the hook? "Okay, gang, let's go. Places, everyone."

130

For the rest of the morning, it was all business. Rob handled the cast with professional aplomb, and they responded accordingly. Even the crew seemed to recognize that he was no green beginner; they quietly did as Rob asked. New assistant directors sometimes had a hard time keeping the crew under control—the guys on lights were particularly notorious in this respect—but Rob just breezed through. Nina knew the crew to be an intuitive bunch and wondered if the law-and-order atmosphere on the set was because they respected his authority—or because they didn't yet trust him enough to tangle with him, even in fun.

During a break, she tried to find out.

"You boys are so quiet today," she said, plopping into a chair on a short break.

They looked uncomfortable, somehow. "Yeah. Well, some days are up, some are down," was the delayed rejoiner from one of the old-timers on the lighting crew. But from another one, much younger, Nina heard a muttered remark about not messing with "teacher's pet."

So that was it. In their opinion it was best to lay off Mrs. Meyer's "special friend". . . .

After the full runthrough, Rob asked to see Nina and Christy in private. He gave them a few notes regarding their upcoming big emotional scene, and showered Christy with compliments.

She grinned broadly. "Easy, Rob! If I repeat half that applesauce to Sam Baylog, he'll be down here pounding on Helen's desk and screaming for a renegotiated contract."

"Okay, you're right. I take half of it back. You're only so-so. Go tell him that."

"If I did, he'd light out after you, threatening a lawsuit for defamation of something or other." And Christy went off to her dressing room, leaving Rob and Nina alone.

"Nice work, really nice," he told her. "You and Christy have some great chemistry going. I'm going to recommend the writers beef up her character."

"Good," Nina responded. "I think you're anticipating public reaction. They're going to want to see a lot more of Christy Hall, so we better be ready." She turned to go, but he stopped her—as she knew he would.

"Nina. I can't let the day go by without telling you what a wonderful time I had on Saturday—and without apologizing for getting carried away."

"That's all right, Rob. I understand."

"I don't think you do. It's your own fault, you know. You are positively the most . . ." he searched for the words.

"You better stop while you're ahead. Look, I have to get ready for . . ."

"Nina, please give me another chance to behave better. Have dinner with me tonight? Or any other night? Or lunch?"

Her reproachful look was his answer, and he accepted it gracefully.

"Afternoon tea?" he enunciated carefully, giving it a wonderfully comic British twist.

"Charmed, Lord Dunwiddy, but my social secretary tells me I'm completely booked."

"A pity, Lady Pamela. A great pity."

She patted him on the arm and went to her dressing room, marveling at the fact that even in defeat, the man was utterly charming.

Nina had little chance to mull over further thoughts about Rob Bryant, or about Milly and Terri. For suddenly the pall of recent events seemed to lift, and the cast's spirits soared. The old camaraderie returned and everyone realized it; they celebrated by attacking the day's scenes with gusto.

Even the afternoon prowlings of Lieutenant Dino Rossi and Charley Harper did little to dampen the mood. The daily routine clicked off like clockwork, everyone came in on time, their lines letter perfect. Business as usual. Let the good times roll.

Later in the afternoon, with the show wrapped a few

minutes early for a change, Nina skulked around the murky, closed-down sets waiting for Dino to finish his questioning. It was then that she observed something she wished she hadn't.

In a gloomy corner, their heads silhouetted against a dimly lit panel of simulated brick, Nina saw Rob Bryant and Corinne Demetry. They were engaged in earnest conversation, their faces close. Nina froze. She knew she was spying, but she couldn't resist.

Nina couldn't hear what they were saying, but the body language was universal; words weren't necessary. Rob—back in his natural element—was promoting again, his eyes alive, commanding, his expression supremely confident: amused and amusing.

Corinne, her head tilted up to his, her expression rapt, hung on his every word. Even in the dull light Nina saw the liquid shine of those eyes, the eager wetness of those lips. Corinne offered herself, waited in quaking breathlessness as Rob slowly lowered his head to hers and kissed her. Nina stood transfixed, breathing suspended. A crazy jumble of emotions surged within her breast, including an undeniable sense of betrayal. How could he—so soon after Saturday night?

Then the tide subsided and she saw herself in Corinne, understood just how easy it was to succumb to Rob Bryant's smooth talk.

Then, as the kiss went on and on, she saw the greedy way Rob dropped his hands low on Corinne's body, gently pulling her torso more tightly against his.

Nina whirled and felt her way off the shadowy soundstage. Time to go home, she told herself, her throat suddenly tight. Get out of here. Go find some clean air.

Chessy was waiting in her dressing room. She lifted him with a small grunt and cuddled him briefly. He immediately commenced his diesel engine sputterings. She was amazed to find her eyes suddenly glazed. Was it simply jealousy? Or rage at her own naivete? You'd think, she told herself, at your advanced age, with all your experience—

"Come on, Chessy," she said, taking her frustration out

133

on the luckless puss. "Time for you to go out into the storm."

At dinner, tucked into a cozy booth at Corrigan's, Dino briefly related the scant findings of his afternoon's questioning session.

"This thing has me at my wits' end," Dino said. "The more questions I ask, the less I find out."

"What did Helen say?"

"She fogged me is what she did. At first she told me Milly was mistaken, that she'd never been given advance notice that she'd won the contest. But when I insisted that there had to be something to the story because of what Milly told you the day she died, she got all fidgety." He snorted. "My Roman profile didn't carry the day this time, honey. Someone else must be beating my time—wonder who? Mentioning your name didn't help, either. She had a few choice words for you."

"Par for the course. Then what?"

"Then nothing. I came at her from every possible angle, but she dug in her heels and wouldn't budge from her original line. By the time I folded my hand, she was getting red in the face. She insisted Millicent Gowan was a paranoid misfit, a bald-faced liar, and a victim of her own delusions. Terri Triano had been the front runner from the start."

"What about Horst Krueger? Milly was positive he was on her side all the way."

"Could be. He admitted that he was impressed with her understated manner and her talent. But at the last, he said, the vote went against her. I couldn't help but get the feeling that someone had tied a firecracker to his tail. It wasn't an open election, that's for sure."

"Why would Helen do a thing like that? Change her mind at the last minute?" Nina frowned. "*If* what Milly said is true. I don't figure it. Unless . . ."

"Unless what?"

"Maybe she found out something about Milly late in the game that drastically colored her decision."

"Like what? From what you told me about Milly, she was squeaky clean."

"True . . ."

"By the way, I spoke to Milly's parents. Pretty formidable couple. They took her body back to Illinois yesterday. No information to speak of. There's no link whatsoever between her background there and what happened to her in this 'wicked, wicked city'—their exact words. That interview was one of the toughest I've ever done. The mother broke down repeatedly, kept saying how excited Milly had been about her big break." He shook his head grimly.

"Poor Milly," Nina sighed. "What a terrible waste!"

Dino returned to the original topic. "The only other angle I can come up with is Rob Bryant. Do you suppose he could wield that much influence over his faded blossom? Force Helen to renege on her original decision?"

"Could be. But why? What difference would it make to him which woman won the contest?"

"Well, maybe if he had a thing for Terri, it would be one way to keep her around for a while. If I judge him correctly, he wouldn't hesitate to hold a favor like that over Terri's head, work it into the ground."

Nina didn't want to pursue this particular line of conjecture. "We can't prove that. What about Spence Sprague?"

"At least he was forthright about Terri. He admired the actress but loathed the woman. 'Sewer-mouth' was one of the more charitable terms he used. He wasn't that keen on Milly, either, but he was quick to admit that he voted for her. When I pressed him about Milly receiving advance notice that she'd won, he clammed up, too."

"Which leaves Rob Bryant. You said you were going to lower the boom on him, too."

"He's one cool dude. He got resentful as hell when I introduced comments taken from your testimony; he verged on making some crack about our . . . relationship. But he apparently thought better of it. I'd have read him off, but good."

"He denied Milly's version, I presume."

"But definitely. In the first place, he insisted that he and Milly weren't really that close. If she implied to you that a more intimate relationship existed, she was indulging in some sort of fantasy. He repeatedly denied that Milly had ever told him anything about being conned. I couldn't shake him an inch."

"Then you don't think Rob's connected to Milly's murder?"

"No, not at this point."

"Did you hark back to Terri, see if you could jar something loose there?"

"What's the point? I'm convinced there was no real connection between them. They had casual conversations on the set, at the party, nothing more. I'd pretty firmly established that on the night Terri died anyway."

"Well," Nina said a trifle testily, "if he could knock Milly for a loop as fast as he did, who's to say he didn't do the same with Terri? Trip him up, Mr. Detective. I wonder if they had a hot little thing going—maybe Rob convinced Helen to keep Terri around. It's not as farfetched as it sounds."

It was Rossi's turn to get testy. "Christ, why don't I just turn this whole thing over to you? Let you wear the damned badge. Is that what you want?"

"No, Dino. That's not what I want." At the moment, Nina wasn't sure what she wanted.

He drove her home. There was clearly no way to rekindle the mood of the previous afternoon, and she wasn't sure it would be a good idea just then anyway. A cool kiss at the curb, a brief promise to keep in touch and call you later—and that was all right, too.

What Nina really wanted to do was soak in a hot bath and think about absolutely nothing at all. But as she turned her key in the lock she could hear her phone ringing.

"Hello?" she said breathlessly.

"Nina," the rusty, gruff voice said. "Sounds like you've been running. How'n hell are you? Remember me?"

Nina squealed in delight. "Scottie! How good to hear your voice!" It was Scotty Lane, her old ex-newshawk friend, who'd been hospitalized after a hit-and-run last fall while chasing clues on Nina's behalf. Though the May Minton murder had happened only in early October, it seemed ages had passed since then. After the case was closed, Scotty had gone to Florida to spend some time recuperating with a retired schoolteacher sister.

"How *are* you? That arm of yours? The leg? Back in shape again? When did you get back?" she asked eagerly.

"All shipshape, kid. I got in last Wednesday. And how have you been, darling? Up to your usual tricks, I see. That show of yours must be hexed or something—*two* murders this time. You don't believe in doing things halfway, do you?"

"Please, Scotty." Pain edged her words. "It's no laughing matter. Milly Gowan and I had gotten rather close."

"Sounds like my Nina—everybody's friend. Sorry if I sound flip. You know what I always say: if we didn't laugh we'd drown in our tears. So, tell me about it. Maybe I can be of some help."

For the next twenty-five minutes Nina briefed Scotty Lane on the current status of the two deaths, finding that the mere act of bouncing her ideas off a neutral party, even if she didn't really intend to avail herself of his expert assistance, vaguely therapeutic. It helped her think more clearly, gain some badly needed perspective.

When Scotty heard where Rob had come from, he made a surprising offer.

"Miami, you say? Hell, I've got a lot of connections down there, a couple guys on the *Herald* who are real whiz-bangs. I taught 'em all I know, and they *still* don't know anything." He broke into guffaws at his own joke. "If you want me to get them to turn over a few rocks down there, just give the nod. Rob Bryant, you say? And Helen met him at some Independent TV Producers' Convention back in December? Let me jot some of this down."

"No, Scotty," she protested. "It's not necessary. Dino and his squad are checking through the normal police networks. Something's bound to surface soon. If and when I need something special I'll let you know."

"Well, hell," he grumbled, "it wouldn't be that much trouble. Every little bit helps, you know. You never know when that extra little piece of the puzzle is going to fit."

"Poor baby," Nina teased laughingly. "He's gone and got his feelings hurt now, hasn't he?"

"Well, you froze me out on the Minton case, you know."

"*I* froze you out? Nobody told you to go walking around in front of cars, did they?"

"Walking around in front of cars?" He faked anger. "Now, just one cotton-picking minute there, girl!"

Nina giggled. "Scotty, you nut. I'm so glad you're back. I missed you."

"When are we going to get together? I've been saving my money. I'll buy you dinner. And then we're going dancing. You promised, remember?"

"I remember, darling. And it *is* a date. But not this week. The case comes first. I'll give you a call very soon, that's a promise."

For long moments after Nina hung up, she stood smiling softly to herself. Some people, she thought, can be so damned nice. . . .

Chapter Twelve

Nina arrived at the studio the next morning a few minutes earlier than required, and after a brief stop in her dressing room to deposit her coat and bag, she went directly to the fire door. Pushing it open slightly, she called softly, "Here, Chessy, here, Chessy, here—" She got no further.

The big tom crawled out of a pile of cardboard boxes to the right of the fire door and jumped into her arms, muddy paws and all. "Poor old man," Nina cooed. *"You* want me anyway, don't you? Even if Dino doesn't." She chuckled. "You want some grub, that's what you want."

She cuddled him closer as she returned to her dressing room. "How did I ever get along without you?"

With Chessy contentedly working on a bowl of cat food, Nina joined the group assembling for the day's first line rehearsal. Within minutes it was clear that the happy atmosphere of the previous day still prevailed. Good, she thought, relishing the warm *bonhomie* that had been absent from Meyer Studios ever since the conclusion of the talent search. Let's get back to normal and stay there.

But not for long.

Shortly after 9:30, when they were doing the day's first blocking and timing, they began to be aware of a commotion coming from the direction of the production offices.

"What's going on?" Nina muttered to Christy Hall. They'd been in the midst of resolving the weighty issue of how many steps Melanie Prescott should take toward the door before turning to face the insidiously menacing Audrey Lincoln, and concentration was becoming difficult.

"Just remember, it wasn't my idea," Christy mumbled under her breath, not wanting to incur the wrath of Nick Galano, who had just crawled out of a sick bed and was not in the sweetest mood known to man.

Nina wondered what Christy was talking about, but the question was obviated moments later when the argument erupted from Helen Meyer's office into the hall, and the volume erupted as well. Mrs. Meyer and Mr. Baylog were having a wee disagreement.

"You're outta your mind! You're a crazy lady! You're gonna land in the rubber room!" Sam Baylog shouted.

"You call yourself an agent? You couldn't negotiate a—"

"Agent? Who says agent? Omma *manager*! Don't gimme that agent crap!"

"—snowball in a blizzard! Close-ups are *our* business, not yours, you bird-brained buffalo!"

"You got the terms, take 'em or leave 'em!"

"Get out of my studio! Now! And take that ridiculous coat off my desk before somebody shoots it!"

Mindful of Helen's legendary raccoon, several of the cast were hard put to suppress their giggles—not in the interests of good manners, but because they didn't want to miss anything.

"You threatening *me*? You *threatening* me? Didja hear that, girlie? She *threatened* me, this animal that calls herself a producer! Nobody threatens Sam Baylog! You want trouble, you got it! The only thing you're gonna shoot is close-ups, and plenty of 'em!"

The actors gave up all pretense of listening to Nick Galano and paid rapt attention to the delicious argument. Nick was exasperated, "For God's sake, somebody shut that noise out of here. Close the door!"

But the uproar grew in volume as the antagonists barked their way down the corridor and neared the rehearsal hall. Instead of reaching a crescendo and then diminishing as the pitched battle proceeded toward the street exit, the rehearsal room door burst open and the marvelous mass of Sam Baylog, fur coat and all, filled the doorway.

"Christy!" he bawled at the top of his considerable lungs.

"What is it, Sam?" Christy responded mildly.

"Hang it up! We're walkin'!"

"Go away, Sam. I'm busy."

"I tell ya, we're walkin'. The Meyer broad won't budge. Come on, getcha hat. Who needs this crapola? I got four more jobs lined up for ya."

Nick Galano, fed up with this interruption, opened his mouth to speak, but Christy ended the matter before he could say a word, "Sam, you're making a fool of yourself. I told you not to try this. Now get out of here before I find myself a new agent. We'll talk later—or never." Her normally sweet voice began in low chill and proceeded down to subfrigid. The last two words had icicles dangling from them, and Sam got the message. He regarded the group wordlessly for a moment, then fixed his baleful glare on Nina. "This is all *your* fault, you know!"

With that, Sam Baylog backed out of the doorway. One final explosive exchange erupted, and then two very different pairs of footsteps were heard as Sam lumbered his way toward the street door and Helen's high heels rat-a-tatted back to her office. Moments later there was a mighty crash as the street door was flung open and hurled shut. Then silence reigned.

"What did *I* do?" Nina asked no one in particular.

"All right, I can see we'll have to lay it to rest here and now," Nick said, sighing in resignation. "Christy, what the hell was that all about?"

"You'll laugh."

"We could use a laugh. Enlighten us."

"Poor Sam," Christy sighed. "When he was negotiating with Helen for my contract he wanted some nutty clause about the number of comparitive close-ups I get. Naturally Helen wasn't going to agree to that."

"Naturally. Christy, I know I'm going to regret asking this, but what's a comparative close-up?" It was what they all wanted to know.

"And how is it my fault?" Nina asked in a very small voice.

"That's the really stupid part. Sam had this table worked up. So many close-ups for Nina, so many close-ups for me. I told him to forget it. But you know Sam, always trying to go everybody one better. Sorry for the interruption."

"Oh, I don't think it'll happen again. If I know Helen, she's busy right now issuing an order to have Sam barred from the studio. Now can we get back to work, people?"

Nina's heart sank. She knew, deep down, that Helen wouldn't have much trouble convincing herself that Sam Baylog was right about one thing—Nina McFall was to blame. From Helen's point of view, whenever anything went wrong, Nina was the cause.

Nina wondered wryly if she could persuade Dave Gelber and Sally Burman to write Melanie Prescott out of the script for a while—like a year or two.

Things were looking up again shortly, and by the time Nina returned from a hilarious luncheon at Corrigan's with Angela Dolan, Sylvia Kastle, and Mary Kennerley, she'd decided that Melanie Prescott didn't need to take a prolonged business trip after all.

The runthrough from 12:30 to 1:00 went smoothly enough, and then the two assistant directors gave the actors individual notes before they got into their makeup and costumes. Nick's notes for Nina were very light. She started toward her dressing room, but as she crossed the large rehearsal hall something caught her eye and she deliberately slowed her pace.

It seemed innocent enough: an assistant director was giving some notes to a young actress. But the AD in this instance was Rob Bryant, and the actress was Corinne Demetry—again. What made Nina slow down and take notice was the atmosphere surrounding the duo—the very air around them seemed thicker than elsewhere in the hall. Even though Rob and the beautiful young girl were at least two feet apart, they seemed to be somehow touching. A moment later, when Rob bent over and handed Corinne a piece of paper she'd dropped, their fingers came into contact and lingered unnecessarily.

That does it, she told herself, sitting down at her makeup table and reaching for her eye liner. The man doesn't have a sincere bone in his body! He's out for every woman he can get his hands on, and I'm going to find out the truth. About what? Well, she didn't exactly know—she just knew there was more to Rob Bryant than a silky voice and a boyish grin—and a marvelous tan—and a great body and that fantastic mouth. . . .

Nina was convinced Rob and Corinne were hiding something. After all, they had provided each other's alibis for the time of Milly's murder. Maybe that was worth reexamining, Nina thought, and then groaned inwardly. They also had provided Helen Meyer's alibi! Did Nina really want to get into *that*? No, not really. Not at all.

But she would, if she had no other choice.

Nina found her chance toward the end of the day, when she spotted Corinne alone, taking a rest between dress rehearsal and final taping.

"Almost like old times, don't you think, Corinne?" Nina said, sublimating the resentment eating at her. "The cast is like a family again. Feels good."

"Yes, Nina," Corinne answered, her grin forced. "I can't believe how smoothly things are going."

"What have you been up to, Corinne? Seems like we haven't talked much lately. Anything exciting happening?" Nina asked casually.

"You've been busy," Corinne said in mild accusation. "The two deaths and all. You were preoccupied. You let everything get under your skin."

"Well, after all, working with Milly as I was . . . She *was* getting to be a good friend. It hit me pretty hard."

143

"Feeling better now? Robin and I have both been worried about you. I sure hope Lieutenant Rossi is close to wrapping things up. Is he?"

"Not exactly. Milly's fall, for example. He can't figure how, with all these people on the set that day, nobody saw anything the least bit suspicious. Everybody had an alibi. It's a puzzler."

For a moment Corinne said nothing. Her eyes were everywhere but on Nina. "Yes," she said vaguely, "that *is* strange."

Then, with deliberate purpose behind her words, Nina said, "I worked with Rob Bryant on Saturday, when we were reshooting Milly's scenes. And again yesterday, when Nick Galano was out. He can be quite nice when he wants to be. And he's a very talented director. Aren't you getting the same feeling, Corinne?" She watched the girl's expression intently.

"I *enjoy* working with him," Corinne replied, her expression suddenly animated. "He . . . seems to be very nice. He can be so funny at times. But he has his serious side, too. What I like is the way he makes you feel *important*, like you're the only person in the world. He *listens*."

Yes, Nina thought bitterly. *Tell me about it!* "Oh?" she led Corinne on. "What sort of things do you talk about?"

"Music, art, stuff like that. He knows I'm interested in impressionistic art. It's amazing what he knows about Monet, Rousseau, Cézanne and Renoir. I've learned the most fascinating things."

I'll just bet you have, Nina thought. "Where do you find time for all this talk? On the set I mean? You're certainly not seeing him on the side, are you?"

Corinne's eyes flickered suddenly. "Oh no, nothing like that. We just talk casually now and then during breaks. He always finds a minute or two for me. C'mon, Nina. You aren't serious? Me and Rob? He's practically old enough to be my *father*!" Her cocky grin didn't quite come off. There was something else lurking behind Corinne's eyes, a haunted something Nina couldn't quite identify. *What*? she wondered.

144

"So, how about lunch tomorrow?" Nina asked. "I'll round up Robin. We can catch up on things."

"I have to pass, Nina," Corinne said quickly. "I'll be brown-bagging it tomorrow—some bank business. Maybe later in the week." Nina studied her carefully. She knew Corinne was lying. Maybe a nooner with Rob, a quick run back to one apartment or the other?

"Okay, Corinne. Make it Thursday then. I'll talk to Robin."

Again, her eyes averted, Corinne sidled away. "Gotta run, Nina. Some last-minute stuff in wardrobe before final tape. Catch you later."

Watching her go, Nina thought that Corinne appeared to be somehow diminished—some of her natural sparkle had gone. The girl was definitely worried about something, something infinitely more serious than a shady little alliance with Rob Bryant.

Nina further pondered the change in Corinne Demetry at dinner that evening. It was 7:00 P.M., and Nina occupied a corner table,—alone, at Armando's, one of her favorite neighborhood restaurants. She thought about Dino Rossi, Milly and Terri as she ate a favorite pasta dish, linguine with clam sauce, complimented by a hearty Italian Chardonnay. When she had finished with those merry-go-round speculations, she found yet another phantom—Rob Bryant—waiting his turn.

Thanks to Nick Galano's return, there wasn't much reason for their paths to cross. Yet Nina had been aware of him all day, around the edges of things. He spoke to her only once—hello-and-how-are-you—but there was no real warmth in his greeting. It was just as well, because she really didn't care whether she ever spoke to him again, she told herself.

Once, at day's close, as she returned Chessy to the alley, she caught a fleeting glimpse of him standing near the video-control monitors. He was staring directly at her, but when she glanced up and met his eyes he shifted his body,

145

and looked away. A moment later he walked off without sending her a second glance.

What was that all about? she questioned now. Was it a reaction to Rossi's interrogations? Reaction, also, to the fact that most of Dino's questions had been inspired by the things Nina had reported about her talk with Milly Gowan on the last day of her life? Or did it have something to do with Helen? He had to be aware by now that their relationship was a subject for ridicule.

Nina's thoughts drifted to Helen Meyer. Whatever could the woman have been thinking, to link up with Rob in the first place? She'd already been hurt dozens of times by her indefatigable lecher of a husband, Mortimer Meyer. Criminals aren't the only ones who compulsively return to the scene of the crime, she philosophized. Couldn't Helen see how foolish she looked chasing after a man like Rob? And how, if he really was on perpetual call, did he manage to wedge all these extra events into his busy schedule? Was Helen deliberately closing her eyes to his behavior?

Then, distasteful as the notion was, she found herself trying to imagine what a romantic interlude between Helen and Rob would be like. What web of self-delusion would Helen have to weave to convince herself his love was sincere? Or was she simply so dazzled by his charm and sex appeal that she couldn't think clearly at all?

Enough of such conjecture! It was time to get back to the apartment and attack the next day's script.

A tan Camaro is not a very noteworthy car, which was exactly why the man sitting in the one parked at the corner of West 74th Street and Riverside Drive had chosen it.

He'd been there for nearly an hour, and the cold was getting to him. Fifteen minutes more was about all he could take, he told himself, knowing that at the end of fifteen minutes he'd say exactly the same thing. Some things were worth waiting for.

But he didn't have to wait that long. Only minutes later a cab pulled up to the curb at the entrance to Primrose

Towers and a startlingly beautiful redhead got out. Finally. Christ, look at those legs! What a waste.

The man in the tan Camaro tensed only slightly. Everything was all ready; he only had to roll the window down, lean out, and do it. Nothing stood between them. Traffic was extremely light and pedestrians were nonexistent on such a bitter night. He figured he'd have five to ten seconds between the time the cab pulled away and she reached the lobby door. Plenty of time, twice as much as he needed.

Goddamn!

The stupid cabbie was just *standing* there, revving his motor. The lousy bastard was waiting to see that she got into the building okay? In *New York?*

All right, he could take them both out.

Too late. The cloud of exhaust from the cab obscured his vision, and then she was inside the lobby.

Calm down, calm down, he told himself. Another chance would come soon enough. What difference would another day make, except for the rental on the crummy car?

Chapter Thirteen

On Wednesday morning Nina was in her dressing room with Robin Tally. Both had only brief scenes in the day's episode, and time hung heavy. The topic at the moment was Chessy, but Nina felt Robin had more pressing matters on her agenda.

"Watch this," Nina said, looking down at Chessy who was going through his ankle-winding routine. She placed a bowl of milk and one of cat food on the plastic mat she'd brought in to replace the newspapers. "Din-din!"

But the cat paid the food no mind. Instead he stared beseechingly up at Nina. "What's the matter with him?" Robin asked. "Isn't he hungry?"

"He's hungry all right," Nina laughed. Then she leaned down and scooped Chessy into her arms. "He's hungry for this." She cuddled the big cat while he nuzzled her face, eagerly rubbing the top of his head under her jaw.

"Oooh," Robin exclaimed, "what a cutie! Does he do that every morning?"

"Every morning. I nearly fell over the first time he pulled it."

"Why not adopt him? I think he'd be wonderful company. Doesn't it bother you to turn him out at night? A dog might get him. He could be run over."

"I hate it," Nina admitted. "I worry about him every minute."

"So, you've got a cat. Any rules against pets at your place?"

"No."

"Well, then? Take him home."

"I'm tempted. But I don't know if I'm up to the responsibility. I'd worry about him clawing my furniture, climbing my drapes. I don't think I'm ready for a lifetime of litter boxes."

"But he's such a gentleman. I'm sure he'd be perfectly behaved."

"There's always a first time. It's like a husband—you never know what you've got until you bring him home with you. Then it's too late."

Robin sent her a quirky grin. "Oh? Was that a message? Are we considering husbands these days?"

"You know better than that. I like my arrangement with Dino the way it is. Besides, he's never once mentioned marriage."

"That does put a crimp in things now, doesn't it?" Robin took a new tack. "How's it going these days? God, when I think about Milly and Terri . . . When is it ever going to end?"

"I hope it has ended. Their deaths were interconnected, I'm sure. And perhaps whoever did it got what he wanted. He'll be content now."

"Got what he wanted? Which was what? And who is 'he'?"

"It could just as well be a she. Dino hasn't got idea one. It's driving him nuts. Every time he thinks he's got a lead it blows up in his face."

Robin's expression was expectant. "I don't suppose you're going to break down and tell me anything about it?"

"Not now," Nina said firmly. "There are too many loose ends. But when we've got something, you'll be the first to know. Maybe you can even help me."

"Thanks, but no thanks! One adventure like that thing at Leatherwing was enough for me. I still have bad

150

dreams." Robin shivered. Then she looked at Nina speculatively. "Mind if we change the subject?"

Nina shrugged. "Be my guest."

"It's Corinne. Have you noticed her lately? She's changed. Something's bugging her. It's like she's on another planet most of the time. And when you ask her what's wrong, she just clams up, or she suddenly has to go someplace."

"She's pulled that on you, too? I thought it was just me. Yes, something is definitely wrong there, and I have an idea what it is."

"Nina, do you know something? C'mon, give!" Robin urged.

Trusting Robin implicitly, knowing that nothing she told her would ever go any further, Nina described the two scenes between Corinne and Rob that she had inadvertently witnessed.

"Our little Corinne?" Robin gasped when she finished her account. "Little Goody Two-Shoes? Kissing Rob Bryant? Letting him feel her up? Risking the wrath of Helen the Hun? I can't believe it!"

Robin was stricken, for she liked Corinne as much as Nina did. "What are we going to do? Should we try to give her some good advice?"

"I don't know, Robin. I've been worried since I saw her and Rob together," Nina sighed.

"What should we do?"

"Nothing at the moment. Let's think about it. We'll come up with something . . ."

It was lucky that Melanie Prescott played only a minor role that day, because Nina's mind certainly wasn't on her lines. As she sat in the rehearsal hall trying to concentrate on the intrigues transpiring in the Marston Corporation's executive suites, her mind was light years away. Just seeing Corinne Demetry looking wan and distressed this morning upset her.

When had all that started? she thought. When Rob Bryant first moved in on the poor kid? And if she was as gaga over him as she'd indicated, then why did she look so miserable?

Nina had a hunch that something entirely different from romance was responsible for Corinne's change in mood. But what? She probed more deeply. According to Rob, he and Corinne were together when the scream was heard. Rushing through the hallway, they ran into Helen who was coming out of her office. One story, three alibis. But scenarios of what might actually have happened began to flash through Nina's mind like a videotape on fast forward.

Maybe Corinne had been mistaken about the time. Maybe she had been with Rob earlier, and then he excused himself for a few moments and then returned afterward, somehow persuading her to say he'd never left—"Darling, I'll explain later, but for now if you don't back me up we might not have a future together."

Or maybe Rob had been with Helen at the fatal moment, but for some reason didn't want to say so and had gotten Corinne to lie for him—"Angel, it'll be better for everyone, especially for us, if you'll just go along with this. I'll explain later."

Or maybe Rob and Corinne hadn't run into Helen at all, and Corinne was lying for Helen, at Rob's urging—"Sweetheart, our future lies in your hands. I'll explain later."

And maybe, Nina told herself, you better stop imagining what might have happened and get someone to explain now.

The opportunity Nina needed came an hour later, when she found Corinne alone in her dressing room.

"Corinne, nice work in that last scene," she lied glibly, slipping into the room and noting Corinne's startled expression. "Do you have a moment for an old friend?"

Corinne feigned congeniality. "Thanks, Nina. What's on your mind?"

Nina had already come to a conclusion about what must be done. And for better or for worse, she must see it through. "*You*," she said simply, settling into a metal folding chair across from the young woman.

"*Me*?" Corinne said, nonplussed. "What about me?"

"Frankly, I'm worried about you. Both Robin and I have noticed that you just haven't been yourself lately, since Milly died."

Corinne's eyes darted around before coming back to meet Nina's. "Hey, haven't we got that mixed up? That's supposed to be *my* line. *You're* the one who's been in the pits over Milly, not me. I'm sorry she's dead, of course, but it's really not my affair. We weren't very close."

"Is that right?" Nina said softly, her eyes probing.

"Is what right?"

"That it's not your affair. I happen to think it is. I happen to think you know more about what happened that afternoon than you're letting on."

Corinne's smile faded just the least bit. But she said, "You're talking in riddles, Nina. Just what are you getting at?"

"Please, Corinne, take this in the spirit in which it's intended. I know what you're going through. I only want to help. I mean that sincerely, with all my heart."

"Going through? What?"

"That thing between you and Rob. I . . ."

"Me and Rob? Don't be silly! I told you yesterday, we're just friends. Nothing else."

"Corinne, listen to me. It just so happens that I saw you and Rob in a really heavy clinch Monday afternoon. It wasn't 'just friends' at all."

Corinne's eyes flashed and her back went stiff as a board. "And just what right do you have to go spying on people?" she flared.

"I didn't do it on purpose. It was purely accidental, believe me. Corinne, honey, are you in something over your head?"

Corinne's face worked agitatedly. Then, gradually, she regained control. "Okay, you saw us. So what? I'm old enough to know what I'm doing. We're in love. What are you going to do about it? One of these days he's going to leave Helen and the show. And I'll go with him, as his wife!"

Nina could have wept. Kids, she thought. They know everything! Would it do any good to reason with her? Nina fought to keep her voice level. "Love is wonderful, Corinne," she said. "But you're not the only woman Rob has been after. He's—"

Corinne's eyes filled with rage. "No, you're just saying that! You're making it up just to turn me against him. You're lying, Nina!"

"Am I? Ask Rob where he was at eleven last Saturday night, who he was with. Who he was putting some very heavy moves on."

Corinne's face crumpled. "He told me he had to be with Helen that night and that we . . ."

"He lied. Didn't you know Helen was in San Francisco all weekend?"

Corinne fell silent. Then, as if trying desperately to convince herself, she croaked, "He loves me, he really does. I know he must have a good reason for lying. He'll explain it to me."

It was here that Nina decided to let Corinne have it right between the eyes. "The same way he explained it to you when Milly died?" she challenged. "When he convinced you to lie for him and for Helen, to give them both alibis? Admit it! Tell the truth for once!"

Corinne shuddered once, twice; Nina thought she was going to faint. But then, the next moment, Corinne's features firmed, her eyes hardened. "Really, Nina," she said, a hard edge to her voice, "you are too much! You may think you can intimidate people with this detective act of yours, but you don't scare me. Is that how you get people to confess? Accuse them of all sorts of ridiculous things, let them think that cop boyfriend of yours is looking over your shoulder? And they just cave in, tell you anything you want to hear, whether it's true or not?"

Her tone was scathing. "I used to think you were my friend, but now I know you really aren't. You're just a prying, opportunistic busybody. You're not even a detective! Go ahead, sic Lieutenant Rossi on me—and I'll charge you with slander! I'll tell him the same thing I told him the first time. I'll tell him that Rob was with me when Millicent Gowan died. And a moment later we both saw Helen coming out of her office. That's the *truth*!"

She leaped up from her chair and advanced menacingly on Nina. The light in her eyes was fierce. "I don't know what you're trying to prove, Nina," she hissed, "but whatever it is, you'd better quit. Now, get out of here. This instant! Before I do something I'll regret!"

Nina made one last desperate attempt to get through to Corinne, "Don't you realize how insanely jealous Helen is? At the awards party she found Rob talking to me, just *talking*, and I swear she could have killed me."

"*Shut up!*"

"There have been other similar incidents with other women. Helen would do *anything* to keep Rob to herself. Don't you know that? You could be in serious trouble, maybe in danger!"

"*You're* the one who'll be in danger if you don't stop meddling, Nina!"

"Please, Corinne," she said just before retreating down the hall, "think this over. I want to help you. If you'll tell the truth, I'll do everything in my power to cover up your part in this. Believe that. I *am* your friend."

Corinne uttered a curse under her breath and slammed the door in Nina's face.

Nina passed the rest of that day in a kind of trance, her mind churning nonstop. Nothing seemed real. There were times when she actually couldn't believe what had happened between her and Corinne. One minute she would think she'd dreamed the whole thing, and the next she was reliving every astonishing moment in excruciating detail. Ambivalence ate at her mercilessly. She was sure Corinne was lying through her teeth; she had covered for both Rob Bryant and Helen. But then again, *how* could she be sure?

And what would Rob do when Corinne went to him and spilled the details of their incredible confrontation? Would he come after her, threaten her as Corinne had? Would he vilify her, dare her to go to Rossi with her idiotic ideas?

Or, she thought more fearfully, would his rage take more subtle forms? Would he join forces with Helen to guarantee that the meddlesome Ms. McFall never interfered in their business again?

But those possibilities vanished when a smiling Rob Bryant stopped briefly at the door to her dressing room and told her that he'd just read the next day's script and he was looking forward to the two big scenes that were waiting for her.

Nina was left in a semidazed state. Just what was going on here? Hadn't Corinne told him? Apparently she hadn't. For there was no way in the world, knowing those details, that Rob could have acted in the relaxed manner he just had.

Again, confused though she was, Nina was undecided about taking the day's discoveries to Rossi. One moment she told herself to wait, to think things through and pass the information along only when her suppositions had reached some logical conclusion. The next she was desperately anxious that the day be over so that she might go home and wait for Dino to rush over and comfort her while she laid the entire ugly day before him.

Abruptly at 2:20, as the cast readied itself for the final taping, Spence Sprague approached Nina, a drowsy-looking Chessy hanging from one arm. "This is your last warning, Nina," he stormed. "I told you to keep this cat in your dressing room during final tape. I just caught him on the set, settling down for a snooze on Angela's davenport! Now, lock him up, fast, or he's back on the street for good!"

Nina was instantly alarmed. She took Chessy from Sprague and folded him protectively in her arms. "He *was* locked in my dressing room," she defended. "How he got out, I'll never know." She started upstairs, dark thoughts buzzing in her brain. "Come on, cat," she muttered. How on earth had he managed to escape?

Strange, she thought on reaching her door. It's locked all right. And Chessy was inside, asleep, when I left for dress rehearsal. She inserted her key, turned it.

Everything in the room looked perfectly normal. The light on her dressing table was still on, just as she'd left it. If the cat hadn't gotten out, she never would have given things a second look. But as it was, she stood stock still, staring slowly about the room to see if anything had been moved. Who could have gotten in? How could they get in without a key? The only existing dupes were in Horst Krueger's office. Oh, yes, Spence Sprague had a master key, but she doubted that either man would enter her room. Then who?

Then she had a faint whiff of an unusual scent and saw that her cosmetics were slightly off-kilter, some of them not in their usual places. It instantly became clear that someone had been snooping. What had they been looking for? Good question. There was absolutely nothing here of any value—except for her purse.

My purse! Nina darted to the dressing table, slid open the lower drawer, and saw her bag. She flipped through her billfold, and frowned. Nothing was missing. All her cash—around eighty dollars—was there, her credit cards as well. Even so, it was obvious that someone had rummaged through her purse. Her driver's license was out of place, the credit cards were askew. Her heart hammering crazily, she slid open other drawers and found more signs that someone had gone through her things. Her gloves were on the wrong side, her lambswool slippers were not nested as she always left them.

Nina slowly sank into her chair. What did it mean? Who could have gone to all this trouble? And for what? What could she *supposedly* have hidden in her dressing room that would cause an intruder to take such a risk? And how had he or she gotten in?

The answer would have to wait, for just then the PA system blared. "Full cast," Nick Galano called. "To your respective sets. Final tape in two minutes. Full cast. Move it, gang."

A maddening pressure built up in Nina's brain; she felt like she'd explode if she didn't get some answers soon.

Chapter Fourteen

When Nina gently pushed Chessy into the alley late that afternoon, just before leaving the studio for the day, she was relieved to find the bitter cold had lessened significantly. "See you in the morning, old chum," she whispered, giving him a final scratch under the chin. "Stay warm." He strolled unconcernedly toward the stack of cartons where she had placed an old blanket for him to curl up in. Yet she worried. Maybe Robin was right; maybe she should just accept the inevitable and take him back to Primrose Towers, give him a real home.

She cabbed it to her apartment, alternating concern about Chessy with thoughts of Corinne, Rob, Helen, and the two unexplained deaths. Still undecided about how to handle the situation for Dino's benefit, she had yet to call him.

Once home, she put a Brahms symphony on the record player and soaked herself in a steamy bubble bath. The music was perfect for her mood—dark and heavy. After wrapping herself warmly in a hooded cranberry velour robe, she prepared one of her favorite dinners—broiled loin lamb chops and a spinach salad with a light vinaigrette dressing. She turned the chops and tossed the salad automatically; mentally she was turning and tossing the facts of the case in her mind. She sat down to eat and to think.

She had mentioned the break-in to nobody. And she still hadn't called Dino about her confrontation with Corinne. That would have to wait until she was sure in her own mind that she wasn't making mountains out of molehills. Was she certain the poor girl had really perjured herself on Rob Bryant's behalf? After all, she rationalized fuzzily, just because I think she's lying, does that make it so?

Nina glanced at her watch. Past seven o'clock already? She couldn't devote the entire evening to these thoughts—she needed at least a solid two hours with the next day's script.

But when she heard the weather forecast on the eight o'clock news, all thoughts of both the script and the case left her: a heavy snowfall was expected, to be followed by plunging temperatures.

By nine o'clock she couldn't get Chessy out of her thoughts. Looking down from her window, she saw that it was snowing heavily. The few cars in the streets were moving very slowly; it must be really bad out there. She called the weather bureau and heard a prediction for at least eight inches by morning. And the temperature was already dropping rapidly.

Idiot, she scolded. Why did you desert Chessy in weather like this? Why didn't you risk Sprague's wrath, and just leave him in your dressing room for the night? There was litter; he'd have caused no damage. But, still muddle-headed after the day's crises, she hadn't been thinking straight. Would he make it through the night? Or would she find him in the morning, frozen solid in his box under a foot of snow? Damn it, what kind of a monster are you? Are you going to go get him or not?

That did it. The picture of the animal dead actually caused her eyes to mist. And all because of her selfish concern for her pretty apartment! She threw off her robe, climbed into wool slacks and a sweater, and went to her coat closet. Blast it to hell, how long since she'd worn these clumsy snow boots? The things some people won't do for their pets, she fumed. Where's my quilted coat? Where's that dumb flashlight?

As she drove slowly out of her underground garage, the snow clung wetly to the Mazda's windshield, drastically hindering her vision. The wipers swished nonstop. She dared to squirt from her window washer, but the antifreeze additive wasn't strong enough; she only caused an additional glaze to form. She'd have to drive medium blind until the defroster cut in. Within two blocks the back windows had accumulated enough snow to render her rearview mirror useless; she was forced to rely completely on her side mirrors.

She was thankful the studio wasn't too far away. Barring mishaps, traffic as light as it was, she should be there in ten to fifteen minutes. Five minutes to find Chessy, maybe fifteen minutes to get back. Hopefully they'd both be tucked in for the night by eleven.

It was a good thing she hadn't tried to find a cab. With the exception of one car a block or so behind her, there was no other traffic whatsoever. She pushed the Mazda a little harder now. The heat from the defroster did its work and the windshield gradually cleared.

Ten minutes later the facade of Meyer Productions loomed out of the eerie snowlight. Nina slowed, looking for the drive that skirted the building's western edge and led to the limited VIP parking facilities. Then she spied it through the thick swirling snowflakes and turned in. Fearing that Chessy might be prowling and not in his box after all, she scanned the blowing snow for the sight of an oversized ball of orange fur.

Then Nina caught the helter-skelter pile of cartons in her headlights, stopped the car, and jumped out. A moment later, she went back to rummage in a side pocket for her flashlight. Leaving the headlights on, and the motor running, she hurried toward the fire door. A shrieking wind tore at her scarf, the icy blast making her eyes water. "Chessy," she called. "Here, Chessy! Mama's come to get you. *Heeeere* kitty, kitty, kitty . . ."

The snow was at least half a foot deep already; she was glad she'd found her insulated boots. Another blast of chilling wind smashed into her, and she bent forward against it.

Her heart sank as she got closer to the boxes and saw a set of cat tracks rapidly disappearing in the deepening snow. Please, Chessy, be there! If you've wandered off . . . Her silent pleas were for naught. The box containing the blanket was empty. She tore off a glove and shoved her bare hand inside to see if the improvised cave was still warm. The bedding was cold as ice; Chessy was apparently long gone.

She whirled, staring about wildly. Her heart sank. How would she ever find him now in all this wind and snow? Nina straightened up and shot the flashlight beam around the alley. She saw the dim outline of a parked truck about fifty feet to her right. Thinking that Chessy might have sought shelter under it, she ducked her head down against the slashing wind and started toward it, calling, "Here, Chessy. Come, kitty, kitty!"

Because she was bent double, her free hand shielding her eyes from the wind, she did not see the dark shape that emerged from behind her car, stealthily stalking her from the left, keeping to the deepest shadows.

Nina's heart leaped into her throat; she released a soft, grateful yip of delight. For there, under the truck, huddled next to one of the tires, was Chessy. His big yellow eyes glowed in the beam of her flashlight. "Oh, Chessy," she cried. "You're all right! Come, Chessy. Kitty . . ."

She leaned further down to grab the shivering cat by one of his hind legs and drag him out. He hissed once, but then recognition registered and he went limp, allowing her to gather him in her arms and clutch him tightly against her chest.

"You poor thing," Nina cooed, ducking her face down to his, "you're all wet, all full of snow. Come on—we're going home, where you belong."

Later Nina tried to reconstruct exactly how the next

series of events occurred, but she was never able to sort out the separate details; all were lost in a muddled daze of scouring, pelting snow, the steady shriek of the wind, the opaque shadows that closed in, seemingly possessing a crushing weight of their own.

All at once she was aware of a blur of movement to her left as a dark form emerged from the swirling snow. Nina started, screamed, as a hand fell on her shoulder. Terrified, Chessy dug his sharp claws into her right hand through her glove as he fought to break free. Then, with a terrified yowl he pushed off and shot back under the truck.

Nina had a time-speed image of a masked dark figure— or were there two figures—hurtling at her. An arm whipped around her neck, and someone was bending her back, jamming a knee into the back of her legs. The pain was staggering as the grip tightened across her throat, and she nearly blacked out. She was positive her windpipe was collapsing. Gasping and choking, she fought to project a scream into the night. But it was a futile effort; all that emerged was a strangled squawk.

During the whole thing, her assailant did not utter a sound; it was as though she was being attacked by an apparition, an anonymous phantom from hell. Even as Nina fought with the last remnants of her swiftly fading strength, as blinding flashes of light danced behind her eyes, she swung feebly with her flashlight, striking something but losing her grip. The heavy cylinder skittered off into the snow. She heard a hiss of pain and felt the grip on her throat relaxed just the slightest bit. In that moment, Nina sucked in a searing gasp of frigid air and released a tortured scream. To her it seemed deafeningly loud; surely it would echo over the buildings, down the alley and beyond. It would bring help. But in reality, it was no more than a faint groan.

Then the pressure was back and her larynx felt like it was being crushed. She surrendered to total despair, waiting for death.

At that moment from somewhere in the distance, she

163

heard a rapidly accelerating shriek followed by a guttural cry. Suddenly the grip on her throat loosened and great reviving draughts of air seared her windpipe; Nina tore free and fell forward. She began to run.

As she did so, she caught a sidelong image of the dark figure, hands twisted overhead, straining frantically to dislodge the clawing, hissing animal that had buried its razor-sharp talons in the vital area of the exposed throat.

Nina stumbled, almost went to one knee. She fought to refill her lungs with air, gasping in desperation. As her strength returned, she ran even faster. She glanced back and saw the figure tear Chessy away and fling the howling animal into a snowdrift. Instantly the attacker wheeled and came after Nina, who was halfway up the alley, heading for the wide-open spaces of West Sixty-sixth Street, screaming nonstop.

She broke around the corner of the building, came into the brightly lit snowplain fronting Meyer Productions. She headed straight for the center of the wide thoroughfare, aiming directly at an oncoming automobile. The car's driver touched the brakes, slid sideways and came at her in a floating, slow-motion spin. As it stopped, and the driver rolled down his window to stick his head out, she caught a fleeting glimpse of her would-be strangler retreating into the alley.

"What's the trouble, lady?" the driver called.

"Someone attacked me in the alley," she babbled. Her head ached hideously and she still gasped ravenously for breath. "I went to find my cat, and when I was in there, someone jumped me. . . ."

A few minutes later another car also stopped to help, but by the time Nina led the two men back into the parking lot behind the building, the area was deserted. There was only the echoing whine of the wind and the flashlight lying in the snow. And Chessy, fastidiously licking fresh blood from his paws.

"The guy probably had a car parked nearby. He's long gone by now," one of the men said, and Nina realized it was so. The samaritans saw her safely into her car and waved her on.

Shaky from the ordeal, Nina headed the car north, toward Primrose Towers. Chessy climbed into her lap and she began to relax. "Come on, you old hero," she whispered down at him. "This time you *are* going home. For good!"

In control again, she turned onto Riverside Drive and made a decision. Now, Mr. Rossi, she thought, it's time for that overdue phone call. And I hope I drag you out of a sound sleep!

But she didn't. He picked up on the second ring.

"Nina! Where in hell were you? I've been trying to reach you for an hour." She looked at the blinking red eye on her answering machine and smiled ruefully.

"It looked like a nice evening for a drive."

"Cut the comedy! And what's wrong with your voice? You sound hoarse."

She gave him the headlines, and he blew up like a volcano, as she'd expected. She'd acted like an idiot, she was lucky to be alive, etc., etc.

Nina didn't argue. She knew he was right.

As she hung up her coat and struggled out of the insulated footgear, she suddenly realized she wasn't alone—she had a roommate. But where was he?

"Chessssssssyyyyy?" she called, and was rewarded with an answering "Purp" from the bedroom. She found him there, exploring the depths of her closet.

Okay, old fella, she thought. Play with a slipper. For that matter, play with a Gucci pump. You've earned it!

She went into the kitchen to put out some milk and find some scraps for Chessy, finally deciding to give him her leftover lamb chop as a special reward.

She carefully cut all the meat off the bone, diced it, and then warmed it in the microwave oven before setting the dish on the floor. Chessy, who had been massaging her ankles with his back, inspected the offering, looked up at her as if to compliment her on the cuisine, and settled down to the unaccustomed treat.

Nina thought about making herself a stiff drink, but decided instead on hot cocoa. While the milk was heating, she tried to convince herself that the frightening incident in the snowy parking lot had been nothing more than the work of a chance mugger. She tried very hard to believe that it had nothing to do with the deaths of Terri Triano and Millicent Gowan. She tried like hell.

Chapter Fifteen

Thursday morning found Nina spoiling for a fight, and God help anybody who crossed her path. Not only was her throat stiff and bruised from last night's throttling, but she had slept restlessly—her scare, along with the nonstop ramblings and rumblings of a very disoriented Chessy conspired to wake her every hour or so.

Anyone who thought she'd be so easily intimidated had another think coming. Granted, she was badly shaken, and she'd be extremely wary about venturing out alone at night from now on. But that was a far cry from abandoning the case.

From the moment Nina arrived at the studio she was on the lookout for anyone with signs of a clawed neck. She didn't expect to see anything as obvious as a bandaged throat, but considering the blood she'd seen on Chessy's paws, her assailant had definitely been hurt.

By the time Nick Galano called a break, after the first line rehearsal, she was getting discouraged. Probably due to the continuing cold wave, turtleneck sweaters seemed to be the uniform of the day; Rob Bryant's was deep red, Rafe Fallone's was navy blue, and Bob Valentine's was forest green. And Horst showed up sporting a neck brace! Even the women seemed to be part of the conspiracy; high-collared blouses and scarves were everywhere.

Well, to hell with that for now. Whoever had clawmarks in the neck area would certainly have them for days to come. She'd just wait and watch to see who found a reason for continuous concealment of the throat area. And regardless of the very convenient turtlenecks, Nina couldn't shake the feeling that the previous night's attack was connected to yesterday's explosive run-in with Corinne.

As she moved from main rehearsal to the Marston Corporation set, Nina's walk was not its usual easy stride. And when she spoke there was a gravelly undertone to her voice. "What happened to you?" Nick Galano asked.

"Slipped on the ice," she fibbed, not ready to reveal how close she'd come to death the night before.

"And that made your voice hoarse?"

"I'm coming down with a cold." Then, to throw him off the track, she turned testy. "Are you doubling as a doctor these days, too?"

Galano looked stung. "Sounds like the fall activated your nasty bone, too." And turning away: "Okay, gang, let's get with it!"

During the full group rehearsal, Nina had been quick to home in on Rob Bryant, to check for sign of slash marks courtesy of Chessy on his throat. But her quest was foiled by the red turtleneck sweater. She even thought of catching him at an unexpected moment and snatching the wool cowling away in hope of revealing a welter of bandages beneath. Perhaps the opportunity would present itself as the day went on, though she doubted it.

Once more her detective instinct was frustrated. Again the tedious watchword surfaced: Later. Wait, let Rob Bryant or Corinne Demetry blunder, tip their hands.

Several times during the opening blocking session she attempted to lock eyes with Corinne, to detect some hint of guilt or complicity. But Nina's visual feints were repulsed; Corinne averted her gaze whenever Nina looked her way.

Was one of these damned turtleneck sweaters just a pure coincidence? Nina wondered. Could it possibly be that she was barking up the wrong tree, that her attack had been an isolated event after all? And even if it was connected to the recent deaths, the attacker could still have been a total stranger, a hired thug who'd chosen last night's storm as perfect cover. If you consider yourself even halfway professional as a PI, Nina cautioned herself, don't go off half-cocked.

And yet, there was that insistent feeling about Corinne. . . .

Due to the weather, almost everyone ordered lunch sent in, and Nina retreated to her dressing room to wait and rest. No sooner had she put her feet up when Robin Tally came in.

"What happened?" Robin demanded to know. "You look like you were in a wreck or something."

"I was," Nina said, deciding to take Robin into her confidence, the beginnings of a plan already stirring.

"You mean to tell me that Chessy actually came to your rescue?" Robin said incredulously when Nina finished her story. "An attack cat? A dog, maybe. But a *cat*? Never!"

"I can hardly believe it, either," Nina agreed. "But that's exactly what happened. One minute someone had me in a kind of hammerlock with everything going black. And the next thing I knew, there was Chessy, his claws in the guy's neck, hanging on for dear life."

"Incredible! What a headline. 'Junkyard Cat Saves Mistress' Life.' Now are you going to give that poor thing a home?"

"*Give* him a home? He already has it. You should have seen him last night. If I'm lucky, he's going to let *me* live with *him*."

"Who do you think it was? The guy in the parking area? Holy cow, Nina, this is so exciting!"

"I don't know. Not yet, anyway. But I have an idea." Her voice sank to a near whisper. The dressing room walls were too thin to trust. "Dino said I wasn't supposed to mention this to anyone but . . ."

Robin edged closer in excitement, but suddenly her expression became wary and very suspicious. "Hold it right there. If Rossi said you weren't supposed to tell anyone, why are you telling me?"

Nina's grin was saucy. "Because I've got a little plan I need some help with, and you've been elected."

"Oh, no! I know all about your 'little plans.' If you think I'm going to go prowling back alleys at night with you . . ."

"No alleys this time. It happens right here in the studio. All you have to do is stand guard." Nina briefed Robin on the dressing-room break-in.

"My God," Robin breathed, her eyes wide. "This gets scarier by the minute. What does Rossi think about all this? Isn't he worried about you?"

"Of course, he's worried. He gave me Hail Columbia for going out alone last night, cat or no cat. But other than warn me to back off, there's nothing else he can do. He certainly can't sit a couple of officers on me around the clock."

"'Sit a couple of officers'?"

"That's police talk for a stakeout. He wouldn't be authorized to assign someone to guard me just because of what happened last night."

"But this room was broken into and searched!"

Nina looked sheepish. "Actually, I didn't tell Dino that part."

"You didn't? Why not?"

Nina realized she'd have to give Robin a bit more information to gain her cooperation, so she described her growing feeling that Corinne was somehow connected to the strange events. Robin looked skeptical.

"I'll grant you Corinne has been behaving oddly lately," Robin said, "but what makes you think she was the one who broke in here?"

"I don't. I think it was a man."

"Why?"

"Because as soon as I came in, I smelled something that didn't belong here."

"Well, what *was* it? Don't be so mysterious."

"Cologne. A man's cologne."

"Whose?"

"I don't know, it was very faint. Just a whiff, really."

"Nina, that's not much to go on. Maybe it just floated through the doorway from the hall."

"I know. That's why I have to proceed carefully."

"What do you want to do?"

"Search Rob Bryant's office."

"You're crazy! Why?"

"Because he and Corinne are very thick these days, and I just can't shake the feeling that Corinne knows a lot more than she's saying. That's why I didn't tell Dino about the break-in—he goes on facts, not feelings."

"But what do you expect to find?"

"I have no idea. But if he and Corinne are as involved with each other as I think they are, I just might find something that will throw light on things."

"Nina, if you're so convinced Corinne is the key to all this, why don't you search *her* dressing room?"

"I don't have to."

"Why not?"

"Because she doesn't keep it locked." Robin looked baffled. "I came in a little early this morning and tried the handle before she arrived. It was unlocked. If you were hiding something in your dressing room, would you leave the door unlocked?"

"I guess not. But I wouldn't hide anything in my dressing room."

"Who would? And *that's* why I want to take a look at Rob's office."

Unable or unwilling to try to refute such corkscrew logic, Robin listened as Nina described her plan, suspecting correctly that it was being improvised on the spot. Robin would be called on to do nothing more than stand guard near Rob Bryant's office door. If she heard anyone coming, she was to start to whistle "Strike up the Band" so Nina could clear out in time. They'd have to select a moment when Rob was busy elsewhere, preferably out of

171

the studio altogether. First Nina would try the doorknob. If the door was locked, then she'd have to get into Horst Krueger's office and "borrow" the duplicate key. Next they'd return to Rob's office where Robin would stand guard while Nina went through his personal effects like a minor whirlwind.

"It's insane," Robin protested. "God, what if someone catches us?"

"I'll just tough it out. I'll say that I thought I saw Chessy go into their office, and I went after him."

"But Chessy isn't here. He's at your apartment."

"*They* don't know that."

"And if they wonder how Chessy got into a locked room?"

"Like I said, brazen it out. We're not actresses for nothing. They've got to prove I broke in."

Robin shook her head. "Nina, you have got to be one of the craziest women I've ever come across! And I have to be even crazier to go along with these idiot schemes of yours." She straightened and squared her shoulders. "Okay, sweetie. When do we do it?"

They chose the furor of pre-dress rehearsal as the best time to attempt their break-in. The cast, the production crews, the directors were generally running around like headless chickens at that time. Horst Krueger took a late lunch and didn't return until after 2:00 P.M. Rob Bryant would have to be on the soundstage, supervising last-minute setups, giving the timing analyses a final check; he never returned to his office until after final taping.

No one paid Nina the slightest mind as she flitted down the corridor to the directors' offices. Robin stood a little distance away, ready to stall Rob with questions and/or overloud conversation should he show up unexpectedly. Reaching Rob's door, Nina gave the knob a gentle turn and groaned when she found it locked.

She hurried back down the hall. "Krueger's office," she murmured as she passed an anxious-faced Robin. "And

172

relax, will you? You look like you're about to go into surgery."

Robin again assumed the watchdog role herself outside Myrna Rowan's door, an audience with Horst Krueger was obtained only by going through Myrna. As luck would have it, Myrna was also taking lunch late today. Her office was locked only at quitting time. "Here goes nothing," Nina muttered as she edged past Robin and hurried inside. "Wish me luck!"

Her heart froze as her hand closed on the knob. This will be the day Horst's decided to lock up, she thought pessimistically. But no, the knob turned with ease. She tiptoed inside.

The keyboard was affixed to the inner door of a tall storage cabinet against the west wall. Nina recalled having filched a key once before. Now if only that blasted cabinet wasn't locked.

Lady luck smiled on Nina. The key was in the lock. It took only a few seconds to locate Rob Bryant's hook and remove one of two keys there.

Moments later she and Robin were walking back down the hall, affecting a casualness neither felt. Nina rapped on Rob's door sharply to make sure he wasn't inside. When there was no answer, she inserted the key and turned it. Instantly she handed it to Robin. "Return it right now," she instructed, "while the coast is still clear. Upper left hand corner of the key board. Got it?"

"Got it," Robin whispered, her eyes excited, unaware that she'd been conned into exceeding her advertised role of watchdog only.

"Come back as quick as you can. Stand guard."

Once she'd closed the door behind her, Nina charged the director's desk, and began opening drawers. Her heart hammering like a drum, her hands shaking, she found it hard to concentrate. Just what was she looking for? Where should she search? As she had that night at Leatherwing, when she and Robin had searched Byron Meyer's room, she slid her fingers along the bottom of each drawer while

173

her eyes did a preliminary appraisal of the drawer's contents.

There was nothing out of the ordinary in the top panel: sheaves of TTS letterheads, bond second sheets, yellow foolscap for copies, carbon paper, pens and pencils, manila file folders.

The second drawer contained show-biz magazines and newspapers, note pads, a box of rubber bands. Nina's hopes were dashed. There's nothing here, she thought. All this risk was for nothing. Damn, damn!

The third drawer contained gloves, a baggy driving cap, a scarf. Beneath that—Nina's heart leaped—was a small bundle of letters, snugged by a rubber band. Nina riffled them swiftly and saw the return addresses were from Miami, Los Angeles, and Portland, Oregon. They were in feminine handwriting, all apparently from different women. Some of the envelopes were even perfumed.

Rob, Rob, she mused, what a career you've had! Nina couldn't resist opening just one of the letters. The dateline was three years ago. "Dearest Bobbylove," it began, and ran downhill from there, a cavalcade of intensely gushy sentiments, all telling Bobbylove how he was the treasure of her life and that his Lucywoo would do anything at all for her darling. . . . This is no time to start gagging, Nina told herself, replacing the letter in the bundle. It might be interesting to go through Rob Bryant's old letters some other time, but not at the risk of being caught.

Nina returned the bundle to the drawer, paused for a moment, then snatched them out again. Something had caught her eye. She drew out the envelope just beneath "Lucywoo's" soggy note and stared at it. There was nothing on the envelope except the single word "Rob" but bells were going off in Nina's mind. There was something about that handwriting . . .

She jerked her head up sharply at the realization that Robin, at the end of the corridor, was whistling "Strike up the Band." Someone was coming!

Nina made a fast decision. She stuffed the envelope into her blouse, thrust the rest of the letters back into Rob's desk

174

and sprang for the door. Breathing a silent but fervent prayer, she slipped quickly into the corridor, closing the door behind her and listening for the lock to spring back into place. Then she sauntered casually down the corridor.

"False alarm," Robin said. "It was only Myrna, and she went the other way. Did you find anything?"

"Nothing unusual," Nina said, not quite truthfully. It was too soon to be certain. The less Robin knew, the safer she was.

Alone in her dressing room, Nina took the envelope out of her blouse and unfolded the note. "My Darling," she read, "You were right, I was wrong. Please forgive. And don't worry about AL—I'll take care of that situation. Trust me. Your own."

She gazed at the words for long moments, then opened her dressing table drawer and searched until she found what she was looking for—the Christmas cards she'd received from the TTS group. She went through them and extracted the one she wanted, putting it on the table next to the unsigned note from Rob's desk. The scrawled message inside the glittering card was brief and the words were different, but the handwriting was identical: "Dear Nina, Best wishes now and all through the year. It's going to be a great one for all of us! Regards, Helen."

Chapter Sixteen

Nina hurried home to freshen up and to check on her star boarder. What havoc, she thought apprehensively, could she expect to find upon opening her door? Chessy was her first pet ever. How much damage could a tough cat do?

The tom was waiting for her when she opened the door, purring happily, dancing around her feet. "Poor old man," she soothed, dropping to her knees to pet him, "did you miss me so much? What have you been up to?"

Apparently nothing, she concluded a few minutes later as she finished touring the apartment, finding nothing amiss.

"You *were* a good boy, weren't you?" she said approvingly. She noted that his paws and the oval-shaped bib beneath his chin were gleaming white. "And so clean, too! You must have been washing all day." Maybe, she concluded, being a cat owner wasn't going to be so bad after all.

Leaving Chessy rumbling happily over a fresh bowl of food, she hurried to shower and change for dinner.

She met Dino for dinner at The Quatrefoil, on West 46th Street, at 6:00. It was unfashionably early, but she wanted to be home in plenty of time to do justice to the next day's script. Besides, she was ravenous. Snooping apparently put an extra edge on her appetite.

Not until drinks had been served and they had given the waiter their dinner orders did she launch into her story, starting with the discovery that her dressing room had been searched and ending with the peculiar note from Helen that she'd found in Rob's desk. "So," she concluded, "what do you make of it?"

His reaction was predictably stormy. "I make of it that I might as well talk to the wall. First you fail to tell me that your room had been broken into, and then you go and stick your damn fool gorgeous neck out on a search for who-knows-what! What am I going to do with you? Don't you care how much danger you put yourself into? Or how much I worry about you?"

Gorgeous neck and how much he worries. Good, he isn't too furious, she thought, and decided to play it light and airy.

"Oh, poo! There was no danger at all. Robin was on guard every minute." So she left out the part where Robin had gone back to Horst's office to return the key. A minor detail.

"Please, darling," he said, dropping his voice to that register that sent a ripple of chills up and down her spine. "From now on, you've got to play it safe. Promise me."

She playfully wrinkled her nose at him. How could she ever doubt the depth of this man's love for her? "Promise. Now, let's take a closer look at this note." She put it on the table. "What does it mean?"

They read it again in silence. "My Darling—You were right, I was wrong. Please forgive. And don't worry about Al—I'll take care of that situation very soon. Trust me. Your own."

"You're certain this is Helen Meyer's handwriting?"

"Absolutely. I matched it against her Christmas card."

"How can we be sure it was meant for Bryant?"

"Dino, it was in his desk among a bunch of other letters,

178

and it was in an envelope with his name on it." He really could be exasperatingly thorough at times!

"Okay, I can accept that the note is from Helen to Rob. So who's Al?"

"I've been trying to figure that out. I don't know anyone named Al."

"Apparently Helen and Rob do."

"Well, we've got to find out!"

He began to laugh at her. "I guess you're going to have to just come right out with it and ask. Demand the truth. They'll understand."

Warming to the game, she turned to address the empty chair across the table. "Excuse me, Helen, but I was poking around in your boyfriend's desk the other day—having broken into his office there really wasn't much else to do—and I found this silly note you'd written him. Naturally, since it wasn't addressed to me, I read it, and it mentions someone named Al. So I'd like an explanation. Who is this Al, and why haven't I heard about him before?"

She turned back to Dino, who was having a convulsion. "Is that what you meant by 'playing it safe'?"

"Perfect. I'm sure you'll find out everything you want to know. Seriously, you ninny, there *is* something you're going to have to do."

She waited expectantly.

"Return the letter to Rob's desk."

"*What?*"

"For one thing, it doesn't tell us anything. And for another, it could never be used as evidence."

"Why not?"

"Because, my little burglary expert, it was illegally obtained."

"You're kidding!"

"Nope. First chance you get, put 'er back. Now I've got something for you. It looks like some of Bryant's directorial credits are phony."

"You're kidding!" Nina said again. "Regardless of anything else, he really is a *very* good director."

"That may be, but we're having some trouble tracing his

179

whereabouts before he met up with Helen and Horst at that Miami convention."

"Maybe I should let Scotty Lane ask his Florida pals to do some checking after all."

Dino agreed, and their appetizers were served—baked clams Casino for him and prosciutto with melon for her. Over the food, they made plans for the weekend. Having been cheated out of so many weekend trips, they decided this time to tell no one where they were going—meet at LaGuardia Airport the next evening at 7:00, and take a flight to Washington, D.C. Not to see the monuments, not to tour the Smithsonian, not to wander the galleries—just to get the hell away from it all for two days.

"Of course, I'll have to let Mrs. Bartolucci know where we are, just in case." Nina agreed. Dino's housekeeper was also in charge of Peter, Dino's twelve-year-old son, and it would be unthinkable for her not to be able to reach Dino at all times. As for Nina's "family," she'd ask the doorman to look in on Chessy once a day over the weekend, to change his water, and give him fresh catfood.

As the entrees arrived—steak pizzaiola for two—Nina basked in happy anticipation of two days of utter privacy. They might never even leave the hotel room, if she played her cards right. . . .

They left the restaurant at 8:30, having lingered over coffee and liqueurs until the theatre crowd was gone. Although much of the snow had melted, the vicious cold was back and patches of ice here and there made the footing treacherous. Nina had to grab wildly for Dino's arm to avoid falling just as she was stepping into the taxi. The giddy moment made them both laugh.

Dino gave the cabby Nina's address and a folded bill. "See you tomorrow at the terminal, darling."

"Be careful, love."

As the taxi rolled down 46th Street, Nina turned and looked through the rear window. Dino was standing there, watching, as she knew he would be. He'd wanted to see her all the way home, but she knew perfectly well that if he did then she'd ask him to come up for a moment, and one thing would lead to several others and she'd be up until all hours working on the next day's lines.

No, they'd just have to wait until the next evening. Discipline is good for the soul, or something like that. . . .

"Here you are, lady. Careful of the ice. You want me to walk you into the lobby?" Dino must have given him a very nice tip.

"No, I'm fine. Thanks anyway. Good night."

"'Night."

But she wasn't fine, far from it. As the taxi departed, Nina took two steps and felt her left foot skidding out from under her. Without Dino to hold onto, this time it didn't seem so funny. The patch of ice was particularly smooth, and Nina's right arm shot out in a reflexive attempt to balance herself. But it was hopeless—her left foot only slid away faster, and a hot pain sprang up in her ankle as she strained too hard to remain upright. In a blurred flash she fell onto the sidewalk, feeling pain all along her left side.

Which was a very good thing, or the bullet that shattered one of the heavy glass doors to the Primrose Tower lobby would have shattered her skull instead.

It took only a moment for Nina to realize what had happened. Resisting the urge to try to stand and run, she forced herself to roll quickly, over and over, toward the curb. The cars that were parked there would provide some shelter.

She reached the edge of the sidewalk and froze, trying to figure out what to do.

The figure holding the rifle with the telescopic sight was also trying to decide what to do. Where did she go? There was only one place. She must have crawled under one of those cars.

That's where she was—Nina squirmed her way under a good-sized station wagon, not regretting for a moment the damage done to her second-best mink.

A moment later, more shots rang out and she heard the tear of metal as the bullets bored into the body of the car.

She gasped as she realized someone was trying to hit the gas tank and blow the car up. She'd be incinerated! Better get out of there and run for it. She'd have more of a chance running than lying there waiting to be burned alive! *If* she could run.

The strange noise she thought she heard coming from a distance turned out to be her own voice, shrieking out of control. Then she heard something else—footsteps. Someone was running toward the car. Someone was going to crouch down, thrust a gun at her, and blow her head off! She closed her eyes and the screaming reached new heights.

Nina began to jerk and twist in hysteria as a strong hand closed around one of her ankles. In this last moment of utter terror, her voice failed completely and there was only the sound of the wind.

The hand tugged, at first hesitantly then more urgently. And she heard a voice.

"Come on, come out of there, will you? Lady, are you all right? Holy Christ, it's Ms. McFall!"

Unclenching her eyelids, she peered out and saw the familiar face of the Primrose Towers doorman, Willy.

"Are you hurt, Ms. McFall? What happened?"

"Willy? Oh Willy! Please help me get inside. Hurry!"

She crawled out from under the station wagon and got to her feet with much help from the frightened Willy.

"Let's get inside, quick!"

"Yeah, now lean on me, Ms. McFall. What happened?"

But she couldn't really tell him what happened. She'd fallen on the ice and then all hell had broken loose.

"Soon's I heard that glass door breaking I called the cops, Ms. McFall."

No! The last thing she wanted now was to have to talk to the police. She knew what she had to do, and it had nothing to do with policemen.

"Willy, get me into the elevator—hurry! Now listen, you've got to do me a favor. I'll explain later. If anyone asks, I came home ten minutes ago and went upstairs. You never saw me under any car. I was not present when the shooting happened. No one was. It was just a crackpot sniper anyway, and I don't want to spend hours giving statements to the police. Okay? *Promise me!"*

The baffled Willy promised, and apparently performed his role acceptably, since no one rang her bell.

Upstairs, curled into a terrified ball with Chessy, Nina waited until the shaking subsided and then decided that the best cover for the moment would be silence. Of course, Dino would have to know about the incident—eventually.

Chapter Seventeen

Nina walked on eggs all day Friday, edgy as a squirrel. She was almost grateful to be on call today. Otherwise, she'd have locked herself in a closet, imagining her relentless persecutor breaking down doors, coming through windows—finding *some* way to polish her off for good. But at the studio—safety in numbers and all that. She had not called Dino to report last night's attempt on her life. She firmly intended to, but consumed with determination to return the note to its place in Rob Bryant's desk and to execute a new plan as well, she decided to kill two birds with one stone, so to speak.

As if Nina's confidence wasn't shaky enough, the normal routine on the set quickly deteriorated into a shambles. For one thing, Robin Tally was written out for the day and would not be available to act as sentry for Nina's repeat visit to Rob's office, nor for the second part of her plan. Then Bob Valentine had been rushed to the hospital overnight with an inflamed appendix; he would be out for about a week, which meant a fast rewrite of today's episode and a totally new scene to learn.

Then at about 11:00 A.M. Helen Meyer had made a surprise appearance on the set, apparently planning to linger indefinitely. This put Spence Sprague and Horst

Krueger on edge, and they were short with their assistants, who in turn dumped on the next people down the line. The actors, having no underlings to torment, snarled at each other.

In the midst of all that, a commotion erupted at the front door when the burly Sam Baylog tried to bully and shove his way past the guard, who'd received instructions to bar him permanently from the studio. A mighty crash brought the incident to a close as Baylog, in a fury, upended the guard's heavy old wooden desk and the police were summoned to eject him.

The only positive development came at lunchtime, when Rob and Helen went off together, leaving Nina with the opportunity she needed.

Ten minutes into the lunch period, the studio was unusually quiet, and Nina walked noiselessly down the corridor toward Horst's office. She rounded the corner and entered the anteroom where Myrna's desk stood—and came face to face with Myrna, who was just loading a fresh ream of paper into the copying machine. Damn!

"Hi, Nina. What's up?" Myrna said, pushing the start button and watching carefully as the machine began to warm up. "One of these days this thing is going to break down in the middle of an emergency script change, you'll see. Then maybe we'll get the kind of copier we need."

The machine in question, as though to put the lie to Myrna's comments, began to feed paper smoothly into place, sheet after sheet.

"Looks okay from here," Nina offered.

"It's going to jam. I know the signs. So—everybody's got a problem today; what's yours?"

"Nothing urgent. But I think the deductions on my last paycheck were fouled up," Nina said in desperation. "When you get a chance, will you take a look?"

"No problem. Make a deal with you. I'll go check on it right now if you'll keep an eye on old Betsy here. If there's a jam, just push this button so it doesn't overheat. I'll clear it when I get back."

And off she went to the bookkeeping department. On

her way toward Horst's office, Nina patted Betsy lightly. "Let's just ignore each other, Betsy, okay?" she murmured. "You do your thing and I'll do mine."

In less than five minutes Myrna was back, radiating irritation. "There's nothing wrong with your deductions," she snapped. "They're perfectly okay."

"Well, that's a relief. I don't know what my accountant was talking about. And speaking of perfect, your friend Betsy here has been humming like a top. Thanks, Myrna."

Nina eased her way back down the corridor. Clutched in her palm was a duplicate key to Rob Bryant's office, along with a duplicate key to Helen Meyer's.

For a wonder, considering the way the day had begun, the final taping went off without a hitch and was completed exactly on schedule, at three o'clock. Immediately thereafter, the studio began to empty for the weekend. Normally Nina would have been in the vanguard of the exodus, Monday's script clutched in hand. But today she had three things to do before leaving: return Helen's note to Rob's desk, search Helen's desk for a clue to the mysterious Al, and return both duplicate keys to the panel in Horst's office.

Nina was glad she'd gotten up early enough that morning to pack for the weekend before leaving for the studio. Now all she had to do was return to the apartment, take a quick shower, dress, feed Chessy, remind Willy to look in and change the catfood and water, and leave. It she could be out of the studio by four-thirty, there should be plenty of time to do all that and meet Dino at LaGuardia at seven o'clock.

She picked up Monday's script from Myrna, who already had her boots and scarf on. Good sign: that meant most of the cast had gotten their scripts and she'd probably leave soon. Walking back to her dressing room, Nina was aware of the silence that had descended on the studio, and firmly ignored the creepy feeling it gave her. All she had to do was sit perfectly still in her dressing room, with the lights off, for about ten minutes. Then, with the coast clear, she'd pay her planned visits, replace the keys, and leave. What could go wrong?

The same thought was echoed by the bulky figure sitting silently behind Melanie Prescott's office set.

At first, for Nina, nothing did go wrong. With her coat on and all ready to leave, she entered Rob's office and slid Helen's note back where she'd found it, in the bundle of letters from Lucywoo and the others in the third drawer of his desk. Closing the drawer, she wondered why he kept all those old magazines from around the country and took another quick look at them. They yielded no immediate information, but as she was returning them to position she noticed a flat white envelope at the back of the drawer. Nothing was written on it, but it was so dog-eared it must have been opened and closed many times.

Nina looked inside and found what appeared to be Rob's spare Social Security cards. But there were four, and as far as she knew, only one spare was issued. Of course, more could always be requested, but why so many? Was he paranoid about losing them? She took them out and a moment later was frantically copying names and numbers onto a blank pad, for they weren't Rob's cards at all. Each belonged to a different person: Niles Nordland, Clinton Sundberg, Alfred Vogel, and George Peterson.

Alfred Vogel? *Alfred*? Was this the Al in Helen's note?

Moments later, with the list of names tucked into her purse and Rob's door locked behind her, Nina was headed toward Helen's office.

But she didn't get there. As she rounded the last turn in the corridor leading to Helen's office, Nina was suddenly seized from behind in a grip that both immobilized and silenced her. The arm thrown around her waist froze both her arms, and the other hand firmly clamped her mouth shut. She struggled fiercely, her throat tortured by the useless effort to scream.

"Sh! Sh!" the voice at her ear whispered urgently. "It's

188

me! Be quiet! Don't make a sound. Somebody is in here—a prowler, I think. We've got to get out!"

The viselike grip loosened enough for her to turn her head, and she saw it was Rob who had grabbed her. She also saw that he was terrified. Satisfied that she realized who he was, he released her entirely, holding a finger across his lips. She stared at him in confusion.

"I came back to pick up Monday's script." He was whispering so softly that she had to read his lips to understand what he was saying. "And I spotted somebody sneaking around. Then I saw you. Sorry I scared you; I didn't know what else to do. What are you doing here anyway? Never mind, let's just beat it."

Nina nodded in agreement, sharing his anxiety to escape.

He took her by the hand and they began to tiptoe down the corridor, away from Helen's office. At the door to the main rehearsal hall, Rob's grip on Nina's hand tightened and he froze, motioning her to do the same.

He slowly turned the knob and opened the door slightly, putting his eye to the crack. Nina moved closer to take a peek.

Peering through the gloom at first she saw nothing unusual. But then something shifted and she knew with a sickening chill what she was looking at. That large blurry outline was someone sitting at the far end of the room. And a moment later, when the bulky figure stood up like an awkward fur-bearing animal, she knew who it was. Sam Baylog had returned and somehow gotten in.

Nina and Rob softly closed the door and looked at each other in fright. The man's violent temper was legendary, and his strength had been displayed only that morning when he overturned the guard's desk. Rob beckoned and Nina followed.

They slipped through the first unlocked door they came to, which proved to be a spare dressing room, and had a whispered conference in the dark.

"It's Sam Baylog!" Nina said.

"Yes, it's Baylog. I don't know what he wants, and I don't want to find out."

"Let's call the police," Nina suggested.

"No, not from inside. He could hear something and come after us. Let's get out first and find a phone booth."

"Okay, good."

"But not through the front door. We'd never get past him. Do you know another way?"

Nina thought of the maze of corridors on the level below and knew there were emergency exits down there.

"We'll go through the boiler room."

"You'll have to lead."

"Okay. Follow me." She took his hand automatically.

"Nina, go very slowly. Don't make a sound."

"Right."

Inch by inch, they made their way toward the firestairs that would lead them down to the basement.

In the rehearsal hall, the bulky figure smiled. Those two thought they were being so clever. . . .

Chapter Eighteen

It was getting dark quickly now, and Dino Rossi was beginning to worry. From his desk at the station house, he'd been calling Nina's apartment every five minutes or so for more than half an hour. No answer—she'd apparently forgotten to turn on her machine. Where the hell was she? Keep cool, he told himself. She probably stopped on the way home from the studio to pick up some things for the weekend.

Sure. Such as what? Anything! Toothbrush, a new lipstick, whatever women needed. Pantyhose. They were always running out of pantyhose. Yeah.

He tried Nina's number again and hung up after the eighth ring. Maybe he'd just better sign out early and run over to her place, intercept her as a surprise so they could go to the airport together. That was a better arrangement anyway.

But before he could act on the idea, his phone rang.

"Rossi," he barked into it, hoping it would be Nina. But it wasn't.

"Hey, Rossi, how are ya?" the crusty no-nonsense voice crackled through the receiver. "Scotty Lane here. Remember me? Nina's pal?"

Dino remembered Scotty, all right; he was the retired

reporter who had played an important role in solving the Minton case last fall. "Scotty, has something happened to Nina?"

At Dino's question, Scotty's easy tone vanished instantly. "I don't know, pal. That's what I'm calling to find out. I've been trying to get in touch with her for an hour now, and I can't raise her anywhere. She's not home, and the studio must be closed down for the weekend; all you get there is one of those stupid recordings. Something going on?"

Dino briefed Scotty on the plan to meet Nina and spend the weekend in D.C.

"Well look, you'll probably talk to her before I do, so tell her I found out some interesting stuff about her playmate Bryant." Scotty knew his audience; he just waited for Dino's next question.

"What stuff? You better tell me about it—it could change everything."

"Whatever you say, chief. This guy Bryant has some very peculiar items in his background. Nina said to hold up on checking him out through my Miami contacts, but I went ahead and nosed around anyway. I just didn't like the sound of it."

"Good. What did you find out?"

"One of my friends made a few strategic calls to somebody on the *Miami Vice* set, where this guy Bryant is supposed to have worked. Well, he worked on the show, all right. But not as Rob Bryant. Down there, they knew him as Niles Nordland. Ring any bells?"

The name meant nothing to Dino, but the fact that Rob Bryant had used an alias made him highly uncomfortable.

"Anything else, Scotty?"

"Yeah. This friend of mine started to dig, don't ask me how, and he came up with a widow named Lucy Montoya who'd followed Bryant all the way from Oregon. Claims Bryant took her for ten thousand. Only then he wasn't Bryant, and he wasn't Nordland, either. In Portland he was known as George Peterson. She's really after his ass. Any

192

time we give the word she'll fly up here and sign a complaint."

"Scotty, I have to find Nina right now!"

The intensified note of worry in Dino's voice frightened Scotty. "Yeah, sounds like you ought to do that. I know about her tendency to run off and do things on her own. Lemme help?"

Within minutes, Dino had dispatched an unmarked car to pick up Scotty. He also left orders for Charley Harper to meet him at Rob's apartment building and for Bruno Reichert to try to locate Spence Sprague, Horst Krueger, and—most particularly—Helen Meyer at Leatherwing. If anybody knew where Bryant was, it would probably be Helen Meyer; finding Rob fast could be at least as important as intercepting Nina, probably more so. Just in case, he also contacted the airport police and left word for her there.

Then he grabbed his coat and ran out of the office.

The basement of Meyer Studios was gloomy, dark, and cold, and Nina was very glad to be there at the moment. Still holding firmly onto each other's hands, she and Rob had proceeded with extreme caution down the firestairs and into the maze of corridors that connected a bewildering assortment of murky rooms. Only a glimmer of light filtered down from the few filthy windows that were set high in the walls, at sidewalk level. Nina had no idea where she was headed; she was just glad to be putting more distance between her and the menacing Sam Baylog.

"Where are we going?" Rob whispered.

"Looking for a fire exit. I can't see a thing. Do you have a lighter?"

He did, and the flickering light helped them find their way. It also helped them see the huge waterbugs that skittered across their path every few feet. At the first of these, Nina almost released a shriek that would have brought the entire building down on them, as well as Sam Baylog. From then on, she kept her tongue firmly between

193

her teeth and tried not to look at the floor. Some things were better left unseen.

They went through a steel-framed doorway and found themselves in a huge chamber, empty except for a few abandoned pieces of old office furniture. Nina judged they were probably directly beneath the office area, which made her remember the peculiar things she'd found in Rob's desk. She also remembered that she was supposed to meet Dino at LaGuardia Airport at seven o'clock.

"What time is it?" she whispered.

"Got a date?" he asked, seemingly amused by the question.

"What *time* is it?" she repeated, annoyed by his tone.

"It's almost five," he said, bringing the tiny flame close to his wrist.

"Come on, let's find a damned door and get out of here," she said. Her determination to escape the building was rewarded by the discovery of a steel door, marked Exit. It was exactly what they were looking for—and it was absolutely immoveable. No matter how much pressure Rob put on it, he couldn't get it to budge.

"Now what?" he said, abandoning his efforts.

"Now what?" she repeated idiotically, and then felt a fresh resolve to get out safely. "Now we go back upstairs and do what we should have done in the first place—find a phone and call the police."

He seemed about to offer a different suggestion, but just then the eerie silence of the building was shattered by a series of crashes from above, as though someone was smashing furniture with a vengeance. They froze once again as the noise continued spasmodically for a few minutes, then ended in heavy footsteps that sounded to Nina as though someone was running toward the front door.

The silence that followed had a finality about it, and they decided to make their way slowly back through the corridor and up the firestairs. At the top, they paused and listened for long moments. Nothing.

Rob put his hand out and slowly began to turn the knob.

Instantly the door was thrown wide open with a jolting crash and a large blurry figure hurled itself on them. Again Nina had the impression of an animal, a furious bear suddenly released from its cage. Rob's lighter went out, and Nina felt herself shoved hard against a wall, gasping for air as the figure lunged at Rob.

"You bastard! You rotten lousy stinking sonofabitch bastard!" the attacking figure shouted hoarsely, flailing away at Rob.

Helen! It was Helen Meyer, enormous in her raccoon coat, who was raining blows on Rob's head, shoulders, chest, anywhere she could reach as her voice spiraled out of control. "You thought I trusted you, didn't you? You slimy shit! You've been sneaking around behind my back with this cheap whore! Haven't you? HAVEN'T YOU? And the other ones, too! I'll give you what they got! I'll kill you! I'll scratch your eyes out!"

The verbal abuse poured out of Helen in a raging torrent, and Nina listened in fright as the older woman reviled Rob in terms and combinations she'd only dimly known existed. Helen was so out of control that much of her raving was unintelligible, but her energy was inexhaustible. It seemed she wouldn't rest until she'd cursed Rob Bryant to death.

Nina groped her way to a light switch and turned it on just in time to see Helen shove Rob away from her in a fresh burst of strength and fumble for something in her purse. Rob lunged at her and knocked the purse out of her hand as Nina finally found her voice and screamed. Helen had a gun! She was actually going to pull out a gun and shoot them both! Was that what she meant when she said "I'll give you what they got?" But Terri and Milly hadn't been shot. . . .

"Nina," Rob gasped, holding on to the wildly struggling and babbling Helen, "she's insane. I can't let her go—she'll try to kill us both!"

"What's the matter with her?" Nina gasped.

"She's jealous, for Chirst's sake! She thinks I've been screwing around with you and every other woman on the

195

set. Find something to tie her hands until she calms down. There's some electrical tape over there—get that. Hurry up. *Please!* God, she's so strong! You don't know what she's capable of."

"I'm starting to realize."

Nina brought the tape to Rob and helped him while he bound Helen's wrists together and forced her down into a chair in the spare dressing room. But the fact of being overpowered only added more fuel to Helen's fury, and her volume actually increased as she continued to revile them both. Finally Rob shrugged and taped her mouth shut.

Silenced at last, the disheveled and heavily sweating Helen looked wildly from Rob to Nina and back again. Her eyes rolled madly, demanding release.

Nina was aghast. She'd never before seen anyone go completely wild, and she was thoroughly frightened by the sight of the usually civilized and always elegantly dressed woman who was now bound and gagged, her hair a tangled mess, her makeup smudged with tears and spittle.

"My God," she said half to herself. "What are we going to do?"

"Let's collect our thoughts while she calms down. I've seen her in a rage before, but never anything like this. You can't even talk to her until she calms down." Nina continued to stare at Helen. "You look like you could use a little freshening up yourself," he suggested, and Nina suddenly realized she was very much in need of the ladies' room. "Go on, wash up. I'll stay here with her until you come back. Then we'll decide what to do."

"Yes, good idea. I won't be long."

Nina backed away from the writhing figure in the chair and hurried along the corridor to the ladies' room, turning on lights as she went. After a thorough wash she ran a comb through her hair, applied fresh lipstick, and studied herself critically for a moment. She wanted nothing so much as to go home, jump into a hot tub, and stay there for the weekend.

The weekend! Dino! She glanced at her watch. It was almost a quarter to six! Even if she just abandoned Helen and Rob and ran out of the studio right then, she'd never make it to La Guardia by seven! She had to get to a phone and try to reach Dino immediately.

She gathered up her purse and rushed out of the ladies' room—and right into the arms of Rob Bryant, who was waiting for her with a very strange expression on his face.

Chapter Nineteen

"Rob! You startled me. How's Helen?"

"Not bad, considering her age."

His meaning wasn't immediately apparent to Nina. "Yes, all that struggling and screaming would take its toll on anyone. . . ."

He laughed easily. What was so funny?

"Why don't we see how she's doing?"

"Yes, good idea, Nina. Let's just look in on Helen."

They returned to the spare dressing room, and Nina gasped at what she saw. During her brief absence in the ladies' room, Rob had retied Helen's hands behind her and bound her legs to the chair.

"Rob, was that necessary?"

Still gazing at the whimpering Helen, Rob smiled fondly. "Oh yes, absolutely necessary. She's fairly strong, you know. And we don't want to be interrupted, do we?"

He turned to Nina, the fond gaze dissolving into a look of sheer lust. Nina resisted the impulse to scream and run for the door; she knew she'd never make it.

"I guess we don't," she whispered.

"Don't worry, we're not going to be. I've made sure of that. And now, we have the place completely to ourselves." He seemed to be waiting for a response.

"And since it's such a big place," Nina said in as casual a voice as she could manage, "why should we stay in this cramped little room? Let's be comfortable."

He considered a moment, glancing at Helen as though to reassure himself that she was safely out of commission.

"Yes, you're right. Let's go into your office. I like the furniture there."

My office? What is he talking about? Nina thought. I don't *have* an office.

He took her by the arm and she allowed herself to be led down the corridors toward the soundstages where the sets were.

"There," he said gently, easing her into an upholstered chair on the set that represented Melanie Prescott's office at the Marston Corporation. "Now we can really get to work."

"To work?"

The question seemed to anger him. "Yes, Nina. To *work*. What do you think we're here for?"

"Of course. I'm delighted that you want to work. My work is the most important thing in my life," she babbled, trying to suppress her growing terror.

He reached out and tenderly ran his fingers along the line of her jaw. "Yes, yes, oh yes . . . ."

"Rob, do you remember a conversation we had not too long ago, when you said that you wanted to take me out to dinner again so we could get to know each other better?"

"Certainly I remember it. I remember everything."

"That was a very important statement. I just wish I'd realized it at the time. You were right—we *should* have gotten to know each other better, so . . ."

"We're going to, Nina. We're going to get to know each other a lot better."

"That's good. Rob! Especially since you want to get to work. Let's have that dinner now, and while we eat we can talk about all sorts of things."

He stroked her cheek in silence.

"Would you like that, Rob? Rob?"

"Ah, Nina. You're so very beautiful. And you must think I'm so very stupid."

Careful now, very careful. Don't tense up. Stay *relaxed.* "What do you mean?" She uttered the question with a friendly amused laugh.

"What do you mean?" he repeated, mimicking her tone precisely. "I mean *you're* the stupid one!" He suddenly grabbed Nina by the shoulders, hauled her out of the chair, and pulled her across the set to Melanie Prescott's sofa. "Did you think I was going to let you trip me up?" he challenged, throwing her down onto the sofa.

"That was the problem!" she said, abruptly changing her tactics. "You were too clever. I couldn't catch you! No one could catch you. You didn't leave any evidence, did you? But I knew, I *knew* right from the start!"

He glared at her for a moment, all pretense at warmth gone. "That's bull. You didn't know a damn thing."

"I knew," she insisted. Anything to keep him talking . . .

"You knew nothing," he said. "If you knew so much, why'd you go down into the basement with me just now?"

"You fooled me into thinking it was Sam Baylog who was prowling around, not Helen."

"Baby, if you knew I was the one you were looking for, you'd have run right into Sam Baylog's arms and begged him to protect you. So don't hand me that line of crap, because you don't know anything. Do you?" She looked at the floor. "*Do you?*"

The iron grip Nina had on her nerves and willpower was beginning to loosen. And when she looked up at him it slipped several notches further; he had taken the roll of electrical tape out of his pocket and was beginning to unwind a length of it.

"I know a lot, Rob. More than you'd imagine," she said quietly.

Infuriated, he dropped the tape and pulled her to her feet again, holding her roughly by the shoulders. "Okay, tell me what you know, you lousy liar! Tell me right now, while you can still talk!"

201

"I know about you and Terri."

His eyes widened.

"I know you killed her—Milly, too."

The flat statements took him by surprise. He relaxed his grip on Nina's shoulders and she sank back down on the sofa, glad for a way to hide the fact that her knees were shaking.

"Just think of all the trouble you'd have saved yourself," he sneered, "if you'd kept your nose out of things that don't concern you. You and that boyfriend of yours. Now it's too late." He paused, stroked her face again, ran his fingers across her lips. "What were you trying to prove?"

"Milly was my friend. I just couldn't see her killed and do nothing about it."

"Your friend, huh? Sounds just like you. True blue, loyal to the end. A regular Pollyanna. And what about Terri? Didn't you care about her?"

"She was different," Nina said, baiting the hook again. "I could take her or leave her."

Rob chuckled. "Welcome to the club. Same here. Bossy, interfering bitch. Couldn't leave well enough alone. Just like you. If she'd stayed out of my business . . ."

"She was your wife," Nina said, making a wild stab in the dark. "She deserved better."

"My wife, huh? So you know that, too. And how, may I ask, did you find out about that?"

"The same way I found out about the other women—in Miami and Los Angeles—" Oh God, where did poor old Lucywoo live?—"and Portland, Oregon. Do you have the same thing in mind for Helen? I don't think she'll be that easy to get rid of."

His eyes narrowed; momentarily he went silent. Then, "You're smarter than I thought."

"I have my moments."

"Well, you're running out of moments—real fast!"

Even at this moment, staring death in the face, curiosity was still rampant in Nina's brain. "Why?" she asked. "Why did you kill Terri?"

"You haven't figured that one out? Because she was in my way. She was getting to be a drag."

"She *was* your wife, wasn't she? Among others?"

"Yeah. Back in nineteen eighty-five. Mrs. Freeman Collier. That was the name I used with her. Names were never a problem for me—I once developed a very close relationship with a very homely lady who worked for Social Security. She produced a new name for me whenever I wanted one, complete with card and number. When I was finished with it, she just deleted it from the system. That was her one talent; in all other departments she was a flop. Christ, how I paid for those aliases. . . . Anyway, Terri went back to her maiden name after we split. Did you know we were together almost two years? For a while, at the beginning, I was convinced I really loved her; for once there was no money involved. But women change; they get to be a hundred-pound chain around your neck. So I skipped, headed north."

"To Oregon?"

"To Oregon—a rich widow. I scored almost forty big ones off her before I checked out. She kept trying to turn me into a pillar of the church. The church! Can you feature that?"

"Frankly, Rob, I can't." Her brain was clicking madly, pieces of the puzzle dropping into place. "How did Terri get on your trail? How did she find you?"

"She didn't. It was a freak, a rotten accident! Here I was in New York, just getting into my new job on *The Turning Seasons*, and didn't she show up, some half-assed finalist in a dippy talent search? When she came waltzing into the studio, I nearly passed out on the spot."

"How did Terri take it?"

"She was cool. Terri always was a smart cookie, quick on the uptake. She just gave me one of her cool smiles and kept a straight face. Then the shit really hit the fan."

Terri Triano, Rob went on, had quickly assessed the lay of the land, had seen a way to use it to good advantage, to really stick it to her ex-husband. Catching him alone, she told him that he'd be smart to get in touch, and quickly.

They went to dinner, and she laid out her blackmail terms. Fifty thousand dollars in cash, or she'd go to Helen Meyer and blow the whistle loud and long.

Rob begged for time to get the money, but he had no real intention of paying it. He needed time to come up with a plan to get rid of his ex-wife for good. A stalling action had commenced.

"What about Milly?" Nina intervened. "As I told you, she said *she* was the first choice in the contest and that she was mysteriously yanked at the last minute. You knew about that, didn't you?"

"It's true," Rob said, smiling blandly. "I knew. And she did win. But I fixed it with Helen so Terri got the role."

"But why? I'd think, if she was a threat, you'd want to get her back to Los Angeles as fast as you could."

"Terri was slippery and tough; I didn't trust her for a damned second. I wanted to keep her where I could keep an eye on her." He smiled evilly. "Until I was ready to get rid of her."

"And so you twisted Helen's arm?"

"Oh, Nina, you are something else! Sure, I put the screws to the old bat." He winked. "Or rather, I *didn't* put the screws to her. She caved in that same night until I did."

"Poor Milly," Nina said softly. "What a way to lose out."

"It's a cruel, cold world, isn't it?"

"You are contemptible, Rob!"

"Aren't I? But wait, honey. You haven't seen anything yet. The night is young." He leaned toward Nina, covering her mouth with his lips.

"No . . . don't," Nina gasped, edging away from him on the sofa. "How did you do it?" she said, anxious to distract him. "Kill Terri? Nobody . . . not even Dino, the medical examiner . . . can figure it out. We're sure it was murder, but we don't know how it was done."

"You never will." He smirked, pride in his expression. "Correction: *They* never will. I can tell you, because you'll never get the chance to tell anybody. I suppose you knew that Terri was on drugs? It was one of the underlying reasons I decided to get out. She was on a designer drug,

Sentanyl; she couldn't kick it no matter how hard she tried."

"Yes, the ME determined that. She had needle marks all over her arms. But there wasn't enough residue in her system to prove that she'd overdosed on anything specific."

"Right. That was another thing: I was supposed to become her pusher besides. Could I find her some Sentanyl? But her last rush wasn't from Sentanyl; she only thought it was."

When Rob realized that Terri was still hooked, he told Nina, it occurred to him that there was the perfect opening, a tailormade way to eliminate the blackmailing bitch. But he could never get Terri to overdose. She was too savvy, too much in control.

Then he heard of an oddity called thrombin, a substance which is naturally produced by the body and influences the clotting function of the blood. Oblique questioning of a female medical student he'd recently bedded provided the precise angle he desired. Additional thrombin, she told him, is sometimes given to people with hemorrhage problems. But when given in four and five milligram doses, it induces too much clotting. The result, in a matter of ten to fifteen minutes, is a huge clot that soon moves to the brain and triggers an almost certain fatal stroke.

Despite her mounting repugnance, Nina couldn't help but feel awe at the ingenious plan. "Incredible," she breathed. "And there's no way it can be traced?"

"That's the real beauty of it. There's no way anyone can prove that thrombin was artificially induced. After all, it's a normal substance, always present in the human body."

"But where did you get the stuff? Aren't doctors the only ones authorized to buy it?"

Rob laughed contemptuously. "There are doctors and there are doctors. Just wave enough money at the right one, and some of them would sell their mothers!"

Nina's pulse hammered crazily. If only Dino could be in the corner somewhere, listening to all this! He'd never believe it otherwise. "But how did you get Terri to use it?

205

And why at the party; with all those people there? It sounds insane."

"You really *are* stupid, aren't you? It wasn't supposed to happen at the party. I was with her on Friday night and she was pushing hard for a down payment on the fifty thou. She was also in bad need of a fix, so I gave her a vial of Sentanyl in the restaurant. Right away she went into the john and shot up."

"And the thrombin?"

"I didn't give her that until we got back to the hotel. I figured she'd do it the next morning, and that would be that. They'd find her dead in bed. But it didn't happen that way at all. How was I to know the dumb ditz was going to hold off all day and then get all hyper and nervous over the presentation of the award, and the press coverage, and all that junk?"

Nina finished the story for him. "So she went into the women's room at the Tavern on the Green, and used it then. She was at dinner, waiting to deliver her acceptance speech, when it hit. Apparently it took a little longer than usual to take effect."

"Apparently. But who was keeping tabs? Not me. It was a surprise to me when she keeled over, even though I knew, the minute it happened, what she must have done."

Nina lapsed into stunned silence.

"See, Nina? See how little you really know?" His hands were sliding along her arms, up to her shoulders, starting to move downward.

Her eyes haunted, she asked, "Why Milly, too? What part did she play in all this?"

He pulled a sarcastic face. "An innocent bystander, I suppose. But she knew too much. As long as she kept her mouth shut, I was willing to let things slide. But when she started to talk, she had to go."

"How do you know she said anything?"

"Give me a break, Nina! Those questions your detective friend asked me. That talk about the funny phone calls Terri was getting, the fact that she was out on Friday night. Where else could that have been coming from? So I figured that maybe Milly knew more than was good for her. I couldn't help wondering just how much Terri had told her, how much she really knew about our relationship, or what she was telling you. And once the police got their noses into that . . ."

"Isn't that a rather flimsy motive for murder?"

"Is it? Are you sure Milly didn't give you a little something that last day? An envelope, a little package?"

"A little package? What are you talking about?"

"As I told you, Terri was a very cagey lady; she could be terribly suspicious. She once warned me that if anything ever happened to her she'd find a way to reach back from the grave, to let the world know about it. A letter hidden somewhere, left with someone . . ."

"That's ridiculous. It's like something out of an old pulp novel!"

"Maybe. But I wouldn't put it past Terri—she was that kind of woman. I even persuaded Milly to let me go through Terri's stuff first thing Sunday morning, before the cops got to it. But there wasn't anything there."

"You did?" Nina's head spun; this was all coming too fast for her. "Why would she let you in, allow you to go through Terri's things? Milly never told me that."

"Not yet she hadn't." A smug smile. "As for her letting me in, you ought to know the answer to that one, Nina. I *do* have a way with the ladies, wouldn't you agree?"

"Indeed you do," she said, remembering.

He winked. "Damned right. Now you know why Milly had to go?" A rabid expression crept into his eyes. "She had that letter; she'd hidden it somewhere. She was just biding her time before she laid it on me. Along with some brand new blackmail demands of her own. And now she's gone. Nobody will ever find the letter."

Nina blinked, staring at Rob intently. It was almost as if he was going into a psychotic trance. "And that's why you broke into my dressing room. You thought Milly had given this imaginary letter to me? If I had such a letter, why would I bring it to the studio? Why wouldn't I turn it over to Rossi immediately?"

Her deliberate insolence had strangely little effect on him. He seemed almost to be listening to something else. "Yes, that's right. Why wouldn't you . . . But I had to kill her after I saw the way you two always had your heads together . . . Sooner or later she'd pin something on me. . . ."

Nina was getting desperate for ways to keep him talking. She wondered what time it was but dared not look at her watch.

"And now that Milly is out of the way, you have only Corinne to worry about. By the way, what are your plans for Corinne?"

He grinned easily. "The usual. Screw her black and blue until I've had enough, and then move on to someone else. That Christy Hall might be worth the trouble. Pretty little thing . . ."

"But you're forgetting something. Corinne lied for you, didn't she? You got her to say she was with you when Milly died. How did you do that?"

"Same way I do everything. I just ask a woman for a favor at the right time, and I get what I want."

"Aren't you afraid Corinne will go to the police after you dump her?"

He laughed scornfully. "With what? What does she know, except that she told the police a lie? She doesn't know where I really was, or what I was doing, now does she?"

But Nina was certain that Corinne had guessed what Rob had been doing—strangling Milly and throwing her body from that landing. That would explain her edgy behavior during the days that followed. She was feeling guilty about the lie she'd told, and terrified because she guessed the truth. I'll have to square it with the police later, Nina thought, for the moment forgetting her predicament. And then, with a shudder, remembering it.

"Rob, you are truly amazing. Tell me something: how did you manage to get Milly to meet you that day, just before final taping was supposed to start?"

He looked at her pityingly. "Don't you get it yet? My

208

women do what they're told. I *told* Milly to meet me there at that exact minute. And she did."

"But *why*?"

"Because she wanted to hear the same old lines all you stupid broads want to hear."

Nina saw her chance and seized it.

"What lines, Rob?" she purred. "Let me hear them."

A sly smirk began to slide across his face. "You faker! You phony. I knew right from the start what you were all about. You and your don't-touch-me act. Who did you think you were fooling? That night in my car, one more minute and you would have been begging for it. So now, beg!"

Nina played the scene for all it was worth—her life depended on it.

"I really want to hear those lines, Rob, and I want to hear them from you."

"Sure you do. Everyone wants to hear them. You, Terri, Corinne, Milly, Melanie . . ."

Melanie? What's he talking about? Nina thought. Melanie was her character on *The Turning Seasons*. Did he think his attraction extended to fictional women as well? Let's find out where this leads. A bit of paraphrasing from the previous day's script might be useful.

"Yes, especially me—Melanie."

"Melanie?"

"I need to hear you say those things more than I need food and shelter. You know that, don't know? You could be my life, my salvation. But you're being cruel. Are you saying those things, those wonderful, wonderful things, to someone else? Is it Audrey? It *is* Audrey, isn't it? Yes, I can see it in your eyes, your wonderful, wonderful eyes! Oh please, don't betray me with Audrey!"

She was running out of steam. Rob was looking around the set as though he'd never seen it before.

"Audrey isn't here," he said quietly, giving Nina fresh fuel.

"Let's get her here! Let's bring her in and finish this thing once and for all! I'll show you why she isn't worthy of your love, I'll prove to you that Audrey Lincoln is a lying little tramp, no better than . . ."

She stopped. Audrey Lincoln? A.L.? Was *that* who "Al" was?

But the hesitation was fatal. Rob suddenly lashed out and slapped Nina across the face, sending her reeling back onto the sofa. A moment later he was swiftly wrapping electrical tape around her wrists. The little strength she had left was useless against his incredible power.

"You're wasting my time with this, Nina," he said, once again exuding the familiar boyish charm. "You want to play a little scene? We'll do it. Places!"

Roughly he thrust her flat on the sofa and wrapped several thicknesses of electrical tape around her ankles and across her mouth. Then he ran off the set and down the hallway. In a moment, Nina heard the sounds of scuffling, and then Rob reappeared, almost carrying Helen. He dragged her across the set and dropped her onto the sofa beside Nina.

"Okay, let's rehearse. You know the new scene, Nina? The one where the lady executive finds her boyfriend alone with the redhead and shoots her, and then turns the gun on herself because she can't face the consequences?"

Nina could only stare at him in horror.

"Or maybe that's not such a good idea. Maybe it's the scene where the actress and her boss are alone in the studio and a prowler comes in and kills them both. Yes, that's much better—no messy personal angles to deal with. And what a struggle you two are going to put up! I've been itching to smash this place to pieces for weeks now . . ."

With that, he picked up Melanie Prescott's desk chair and hurled it against the window wall of the office set. The noise was deafening as the wooden walls splintered and shattered. Goaded on by the sounds, Rob raced around the set hurling props and furniture, breaking picture frames, vases, desktop equipment, chairs, and everything not bolted down.

The noise aroused Helen, who came out of her stupor and began to moan in fright. Rob rushed over to her and took her raddled face in his hands. She looked as though she'd been through a war. Then he shifted his gaze to Nina.

"Come on, throw yourself into the part! You're supposed to be such a great actress, now act! What's the matter, not in the mood? Want some mood music? Need a little makeup? Wait right here!"

Again he rushed from the set, and Nina struggled to loosen her bonds, but it was useless. If only she could get Helen to turn around and use her tied hands to . . .

A single loud cry came from the hallway, followed by a heavy thud. Then silence. Nina stared at the door, listening to the heavy footsteps that were approaching.

It was Sam Baylog, and he was dragging something along behind him—Rob Bryant's unconscious body. Nina fainted.

Nina opened her eyes to find Baylog shaking her by the shoulders. "Come on, wake up! Listen, you people are really nuts. I came back here to tear up the joint a little so you'd know I don't kid around. But I heard how this scumbag works, and there's no way he's gonna treat my Christy that way." Baylog turned and addressed Helen, who was wide awake now, goggle-eyed. "You can forget it, Mrs. Meyer, we're walkin! You don't like it, sue me!"

And with that he turned and lumbered out.

His footsteps receded into the distance, and they heard the front door slam. Struggling frantically to free herself and Helen before Rob regained consciousness, Nina rolled off the sofa and landed on top of his legs. The jolt aroused him, and both women stopped struggling and simply watched in mounting horror.

Slowly and deliberately, but still with that damned boyish grin, he walked over to Helen and pulled out a pistol, aimed it directly between her eyes, and fired. Nina's eyelids involuntarily closed hard as the wall behind the sofa turned red.

Then he turned and aimed the pistol at Nina.

Chapter Twenty

Again she heard footsteps approaching in the hall. But this time it wasn't Sam Baylog, it was Morty Meyer! Never mind that Morty had been dead for months—there he was.

"Hey, Nina," he called. "Come on, open your eyes!"

She did as she was told. After all, dead or alive, he was the original Meyer of Meyer Productions.

"Hello, Morty," Nina said, speaking easily right through the electrical tape over her mouth. "What a surprise."

"You know me, kid. A bundle of laughs." He turned his attention to Helen's body, sprawled on the sofa. "Baby, you look like death warmed over," he said in mild reproach. Then he looked back at Nina and wiggled his eyebrows. "Not bad, huh?"

Nina started to giggle, and the giggle turned into a low laugh that built quickly and erupted in a wild burst of hysteria.

"Okay, okay, it's okay, come on now, it's okay." The words were soothing and reassuring but it was no longer Morty's voice. Someone's arms were around her and he was rubbing her back the way a father might. Nina opened her eyes and snuggled as close as she could into Dino's bare chest. From his position at the foot of the bed, Chessy regarded them doubtfully.

"Oh, I was dreaming again," she whispered.

"I know—you've been moaning for a while. But now you're awake and everything's okay."

She lay back in his arms and looked around her bedroom, savoring the familiar warmth and comfort. She wanted to put the whole hideous episode behind her, but a million details crowded into her mind, demanding attention.

She could see herself back in the studio with Rob, tricking him into talking, stringing him along, playing for time until the moment she ran out of ploys and he smashed up the set. Then he went truly berserk and started to babble about mood music and makeup. Had he actually gone off to find some makeup for the death scene?

"Dino?"

"What, love?"

"Was Sam Baylog really there?"

"Yes, he was there all right. And we found out that he really did trash Helen's office, as a way of scaring her. But why?"

"So she'd agree to give Christy Hall more close-ups."

"You show business people are all cuckoo!"

"But he was there, *really there*, right?"

"Right."

"I guess I asked you that before, didn't I?"

"Last night. At the diner."

"I forgot about the diner, too. How did we get there?"

Dino sighed and burrowed deeper under the covers, cradling Nina in his arms while he again recounted the last moments of a dizzying day.

When he arrived at the studio with Harper, Reichert, and Scotty Lane, they collided with Sam Baylog on his way out, grumbling about the idiots inside, rehearsing some crazy scene. Dino lost control of himself and pinned the lumbering giant to a wall, demanding to know where Nina was.

Baylog led them to the splintered remains of the Melanie Prescott office set just as Rob was regaining consciousness from the massive agent's single walloping punch. While

Harper stood guard over Rob, Dino released and revived Nina as the others took care of Helen. Bit by bit the story took shape. When it became clear that it was Rob Bryant who'd attacked Nina in the snowstorm and then had tried to finish her off with a rifle, Dino had to be restrained by Harper and Reichert from beating him to death on the spot.

After a long stop at the station house so Helen and Nina could file formal complaints against Rob and have him placed behind bars, probably forever, Dino took both women and Scotty to an all-night diner. Ravenous hunger had overtaken everyone except Helen, who downed Manhattan after Manhattan while the other three demolished huge steaks. In any other city but New York, they would have drawn stares: the ravishingly beautiful but groggy and disheveled redhead, the startlingly handsome detective, the woebegone and woozy *grande dame* with the beginnings of a magnificent shiner, and the dapper little retired newspaperman. But in New York, no one noticed.

Finally, appetites satisfied, Dino put Scotty and Helen into an official car for the long ride home—Scotty had volunteered to see Helen all the way to the front door of Leatherwing; the car would then take him back to his home in Greenwich Village.

As for Nina and Dino, they went directly to her apartment where two very tired people took one very long shower and then collapsed into bed, displacing a disgruntled Chessy, who now sat at the foot of the bed in the early morning light, watching his person doing funny things with her mouth to that other person's mouth.

Whatever they were doing, they did it for a long time before any more words were spoken.

"It was so awful," Nina said at last. "Poor Helen—I feel so sorry for her! Imagine having to listen to your lover talk about murdering you!"

"He did the same thing to you."

"Yes, but I hadn't deluded myself into thinking that I was in love with Rob. Helen was."

"She's alive, isn't she?"

"I suppose you might call it that. But inside, I think it's

going to take her a long, long time to recover from the wounds she received last night—and I'm not talking about her bruises."

"I'm sorry, but I can't get all worked up over it," Dino said. "She found out the truth in time. Hell, she could have ended up married to that leech! He'd have taken her for everything she had. I repeat: she's alive." His voice became hushed. "And *you're* alive, darling. That's what matters. God, when I think of what might have happened!"

Nina's throat tightened, and she clung even more desperately to him. "Darling, I don't think you know what that does to me—to know you care that much."

"What do I have to do?" he said, his voice husky. "Rent a billboard? You ought to know how I feel by now."

"I do. But a woman likes to hear it just the same."

Nina chose that tender moment to advance a touchy cause. "Dino, darling?"

"Yes?"

"What are you going to do about Corinne Demetry? Isn't there some way you can overlook her false testimony about Rob Bryant? It was wrong, I know, but she's just a kid, one of Rob's victims. He has this way with women . . . She was out of her depth, that's all. Please, Dino? Couldn't you bend the rules a little?"

"Nina," he grumbled softly, nuzzling her bosom, "you are such a sucker for every sob story you hear. Christ, the woman's partially responsible for nearly getting you killed!"

"Please, love. She's my friend. I'm sure she'll be feeling bad enough as it is, without having criminal charges pressed against her. Think about it?"

"Okay, I will. It's against my better judgment, but for you . . . And while we're on the subject of fallout, who's going to take over Bryant's job?"

"I think," Nina said, "that, under the circumstances, Helen might be persuaded to rehire Bellamy Carter. In fact, I intend to give Horst a call and suggest that he put a bug in Helen's ear. I'll tell him to mention my name—I think she'll get the message."

"You schemer. You're about as subtle as a pile driver."
He kissed her again, sliding his lips along the line of her
jaw. It made Nina tingle in all the right places, and she
moaned softly as she ran her nails teasingly along his back.

Rossi managed to resist her blandishments, at least
temporarily. "In case I didn't mention it last night, thanks,
darling. Again. It's a helluva risky way to gather evidence,
putting your life on the line the way you did, but the fact is,
without it we'd never have pinned both murders on
Bryant."

"Thank *you*, darling." Nina sighed, and began sliding
her body against his, her fingertips fluttering on his crisply
furred chest. "It's so nice to be appreciated."

"What's on our agenda for today, sweetheart?" Dino
murmured. "Since it doesn't look like we're going to make
it to Washington."

"Maybe I should get up and cook us a nice breakfast?"

"Maybe you should stay right here. Breakfasts I can
always get. Now, about this 'Nina Special' you mentioned
once—you've definitely got me curious."

"Of course," she said, her eyes smoky. "One Nina
Special coming up." She began to trail tiny, peppery kisses
along his shoulders, then down his chest. Her hands
became more daring, evoking the desired response.

Chessy, still comfortably curled up at the end of the bed,
stopped purring as his real estate began to shake. With
great dignity, he leaped to the floor and headed for the
kitchen. By the time he'd polished off his cat food, maybe
the earthquake would be over. . . .

In Book Four of Eileen Fulton's Take One for Murder . . .

Nina McFall is always glad to hear from her devoted fans, who deluge her with letters, presents, and advice. But lately she's been receiving passionate letters from a man calling himself her "Secret Lover," warning her against the evil intentions of Melanie Prescott's current love interest on *The Turning Seasons*, and swearing that he will let nobody come between himself and his idol.

Nina doesn't take it seriously—until a delegation of fans arrives at Meyer Studios, and shortly thereafter the actor playing Melanie's lover turns up dead in the Hudson River. Now she's sure "Secret Lover" means business. She's also sure he's crazy, since he's obviously confused Nina the actress with the part she plays on the show.

Detective Lieutenant Dino Rossi doesn't buy it, however, and mobilizes his squad to pursue other leads. Then a second murder is committed, and a terrified Nina realizes she must unmask her homicidal adorer before he discovers the *real* love of her life and targets Dino for death as well.